LAWMAN

LAWMAN

LAWMAN

A MURPHY WESTERN

ETHAN J. WOLFE

THORNDIKE PRESS

A part of Gale, a Cengage Company

LIBRARY OF CONGRESS CIP DATA ON FILE.
CATALOGUING IN PUBLICATION FOR THIS BOOK
IS AVAILABLE FROM THE LIBRARY OF CONGRESS

ISBN-13: 978-1-4328-5742-4 (hardcover alk. paper)

Published in 2020 by arrangement with Ethan J. Wolfe

Printed in Mexico
Print Number: 01   Print Year: 2020

LAWMAN

LAWMAN

PROLOGUE

Former First Lady and wife of Ulysses S. Grant, Julia Grant, always took tea when she opened the daily mail. Lately there was a great deal of correspondence that needed her husband's attention.

Most days she drank two or more cups before she weeded through the stack of mail. Much of it she took care of herself unless Hiram's signature was required.

Stuck in the middle of the pack was an official-looking envelope from Mark Twain, who would be publishing Hiram's memoirs sometime next year.

She carefully tore it open and read the letter. Then she stood, left her study, and found Hiram in the backyard where he was working on his memoirs. She sat at the table opposite him.

"I believe you need to read this one, dear," Julia said.

Grant took the letter and read it carefully.

While he read, Julia lifted Grant's coffee mug and took a small sip to make sure he hadn't flavored the coffee with his favorite sweetener, eighty-proof bourbon.

He hadn't, probably because he suspected she would test it.

"A representative of Mark Twain wishes to arrange a twenty-city-tour speaking engagement prior to the release of my memoirs," Grant said. "Half to be held at college campuses."

"Look at the fees, dear," Julia said.

"I see them," Grant said. "One thousand per engagement."

"It's been years since you've lectured, Hiram," Julia said. "It will do you good to get away from your desk for a few months and speak with people."

"But do young people today want to sit and listen to an old gasbag like me go on for two hours?" Grant said.

"Not interested in listening to the man who took Lee's surrender and then became the eighteenth president of the United States? Don't be ridiculous, Hiram," Julia said.

"Last month we attended the baseball game at Cooperstown, remember?" Grant said.

"Of course, Hiram. What of it?"

"There must have been five hundred young people in the stands, and not one of them recognized me," Grant said.

"Hiram, who expects to see the greatest general in American history and the eighteenth president of the United States at such a silly thing as a baseball game?" Julia said.

"As I recall, you dragged me to the game because your nephew is on one of the teams," Grant said.

"Baseball is not important, Hiram," Julia said. "What is important is that you do this speaking tour. Americans must never forget our past and the leaders who shape our future."

Grant grinned at his wife. "Maybe you should do the speaking tour," he said.

"Hiram, please," Julia said.

"All right," Grant said. He glanced at the letter again. "When will this representative be here?"

"The ten o'clock train from Manhattan tomorrow," Julia said.

"Mr. Pope, is it?" Grant said.

"Thomas Pope, sir. I work for Mr. Twain."

"How is old Sam these days?" Grant asked.

"Fine, sir. Just fine."

9

Grant sighed. "So about this speaking tour."

"Mr. Twain believes this tour will serve to make your memoirs, when published, an international best seller," Pope said.

"My terms are two thousand per engagement and expenses for my own private security detail," Grant said.

"Mr. Twain suggests hiring Pinkerton's," Pope said.

"Because they did such a bang-up job with Lincoln," Grant said. "No, I will choose my own security. Anything else?"

Pope grinned. "Mr. Twain said you'd dictate your own terms."

Grant stood up from his desk.

Pope stood up from his chair.

The two shook hands.

"Make the arrangements," Grant said.

CHAPTER ONE

Dressed in blue work pants, boots, and one of Murphy's sleeveless undershirts, Kai set the ax in the chopping block, removed the work gloves, and looked down the road at the approaching buggy.

She wasn't expecting them, but Murphy's parents, Michael and Aideen, often stopped by unexpectedly. Their farm wasn't far from Murphy's, and at least once a week they had dinner together.

When Murphy suggested they move to his farm in Tennessee, Kai had many reservations about leaving New Mexico. Although her father was Irish and German, her mother was half Navajo, and in the eyes of many, that made her nothing but a squaw.

Murphy told her his parents wouldn't care, nor would most folks living in the region.

Kai wasn't convinced until they moved to his farm, and Murphy's parents welcomed

11

her with wide-open arms. Almost immediately, she was part of the Murphy family and treated as such.

As the buggy arrived, Kai walked across the yard to meet it.

Murphy's father, Michael, jumped down and gave a hand to Aideen. She delicately stepped down beside Kai.

"My goodness, dear," Aideen said. "You're covered in sweat."

"A little sweat never hurt a woman none," Michael said. "I recall many a day where you chopped a cord or two while I was off building our farm."

"Where is my son?" Aideen asked.

"He went to the north field to fight with that stump again," Kai said.

"That idiot son of mine has been fighting with that oak stump off and on again for ten years," Michael said. "Why doesn't he hitch a team and be done with it?"

"He said it's personal," Kai said.

"Personal?" Michael said. "Between a stump and my son, it's hard to tell which one is the stump."

Kai laughed and said, "Your son is taller. Come on the porch in the shade. I have lemonade on ice."

A few minutes later, Kai served tall glasses

of lemonade over shaved ice and sat beside Aideen.

"Kai, as much as we love you, this isn't exactly a social call," Michael said.

Kai sighed heavily. "Why can't they just leave him alone?" she said. "He's done enough for one lifetime for these people."

"I know and I understand, Kai," Michael said. "But this telegram came directly from Grant, and my son would never refuse Grant."

Michael removed a folded telegram from a shirt pocket and handed it to Kai.

"They delivered it to the wrong Murphy," Michael said.

Kai read the telegram. "All it says is Grant wants to see us as soon as possible," she said. "Why us?"

"You'll just have to go to New York and find out from Grant," Michael said.

"I better saddle a horse and ride out to him," Kai said.

"Come to dinner tomorrow night," Aideen said.

Kai rode her horse, Bandit, a gift from Murphy and so named for his propensity to steal things when he thought no one was watching, to the north field.

She dismounted a hundred yards behind

13

Murphy and watched him for a few minutes.

Shirtless, Murphy was leaning into the enormous stump. His massive back and shoulders were drenched in sweat and as he strained against the stump, his muscles appeared to be carved from wood.

Slowly, she walked Bandit forward and grinned when Murphy cussed loudly at the unyielding stump.

Kai stopped when Murphy stepped back and said, "You son of a bitch," to the stump. Then he leaned all of his considerable weight into the stump and strained every fiber in his body. Kai watched in amazement as the stump actually rose several inches out of the ground.

Murphy stepped back, gasping for air, then turned and walked to his left, where the field ended at a shallow stream. The stream acted as a divider between Murphy's property and his parents'.

As he walked toward the stream, Murphy removed his boots, pants, and underwear and simply walked into the stream and dove under the water.

Kai removed her boots as she walked to the water. Then she removed her pants, shirt, and underwear. Naked, she stood at the edge of the stream.

Floating on his back, Murphy noticed Kai,

and he stood up.

The sun was on Kai's back as he looked at her.

"If ever I doubt there is a God, one look at you tells me he exists," Murphy said.

Kai rolled her deep green eyes. "Been reading poetry again?"

"Grant told me to tell you that when you're mad at me," Murphy said.

Kai slowly waded into the stream. "But I'm not mad at you," she said.

She walked to Murphy and looked up at him. At five-foot-eight-inches tall, Kai was an inch taller than the average man, but even on her toes, she couldn't reach Murphy's lips.

Murphy lifted Kai, and she wrapped her legs around him. As he carried her to shore, Kai said, "I rode out here for a reason."

They reached shore and Murphy gently lowered Kai to the thick, soft grass.

"Tell me about it later," Murphy said.

Murphy read the telegram and then stood up. "We best head home and pack," he said.

"Can we get dressed first?" Kai said. "You know how easily you chafe."

Murphy laughed and lifted Kai to her feet.

A few minutes later, as Murphy rode his massive horse, Boyle, and Kai rode Bandit,

Kai said, "What do you suppose he wants this time?"

"Could be anything," Murphy said. "The telegram says 'us,' so it might be just a social call."

"A social call, huh?" Kai said. "Better bring a case of whiskey then."

"Let's just wait and see," Murphy said.

"Are you afraid to marry me?" Kai asked as she nestled her face against Murphy's chest.

"For God's sake, Kai, I'm the one who asked you," Murphy said.

"But are you afraid?"

"No."

"I am."

"Of what?"

"Of one day you'll ride off and not come back," Kai said.

"I've officially retired from service, remember?" Murphy said.

"I've heard that before," Kai said.

"Grant isn't president anymore," Murphy said. "He can't reinstate me, and Arthur hates me."

"Because you're a foot taller than him," Kai said. "That doesn't mean he won't use you like all the others have."

"Before we start writing my obituary, let's

16

find out what Grant wants first," Murphy said.

"I'll need clothes," Kai said.

"You have clothes," Murphy said. "Trunks full of them."

"Society clothes, Murphy," Kai said. "The last time we visited Grant and Julia, I was dressed like I just came from the fields."

"And you were still more beautiful than any other woman in the room," Murphy said.

Kai was silent for a few seconds. "Damn that smart tongue of yours," she said and rolled on top of Murphy.

CHAPTER TWO

Murphy rented a buggy in Manhattan, and
he and Kai spent a leisurely two hours riding north to Grant's home at Mount
McGregor.

Murphy parked the buggy in front of the
house and then helped Kai step down. She
wore a long blue dress with a white blouse,
black shoes with two-inch heels, and a
fashionable hat. She wore waist-length hair
under the hat.

As they ascended the stairs, the front door
opened and Julia Grant stepped out to the
porch.

Julia took Kai's hands in hers. "She gets
more beautiful each time I see her, Murphy," she said.

"Flattery makes her angry, Julia," Murphy
said.

"Angry?" Julia said.

As Murphy leaned in to kiss Julia's cheek,
Kai purposely stepped on Murphy's right

foot with her spiked heel.

"Hiram's in his study," Julia said. "I'll make a pot of coffee, and we can talk in the backyard."

As Julia and Kai linked arms and entered the house, Murphy waited a few seconds for the pain in his right foot to ease up before following them.

At the backyard table, Murphy read the schedule of dates for the speaking tour and said, "You've always hated public speaking, General. Besides, you're writing your memoirs."

"Twain thinks it would boost book sales considerably," Grant said.

"Twain? Mark Twain?" Kai said.

"He's a close friend of Hiram's," Julia said.

"Well, how about it, Murphy?" Grant said.

"I'm sorry, General. How about what?" Murphy said.

"Twain wants to provide a security detail of Pinkerton's," Grant said. "I want to hire you as my security detail."

"General, Pinkerton's can give you an army of men," Murphy said. "Besides, from what I can see on the list, the chosen sites are all . . ."

"Dammit, Murphy, yes or no," Grant said.

"I'll need to go shopping," Kai said.

"What?" Grant said.

"What?" Murphy said.

Kai looked at Murphy. "We both know you're going to say yes, and I assume I'll be attending some of the engagements, so I'd like some new clothing to wear so I don't embarrass the general by looking like a farmhand just off the fields."

Julia grinned and stood up. "I need to check on lunch. We're having humble pie and crow," she said.

"I'll help you," Kai said.

After Murphy and the general were alone, Grant removed a thin flask from his jacket pocket and added some bourbon to his and Murphy's coffee.

"She's quite a woman you got there," Grant said.

"I don't disagree with you on that point, General," Murphy said.

"Murphy, I'm dying," Grant said. "Oh, it may take a while, maybe a year, but I'm for sure dying. The only reason I'm writing my memoirs is, Twain assures me the money made from sales will provide for Julia after I'm gone."

"Julia doesn't know?" Murphy said.

"Not at this point."

Murphy sighed. "What's the first date?" he said.

Grant picked up his bourbon-laced coffee and took a small sip with great satisfaction.

After lunch, Grant and Murphy saddled two horses from Grant's stables, and they rode through the hills of Mount McGregor.

They rode to the crest of a hill and looked down upon a green valley from atop their horses.

Grant took out his flask, sipped, and passed it to Murphy.

"What's ailing you, General?" Murphy said.

"Cancer," Grant said. "Deep down in my throat where the doctors can do nothing about it. It's not bad now, but it will become worse over time."

"Julia will have to know," Murphy said.

"She will when the time is right," Grant said. "Look at this country. No matter what the history books may write about me, I did the right thing."

Murphy looked below at the valley of emerald green and took a sip from the flask.

"Kai will probably spend a thousand dollars on clothes," Murphy said.

Grant smiled. "When you own a thoroughbred, showcase it," he said. "Stay for supper

21

and the night. Catch the train in the morning."

"Tell me about Murphy," Kai said when she and Grant were alone at the table after supper.

"I'm not sure I follow you," Grant said.

"He never talks about his life, about the things he's done," Kai said. "He is very kind and loving to me, but he won't discuss his past when I ask."

"A man's past is a man's past, Kai," Grant said. "Talking about it won't change the present or future."

"We are to be married soon, General," Kai said. "Shouldn't I know a bit about my husband's past?"

"When he's ready, he'll talk about it," Grant said. "And I pray you never see the side of Murphy I've seen. Now here they come with dessert."

Murphy entered the dining room holding a large chocolate cake. Julia held a tray with coffee and cups.

"Somebody went to a lot of trouble to make a cake," Grant said.

"To celebrate the beginning of a successful speaking tour," Julia said. "Murphy, will you do the honor of cutting the cake."

In the morning, as Julia and Kai hugged on the top steps, Grant and Murphy shook hands.

"We'll see you in ten days, General," Murphy said.

"I'll have all the arrangements made by then," Grant said. "Kai, you take care of Murphy. And remember what I told you."

Kai kissed Grant on the cheek. "I will, General," she said.

A mile or so down the road, Murphy said, "What did Grant tell you?"

"Marital advice on how best to handle you when you get out of line," Kai said.

Murphy looked at Kai.

Kai grinned. "You know, women talk," she said.

Murphy shook his head. "Wonders never cease," he said.

CHAPTER THREE

Murphy stood offstage at the University of
Virginia and watched as Grant spoke to a
packed house in the auditorium.

This was the fifth stop on Grant's tour.
Each engagement was standing room only.

What Murphy noticed was that Grant had
the ability to make each stop on the tour
seem brand-new. He rarely repeated himself, and he provided vivid and striking
details about the war and his presidency.

Much of the content Murphy knew firsthand. A great number of the intricate details
he was hearing for the first time. After he
spoke for one hour, Grant opened the floor
for questions, and that lasted anywhere from
one hour to two.

Julia Grant and Kai sat in the first row on
the left side. Kai wore one of the new outfits
she'd purchased in Manhattan three weeks
ago. She looked, to Murphy, to be very
uncomfortable wearing such high-fashion

clothing.

As Grant spoke, Murphy kept a close eye on the auditorium. It was shaped as an amphitheater, so sound resonated to the rear balcony. Grant's rich voice reached every ear in the room, and every eye was trained upon him.

Murphy scanned the faces in the auditorium. It seated six hundred with an additional two hundred in standing room along the balcony wall.

When Grant pointed to someone, that person stood and asked his question, then sat while Grant answered it.

The first five rows were reserved for faculty.

Grant didn't take questions from them until the end, because he was interested in the minds of the students. After forty-five minutes of answering questions from students, Grant turned his attention to the faculty.

Grant pointed to a well-dressed man with a thick beard.

"What is your question, sir?" Grant said.

The man stood.

The moment the man was on his feet, Murphy's senses kicked in. He stepped forward when he saw the man's face twitch.

The man reached inside his jacket.

Murphy was already walking onto the stage.

The man drew a pistol.

Murphy had his Colt out and cocked the hammer.

"The South shall rise again!" the man shouted and cocked the hammer on his pistol.

Murphy stepped in front of Grant, fired his Colt, and shot the man, dead, in the heart.

The auditorium erupted into chaos.

Grant watched the man draw a pistol.

Grant never moved a muscle. He had no need to panic. Murphy was there, and Grant never doubted for one second that Murphy would kill the man.

Julia Grant turned to look at the man her husband had called upon. He was about twenty seats to her left.

The man stood and shouted, "The South shall rise again," and pulled a pistol from inside his jacket.

Julia looked at the stage. Her husband remained seated and never moved while Murphy did what Murphy did best: he shot and killed the man.

Seated to Julia's right, Kai turned to look at the man Grant called upon.

The man drew a pistol and shouted at Grant.

Kai looked at the stage where Murphy was walking quickly to protect Grant. As Murphy stood in front of Grant, he fired his Colt pistol and killed the man with his gun.

Murphy didn't flinch, hesitate, or waver in his actions.

He simply shot the man dead where he stood.

As Murphy stood in front of Grant with his Colt in his right hand, Kai understood a little bit about the side of Murphy Grant had referred to that morning on his porch.

In the room reserved for Grant's dressing room, Grant sat in a chair and drank bourbon from a glass.

Murphy stood beside him holding his pipe.

They could hear voices in the hallway through the closed door.

"Open the door, you buffoon," Julia said loudly. "My husband is in there."

The door opened, and Julia and Kai

entered. Kai quickly closed the door.

"Jesus Christ, Hiram," Julia said. "I'm worried sick about you, and you're in here drinking bourbon."

"I was nearly killed tonight. What should I be drinking? Milk?" Grant said.

"There was about as much chance of you being killed as of Murphy missing," Julia said. "And give me that glass, or I'll finish the job that assassin started."

Reluctantly, Grant handed the glass to Julia. She set it on the table and looked at Murphy. "And you should know better than to let him drink straight bourbon," she said.

"Yes, ma'am," Murphy said, almost meekly.

There was a knock on the door. It opened, and a man wearing the blue uniform of police with the rank of captain entered. He was followed by three men wearing suits.

"I'm Captain Wallace of the DC Police. These men are my detectives," Wallace said. "We spoke to witnesses concerning the shooting."

"Do my wife and her friend need to be present for your questions?" Grant asked.

"No, sir," Wallace said.

"Can one of your detectives escort my wife and her friend to a safe room?" Grant said.

28

Wallace turned to one of his men. "Sergeant, please escort the ladies to the library and stay with them."

Kai looked at Murphy, and he nodded.

The sergeant opened the door. Kai and Julia followed him out of the room.

Wallace looked at Murphy. "You're the one who killed the assassin?"

"I am," Murphy said.

"Nice shot. Right through the heart from forty feet," Wallace said. "I suppose you couldn't have just wounded him though?"

"And leave him alive to possibly get off a second shot?" Murphy said. "A lucky shot that might hit the general?"

"I see your point," Wallace said.

"Captain Wallace, I've known Mr. Murphy since the war," Grant said. "He headed up my secret service detail when I was president. Please skip all the bullshit and tell us what you know about the assassin."

"Nothing," Wallace said. "At this point we know nothing. He had no identification on him. His clothing could have come from anywhere. His pistol is a Remington .32 caliber, and while not common, it's not an unusual handgun. No one appears to know or recognize him, at least at this point."

"He shouted 'The South shall rise

again,' " Grant said. "What do you make of that?"

"A holdover from the old Klan, possibly," Wallace said.

"Do you actually believe the Klan to be disbanded?" Grant asked.

"I do not, but they haven't been heard from in a while, and their numbers are weak," Wallace said.

"Captain Wallace, where is the body of the assassin?" Murphy asked.

Wallace pulled out his pocket watch and said, "In the morgue by now, being studied by the medical examiner."

"I want to see the body," Murphy said.

"Whatever for?" Wallace said.

"Captain Wallace, Murphy has forgotten more about police work than you will ever know," Grant said. "Please take him to examine the body."

Wallace sighed and then nodded.

"Keep the general protected until I return," Murphy said.

Julia and Kai took tea at a window table in the library. Wallace's detective kept his distance and smoked a cigar at the door.

"I've seen much violence in my life," Kai said. "I spent many years with the Sioux and Navajo before coming to live with my

30

Irish relatives. Most of the time, the violence came with much emotion, especially among the Sioux. Anger, revenge, even hatred. The way Murphy killed that man so easily and without emotion, he might as well have been lighting his pipe."

"Did it frighten you?" Julia asked.

"Yes."

"Has he ever showed anger toward you, raised his voice?" Julia said.

"Never."

"And he never will," Julia said. "Men like Murphy — and Hiram, too — are the protectors of the land, the warriors we need to keep us all safe. To Murphy, violence is a tool the way a hammer is to a blacksmith or a saw to a carpenter. When there is need for violence, Murphy draws what he needs from his toolbox. It's nothing more than, and as simple as, that."

Kai nodded.

Julia reached for the teapot.

"More tea?" she asked.

Grant was smoking a cigar and happily sipping bourbon in a glass when there was another knock on the door.

"I'll get it," a detective said.

The detective opened the door and William Burke, special assistant to the president, entered.

Burke looked at the three detectives left behind by Wallace.

"You three men. Out," Burke said.

"Who are you?" one of the detectives asked.

"That's William Burke, the president's right-hand man," Grant said.

"We're supposed to guard the general," a detective said.

"Do it on the other side of the door," Burke said.

The detectives looked at Burke.

"Gentlemen, Mr. Burke wasn't asking," Grant said.

"We'll be right outside," a detective said.

After the detectives left the room, Grant said, "How are you, Bill?"

"Fine, General."

"Care for a snort?" Grant said.

Burke lifted Grant's bottle and poured an ounce of bourbon into a glass.

"To your health, General," Burke said.

"And yours."

Both men sipped.

"So what brings you to my lecture, Bill?" Grant said. "You worked for me my entire term. You already know everything I'm going to say."

"Arthur asked me to attend," Burke said.

"He's interested in your memoirs and requested you come to dinner tonight."

"Tonight?" Grant said. "You know how much he annoys me."

"Considering the fact that you were almost shot this afternoon, I think a dinner on the taxpayer is in order," Burke said. "I assume Murphy is around here somewhere."

"He went to examine the body," Grant said. "Tell Arthur to set the table for four."

"Four?" Burke said.

"Murphy's new lady," Grant said.

"I'll tell him," Burke said.

"Want another snort?"

Burke looked around quickly. "Where's Julia?"

"Being babysat," Grant said.

"In that case, why not?" Burke said.

CHAPTER FOUR

"This is Doctor Peal, medical examiner for the county," Captain Wallace said as he and Murphy entered the examination room.

Peal, at the examination table, looked up at Murphy.

"Murphy, it's been a dog's age," Peal said. "What brings you to my examination room?"

Murphy nodded to the assassin on the table.

"Him," Murphy said.

Peal looked at the body. "Why?"

"Have you dug the bullet out?" Murphy said.

"It's in the jar on the desk over there."

"It came from my Colt," Murphy said.

"I see," Peal said.

"Well, let's have a look at the body," Murphy said.

Wallace looked at Murphy.

Murphy stood over the naked body of the

assassin. He checked his hands and then feet. "Soft hands and feet and manicured fingernails," he said. "Little muscle tone on his body."

"Meaning?" Wallace asked.

"The man never worked a hard day in his life," Murphy said. "So he was no farmer or carpenter, or at least not recently."

Murphy opened the assassin's mouth and examined his teeth. "How old would you say this man is, Peal?" he said.

"Between fifty-five and sixty, judging by the receding gums," Peal said.

"His teeth are in excellent condition," Murphy said.

"His teeth?" Wallace said.

"This kind of dental work is expensive," Murphy said. "So he was a man of some means. Where are his clothes and gun?"

"Over on the work table," Peal said.

Murphy, followed by Wallace and Peal, went to the work table. Murphy checked the shirt, tie, pants, socks, and shoes.

"The shirt is custom-made," Murphy said. "The suit was made by a tailor in Fort Smith, Arkansas, according to the label. Maybe, Captain Wallace, you can use the label to track the suit to the owner."

Wallace looked at Murphy.

Murphy picked up the shoulder holster

and removed the handgun. "Remington .32, double action," he said. "Can't be many of these around in double action anymore. Contact Remington with the serial number. They might be able to tell you if this man is the original owner."

Wallace nodded. "I shall do that," he said.

Murphy looked at Peal. "Do an autopsy," he said.

"Is that necessary?" Wallace said. "We know what killed him."

"Let Captain Wallace know what you find," Murphy said. "Captain Wallace, take me back to Grant."

Wallace looked at Murphy. He shrugged. "Sure," he said.

"Murphy, it appears we've been invited to the White House for dinner," Grant said when Murphy entered the room.

Murphy looked at Burke. "Your doing?"

"Arthur invited you. The general won't go unless you do," Burke said. "I sent my carriage back to tell the chef to set two extra plates."

"Where are the ladies?" Murphy asked.

"When I told them about dinner at the White House, they ran to the powder room to fix their hair and do whatever it is women do to make themselves presentable," Grant said.

"My carriage should have returned by now," Burke said. "I'll send someone to fetch the ladies."

"Where is Captain Wallace?" Grant asked Murphy.

"He went back to his office," Murphy said. "I gave him some things to think about."

"I can imagine," Grant said.

"Well, then, shall we go?" Burke said.

The private dining room table at the White house held twelve, but was set for just six.

"I was sorry to learn of the passing of your wife, Chester," Grant said. "We only met but once or twice at the formal balls, but she was a lovely woman."

"It was just one of those things," Arthur said. "She is gone, but she still lives in here."

Arthur tapped his chest.

Kai, looking very uncomfortable seated next to Murphy, glanced at Julia across the table. Julia gave Kai a small, reassuring smile.

From the soup and salad, to the main course of roasted lamb, to the dessert of warm apple pie with ice cream, the conversation around the table was light and frivolous.

When the last plates were being cleared away, Arthur said, "Ladies, will you excuse us for a few moments while we talk privately in my den?"

"I shall take Kai on a tour when you men discuss your business," Julia said.

In the den, brandy and cigars were served. Once the server left the room, Arthur said, "So soon after Garfield, the last thing this country needs is to lose Ulysses S. Grant. What do we know about the assassin?"

"Nothing except he said, 'The South shall rise again' before he attempted to shoot," Grant said.

"Klan?" Arthur said.

"I pray not, but you are probably right," Grant said.

Arthur looked at Murphy. "What's your opinion? You shot the man."

"The Klan is a strong possibility," Murphy said. "One I wouldn't rule out. However, I question why now, why the general? He lives mostly unprotected at his home and would make an easy target if the goal was to kill him."

"I think I have to agree with Murphy's assessment, Mr. President," Burke said.

"Well, the assassin is dead and can't speak, so where do we go from here?" Arthur said.

"Captain Wallace is handling the investigation," Burke said.

"I don't see this as an assignment for the Metro Police Department," Arthur said. "They haven't the federal resources for this type of work."

"Maybe if you paired them with the secret service?" Burke suggested.

"Arrange a meeting for the morning with Wallace and the service, and please be present," Arthur said.

Burke looked at Murphy.

"Murphy is continuing with me on the tour," Grant said.

"You're continuing?" Arthur said.

"I see no reason not to," Grant said. "There is a second lecture scheduled for noon tomorrow at the University of Virginia. After that, we go west a bit."

"Well, I'm sure you wish to take your ladies to your hotel," Arthur said. "Hopefully, I'll see you before you move on."

Burke stood with Murphy beside the carriage in front of the White House.

"Would you reconsider?" Burke asked.

Before Murphy could answer, Kai jumped

down from the back seat of the carriage and marched to Burke.

"How many more men does he have to kill for you before you're satisfied that enough blood has been spilled, Mr. Burke?" Kai said.

She linked Murphy's arm and guided him to the carriage.

Murphy untangled himself from Kai's long legs and quietly got out of bed. He stuffed his pipe, added some whiskey to a water glass, and took a chair on the balcony. The room was on the sixth floor, and the balcony faced the Potomac River. The moon was up, and its soft light shimmered on the softly moving waters.

Kai suddenly appeared next to Murphy and took the second chair.

"Are you troubled?" she asked.

"Not troubled, just thinking," Murphy said.

"About the man you killed today?"

"No. About his reasons," Murphy said.

"It has to be the Klan," Kai said. "You heard what he shouted. What else could it be but the Klan?"

"I mean his reasons for trying to kill Grant today. Why not last week, last year, or tomorrow?" Murphy said.

"Hatred isn't a good enough reason?" Kai said. "Many people have hated me in my life for no other reasons other than I'm part Navajo."

"Did anybody try to kill somebody else because they hated you?" Murphy asked.

"Do you mean target someone specifically?"

Murphy nodded.

"No."

"You are thinking of going back to work for Arthur for this, aren't you, you big, dumb son of a bitch," Kai said. "We should be planning our wedding instead of babysitting Grant as he gives his speeches."

"I'm not . . . I didn't say I was . . . all I said was I was thinking. Nothing more."

Kai took the glass from Murphy and took a sip. "Ghastly stuff," she said and gave Murphy back the glass. "You've given these Washington big shots far more than they've ever given you," Kai said. "You owe them nothing."

"Not entirely true," Murphy said. "If I hadn't been on assignment, we would have never met, and I would not be sleeping with a woman who leaves me breathless."

Kai sighed and took the glass from Murphy again. She gulped a sip and then stood. "Come on," she said and took Murphy's hand. "Let's see if I can leave you breath-less one more time."

Murphy stood.

Kai led him back into the room.

"That damn silk tongue of yours," she said as she dropped her nightgown.

CHAPTER FIVE

Three days after the attempt on Grant's life, President Chester A. Arthur was reading legislature at his desk in the Oval Office when there was a knock on the door. It opened and Burke entered.

"Good morning, William," Arthur said.

"I hate to disagree, Mr. President," Burke said.

"Go on," Arthur said.

Burke took a chair facing the desk.

"Captain Wallace is in the wings," Burke said.

Arthur sat back in his chair and sighed. "He has news. Is it good or bad?"

"Worse," Burke said. "Shall I tell you, or do you want to hear it directly from him?"

"Tell me," Arthur said.

"It appears the niece of the British Ambassador — she is a student at the university and attended Grant's lecture — has gone missing," Burke said.

"Missing?" Arthur said.

"She was last seen in the private balcony reserved for visiting dignitaries and such at the beginning of the lecture," Burke said. "She was reported missing this morning when she didn't return to the room she shares with another student."

"Are you saying that the niece of the British Ambassador has been kidnapped?" Arthur asked.

"No, I'm not saying that," Burke said. "Captain Wallace is saying that based upon the ransom note he received this morning."

Arthur silently stared at Burke for a moment.

"Send him in," Arthur finally said.

After Grant's lecture in Chicago, Murphy walked with Kai through the streets while Grant returned to the hotel with Julia.

They walked along the path on the shore of Lake Michigan.

"I can't wait to get out of this city," Kai said.

"You didn't like the museum?" Murphy asked.

"New York smelled bad, Washington and Philadelphia worse, but Chicago is like burning coal mixed with horse manure and slaughterhouses."

44

"Because it is. However, I can send you home for the rest of the tour," Murphy said. "It's only for a few more weeks anyway."

"No chance of that, Murphy," Kai said. "I see how these society ladies look at you like they are devouring you with their eyes."

"I never notice such things," Murphy said.

"And I shall stay by your side to see that you don't," Kai said. "Since we missed lunch, can we have an early dinner at the hotel?"

"I don't see why not," Murphy said.

Holding Kai's hand, Murphy led her back to the hotel.

"What society ladies?" Murphy said.

"Be quiet, or you will have a black eye for dessert," Kai said.

Arthur read the ransom note, which came in the form of a telegram.

The Cost For The Safe Return Of The Niece Of The British Ambassador Is Two Hundred And Fifty Thousand In Gold. Not Negotiable. Will Contact In 48 Hours For Your Reply.

Arthur lowered the telegram and looked at Wallace.

"How did this arrive?" Arthur asked.

"Courier from the Western Union office across the street from police headquarters," Wallace said.

"There is no place of origin for this telegram," Arthur said. "How is that possible?"

"I don't know, sir," Wallace said.

Arthur looked at Burke. "I haven't a clue, sir," Burke said.

"The United States does not pay blackmail," Arthur said.

"Mr. President, shall we get the British Ambassador?" Burke said.

"Yes, send for him at once," Arthur said. "And have my chef bring me a glass of cold milk. I feel a case of heartburn coming on."

Burke left the Oval Office.

"Mr. President, I realize this looks bad for us, but how do we even know they have the niece?" Wallace said.

"Is she missing?" Arthur said.

"Yes, but missing doesn't necessarily mean she's been kidnapped."

"The girl is missing for three days, and a ransom demand arrives today," Arthur said. "What do you think it means, Captain Wallace?"

"Sir, may I sit?" Wallace asked.

"By all means," Arthur said.

Wallace sat in a chair facing the desk.

"What I mean to say, Mr. President, is that maybe they are taking advantage of the fact that the girl is missing to make a phony

46

ransom demand," Wallace said.

"And how would they know she is missing when no one else knew, Captain?" Arthur said.

Burke returned and sat beside Wallace. "The British Ambassador will be here within the hour," he said.

Grant and Murphy sat in wicker chairs on the rear porch of the hotel and drank coffee. Grant smoked a cigar, Murphy his pipe.

"It's a funny thing, Murphy," Grant said. "At the moment I don't feel sick at all, and yet I know I will be dead within a year. To know one's own mortality is at hand serves only to expose the many unaccomplished tasks he will leave behind."

"General, you've accomplished more in one lifetime than a hundred other men combined," Murphy said.

"How will I be remembered, Murphy?" Grant said. "As a butcher or a savior?"

"Probably both, General," Murphy said.

"I think you are correct," Grant said. "Shall we have a snort?"

"Why not?"

Grant removed the flask from his pocket and added some bourbon to the coffee cups.

Alfred Turner the Third, the ambassador to

the United States from Great Britain, read the telegram and then set it upon Arthur's desk.

"You shall pay this at once," Turner said.

"A quarter of a million in gold?" Arthur said.

"America is a wealthy nation," Turner said. "As wealthy as Britain, or even more so at this point in time."

"And we have an unbreakable policy of not negotiating with terrorists or paying ransom demands," Arthur said.

"In that case, Great Britain's response will be the likes of eighteen fourteen," Turner said.

"Did you just threaten the United States of America?" Arthur asked.

"My niece is a British subject abroad in your country, and is entitled to the protection of your government," Turner said. "What would your response be in a reverse situation? You would expect Britain to do everything in its power to ensure her safe return. I promise you that it would be the case."

Arthur sighed heavily and sat back in his chair.

"William, can you contact treasury and . . ." Arthur said.

"I already did, sir," Burke said. "When I

left to hail the ambassador."

"The assassination attempt on Grant was a ploy, wasn't it?" Turner said. "A deception so they could kidnap my niece."

"It would appear so, Mr. Ambassador," Arthur said. "Although I doubt they would have minded if Grant was killed."

"When they contact you again, how will you handle the exchange?" Turner asked.

"That depends upon the where, then when, and the how," Arthur said.

"May I suggest the use of the secret service?" Burke said.

"Don't forget it happened in my jurisdiction," Wallace said.

"May I suggest a cooperative force of US and British Secret Service to handle the transaction?" Turner said. "The embassy has a full squad of her majesty's best men."

Arthur looked at Burke.

Burke nodded.

"Mr. Ambassador, may I suggest that you and I meet with our respective secret service and put together a task force?" Burke said.

"First thing tomorrow morning," Turner said.

"There is no more we can do tonight," Arthur said. "After your meeting in the morning, can you assemble the task force, and we'll all meet here. Agreed?"

After Wallace and Turner left the Oval Office, Arthur went to the small table against the wall that served as a bar, poured an ounce of whiskey into two glasses, and gave one to Burke.

"He's right about one thing," Arthur said. "This could fuel an international incident between our two countries."

Burke took a sip of whiskey and said, "Mr. President, maybe it would be a good idea to telegraph Murphy."

Arthur took his chair behind his desk. "And admit to that man I can't handle my own affairs?" he said. "He thinks I'm a fool as it is."

"It's an option, sir," Burke said. "One I wouldn't rule out."

"What can Murphy do that a team of six can't?" Arthur said.

Burke sipped his drink and said, "Don't sell Murphy short, Mr. President. He doesn't have to like you to die for you — or kill for you, for that matter."

"Let's try my way first," Arthur said.

"Very well," Burke said and placed his empty glass on the desk. "Good night, sir."

CHAPTER SIX

"What do you think of Minneapolis?" Murphy asked as he strolled with Kai by Lake Calhoun.

"Too crowded in the center of town, but out here is very nice," Kai said. "There is a beach with people swimming. Can we swim?"

"We'll need bathing suits," Murphy said.

"I see a store across the street that sells swim attire," Kai said.

Fifteen minutes later, Murphy wore his swimsuit in front of the store while he waited for Kai. His suit was basically a pair of shorts with a sleeveless top. He smoked his pipe while he waited.

When Kai finally emerged from the store, she carried her clothing in a paper sack. "I feel ridiculous in this," she said. "It's like wearing pajamas to swim."

"Maybe so, but it looks pretty damn good from where I stand," Murphy said. "Come on, there are lockers on the side of the store."

After locking up Kai's clothing, Murphy and Kai crossed the street to the lake.

"Want to try the water?" Murphy asked. "It can't be much colder than some of the streams we took baths in."

"Go ahead. I'm going to sit in the sun for a few minutes," Kai said.

"Okay," Murphy said.

He started walking to the water and Kai looked at him. She glanced about at some of the men on the beach. They appeared soft and pale. In comparison, Murphy seemed to be carved from aged wood.

As he neared the water, a young woman walking past seemingly tripped over nothing, and Murphy caught her before she hit the sand.

"How original," Kai said aloud.

Murphy helped the young woman up, and she giggled and blushed at him.

"Really, young lady," Kai said.

The young woman touched Murphy's shoulder and slowly lowered her hand to his arm.

Kai jumped up. "That's enough of that," she said and marched quickly to the water.

"Kai, I was just helping this young lady after she . . ." Murphy said.

"Yes, I saw," Kai said. She glared at the young woman. "Scoot. Go trip over nothing somewhere else."

The woman looked at Kai.

"Still here. Go, go, go," Kai said.

The woman turned and walked away.

Kai looked at Murphy. "And you," she said.

"And me, what?" Murphy said.

"Shut up. Nothing. Let's go for a swim," Kai said.

Seated at the conference table in the Oval Office were British Embassy Secret Service agents Walker, Heaton, and Edwards. They sat on one side with Turner.

On the opposite side of the table sat three men picked by Burke from the pool of Arthur's secret service agents: Hough, Vinton, and Nash.

Arthur sat at the head of the table.

"Mr. Ambassador, Mr. Burke, you are satisfied these six men can handle the job?" Arthur said.

"Soldiers of her majesty's secret service can handle any task before them," Turner said.

"Horse dung, Mr. Ambassador," Arthur said. "Have any of these three men been west of Virginia?"

"I don't see what that has to do with anything," Turner said.

"Chances are the kidnappers will put as much distance from Washington as possible," Burke said. "That means the west. Much of it still unpopulated and hard country. A perfect place to spring a trap."

"Do you mean to imply these people aren't sincere in their motives?" Turner said. "If we meet their demands, why wouldn't they return my niece?"

"Because these men are criminals," Burke said. "They already sacrificed one of their own to get what they want. What else are they capable of? I'll answer that. We don't know."

"I'm afraid I must disagree with you on one point," Turner said. "Had your man not been present, the assassin probably would have shot Grant and in the commotion would have gotten away. The outcome of my niece being kidnapped would be the same."

"That's a possibility," Arthur said. "But Burke's point is well taken. The west is no place for a tenderfoot."

"A what?" Turner said.

"A man who is inexperienced when it comes to an unfamiliar environment," Burke said. "We call them tenderfoots."

"Well, rest assured that my men can handle anything thrown at them," Turner said.

Arthur looked at Burke. "I assume your men are familiar with the west?"

"Quite," Burke said. "Hough is from Arizona. Vinton from New Mexico. Nash from Nebraska."

"Gentlemen, when we receive the next telegram, we shall meet and prepare a strategy based upon their demands," Arthur said. "Stay close to home and be prepared to act at a moment's notice."

Standing in water up to her neck, Kai lifted herself on her toes and kissed Murphy.

"I forgive you," Kai said.

"For?"

"I was having evil thoughts about you flirting with that young girl."

"You forgive me for your evil thoughts?" Murphy said. "And I wasn't flirting with anybody. She tripped."

"You are an idiot," Kai said. "Let's go back to the hotel. I feel like forgiving you again."

"Just don't trip."

"Shut up."

"What do you think, William?" Arthur

asked. "Do you think the man Murphy killed sacrificed himself for the cause, or was it just his bad luck Murphy was there?"

"If I had to guess, I would say he sacrificed himself for his cause," Burke said. "Maybe he didn't know Murphy was there, but after he shot Grant, he had to know he would be apprehended by men in the audience and held for the police."

"The cause being the resurrection of the Klan?" Arthur said.

"If you went by his words, I would agree," Burke said. "But as the man is dead and we can't interrogate him, we will never know the cause of his words."

"Was Murphy right to kill him?"

"Absolutely," Burke said. "The man would have shot Grant for sure otherwise."

There was a quiet knock on the door.

"Enter," Arthur said.

An aide entered the office with a report and set it on Arthur's desk. "From Doctor Peal, Mr. President."

"Thank you," Arthur said.

After the aide left, Arthur picked up the report.

"It's an autopsy on the man Murphy killed," he said.

"Murphy requested it," Burke said.

Arthur opened the report and read quickly.

"It says the man was dying of cancer," Arthur said.

Burke nodded. "The sacrificial lamb," he said. "Willing to die early for his cause."

"It appears so, Mr. Burke."

"I suspect that Murphy thought of this, and it's why he ordered the autopsy," Burke said.

"It appears so, Mr. Burke," Arthur said. "What is your opinion, William? Can that team of six handle such a task?"

"No," Burke said.

"That's plain enough," Arthur said. "Mind telling me why you feel such?"

"These men are good, probably the best both governments have to offer," Burke said. "They are well trained agents willing to give their lives to protect you and Ambassador Turner. What they are not is a Regulator. Do you know what a Regulator is, Mr. President? A Regulator is a killer of men. There is no other way to say it. And Murphy is the best Regulator this country has ever produced."

"Thank you for your opinion, William," Arthur said. "Before I resort to such tactics, we shall give the team the opportunity to do the job first."

"Understood, Mr. President," Burke said.

After making love, Murphy and Kai huddled under the covers and enjoyed a quiet moment together.

Finally, Kai said, "You need a best man."

"What?" Murphy asked.

"For the wedding," Kai said. "Your father has agreed to walk me down the aisle, but you need a best man to stand beside you."

"That would be Burke, I suppose."

"Did you ask him?"

"No, but . . ."

"Send him a telegram," Kai said. "Tell him we will be home in two weeks, and you'd like him to be the best man."

"We need a set date, don't we?" Murphy said.

"Your mother and I will handle that and other arrangements."

"My mother?"

"You remember your mother, the woman who gave you life?" Kai said.

"My father walks you down the aisle, my mother plans things, and Burke is the best man. What do I do?" Murphy said.

"You show up and say 'I do,' " Kai said. "That's what you do."

"Why wouldn't I?" Murphy asked.

Kai sat up. Her cheeks were suddenly

flushed and her eyes dark and stormy. "Burke is going to ask you to go back to work. We both know that," she said.

"We don't know anything of the kind," Murphy said.

"As soon as they mess up whatever it is they are planning, Burke will come calling on you, hat in hand," Kai said. "And you will ride off to kill or get killed. Where does that leave me?"

"A fairly well-off widow," Murphy said.

Kai glared at Murphy. Then she balled her right hand into a tight fist and punched Murphy in his right eye. "Don't you ever say that again," Kai said. "Ever."

Murphy touched his right eye with a finger. "I was just fooling about, Kai," he said.

"I spent many years with the Sioux and Navajo," Kai said. "I lost my husband because he was a lawman. I lost my children. I never thought I would find love again, so if you want to go get yourself killed, then go get yourself killed. Just don't test the Navajo in me. You won't like the results."

Murphy blinked tears out of his right eye. "I sure won't," he said.

Kai looked at Murphy. "Don't be a baby," she said. "We need to get dressed. The Grants are expecting us for dinner."

■ ■ ■ ■

Burke sat at his desk inside the White House, sipped whiskey, and thought about the men who kidnapped Turner's niece.

They had the upper hand. They would dictate terms. They would, in all likelihood, kill the agents sent to deliver the ransom money.

And most definitely kill the niece.

As he sipped whiskey, Burke thought about the motive of the men behind the kidnapping.

Was it really the Klan?

Or a scheme to get rich using the niece and the sacrificial lamb Murphy killed?

Sending the six agents was a mistake, but Arthur was the boss, and it was a mistake he would have to learn from.

Burke dreaded having to ask Murphy for help.

Burke knew it would come down to that.

He finished his drink and left the office.

After Murphy seated Kai at the dinner table, he sat across from Grant and Julia.

"Where did you get the black eye, Murphy?" Grant asked.

"We were discussing my returning to work

for Arthur, and Kai let me have a right hook as an answer," Murphy said.

Grant looked at Kai.

Julia Grant turned her head to hide her grin.

Kai looked at Murphy. "I told you not to be a baby," she said.

Grant cleared his throat. "Well, let's see what's on the menu," he said.

CHAPTER SEVEN

Burke handed Arthur the telegram.

Arthur read it twice before he set it aside.

"Why Utah?" Arthur said.

"I looked at a map," Burke said. "The region is part of the Colorado Plateau that spills over to the Utah-Arizona border. It's desolate, unpopulated, and the ideal location for a trap."

"Get the British Ambassador," Arthur said.

Alfred Turner studied the map on Arthur's desk.

"Why these coordinates?" Turner asked. "What's the significance?"

"For one thing, it's a totally desolate area," Burke said. "Peaks as high as a thousand feet, desert canyons. It's an ideal place to ambush somebody."

"Is that what you believe this to be, an ambush?" Turner asked.

"I do," Burke said.

Turner looked at Arthur.

"I can't say as I'm convinced of that just yet," Arthur said.

"And why is that?" Turner asked.

"If it's an ambush, they lose their ability to make a second demand for more money," Arthur said. "Are you familiar with the Brothers Grimm?"

"Yes, of course," Turner said.

"Well, in this case, your niece is the golden goose," Arthur said. "Kill the goose, and your gold supply dries up."

"Yes, I agree," Turner said. "Shall we assemble the men?"

"Let's do this in the conference room," Arthur said.

The six agents, Turner, Burke, and President Arthur stood over the conference table and studied the large map Burke provided.

"Before we proceed, I need to ask if any of your men wish to back out of this assignment," Arthur said.

None did.

"Any married men?" Arthur asked.

There were no married men in the group of six agents.

Arthur looked at Burke. "Proceed, Mr. Burke," he said.

"You've all read the telegram," Burke said. "Please examine the exact coordinates designated on the map."

All eyes went to the map.

"The railroad can take you as far as Blanding in Utah," Burke said. "In Blanding, you will be met by a patrol of army cavalry who will provide a covered wagon for you to transport the ransom. The wagon will be equipped with the latest model Gatling gun. You will each be provided with a long-range sniper rifle and ammunition. You may bring your own personal weapons, of course. Questions?"

"I've been to this valley," Hough said. "There are a thousand places to set up an ambush."

"I suspect that is the very reason the site was chosen," Burke said. "If you wish to back out of this assignment, now is the time to do so."

"Before any of you make that decision, let me tell you what I believe," Arthur said. "This is a test run to see if we will deliver the ransom. I believe more demands will follow before they release the ambassador's niece. The instructions are quite clear. Leave the ransom and return in twenty-four hours to pick up the niece. If they planned an ambush, I don't think they would have arranged it so. As to the location, what better place to pick up your ill-gotten gains than a desolate canyon days away from the nearest town."

"Well said, Mr. President," Turner said. "And I assure you that none of her majesty's secret service will ever retreat from their duty."

Arthur looked at Burke.

"It appears we have a team, Mr. President," Burke said.

"Very well," Arthur said. "I suggest all six of you study the map and route you will take by wagon until you see it in your sleep. Mr. Burke will make travel arrangements and secure expense money for the trip. I suggest you six men vote on who should be your squad leader. Now please excuse me. I have a long list of meetings scheduled."

After Arthur left, Burke said, "I've made arrangements for a private railroad car to take you directly to Blanding. If any man needs a horse, please come with me after this meeting."

Well after dark, Burke and Arthur shared a drink in the Oval Office.

"Am I doing the right thing, William?" Arthur asked. "Am I saving the life of a young girl and preventing an international incident, or am I sending six good men to their deaths?"

"We will know soon enough, Mr. President," Burke said. "There is nothing more we can do except to allow the team to do its job."

Arthur sighed openly.

"Another drink, William?" he said.

CHAPTER EIGHT

Burke and Turner stood on the platform at the Washington, DC, railroad yard and watched as the six men loaded their horses onto a large boxcar.

"I can only pray my niece is still alive and this mission will be successful," Turner said.

"I have the same feelings," Burke said.

The six secret service agents walked to Burke and Turner after their horses were loaded into the boxcar.

Hough, because he was somewhat familiar with the canyons, was selected as team leader.

"We are ready, sir," Hough said to Burke. "And don't worry, Mr. Ambassador, we are fully prepared to give our lives to save your niece."

"Godspeed to you all," Turner said. "And I pray it doesn't come to that."

"The train will run express through the night, and you will arrive in Blanding by morning," Burke said. "Telegraph me the moment you arrive."

"We will, sir," Hough said.

The six agents boarded the train. Burke and Turner watched as the train slowly rolled out of the yard.

"I hope my lads don't do anything to embarrass the queen," Turner said.

"They're good men, Ambassador," Burke said. "All six of them."

Turner sighed. "Shall we get a cup of tea?" he said.

The six agents sat in first-class seats in the lone car as it made its way south from Washington and into Virginia.

"A quarter of a million dollars is how much in English money?" Hough said.

"I'm not sure," Walker said. "I believe one pound is about four dollars and fifty cents American."

"Any way you look at it, it's a whole lot of money," Nash said.

The sliding door to the car opened and the conductor entered. "The dining car will be open for lunch at noon," he said. "There is one sleeping car with six bunks for those who wish to get some sleep. Dinner is served between six and seven p.m. Unfortunately, liquor is forbidden on this trip by orders of Mr. Burke. Are there any questions?"

"Is there a table where we can play some cards?" Nash asked. "We need something to do to pass the time."

"Mr. Burke anticipated the need for just such activity," the conductor said. "The gaming car is one car past the dining car. I'm sure you will find it satisfactory."

Hough stood up. "Let's go, boys," he said. "I don't fancy sitting around with nothing to do until morning."

Burke detested English tea, but he gracefully sipped a cup with Ambassador Turner in Turner's office at the British Embassy.

"I have to admit I am still baffled as to how they managed to send telegrams without a location of origin," Turner said.

"I imagine someone with extensive knowledge of how the telegraph operates could manage to send and receive telegrams without divulging a location," Burke said.

Turner picked up a round biscuit from the plate on his desk and took a small bite. "I suppose in today's modern world anything is possible," he said.

"Well, Mr. Turner, I'm expected back at the White House," Burke said. "I shall report any and all news to you as soon as I have some."

"Mr. Burke, my niece is but nineteen years old," Turner said.

"I know," Burke said.

At his desk, Burke read the complete file on Elizabeth Turner, the niece of Alfred Turner. Daughter of Albert Turner, a member of the British Parliament, she came to Washington two years ago to enroll in the university.

Burke looked at the photograph Turner provided. She was a tiny thing with blond hair and green eyes. She had excellent grades in London and superior grades in America.

She would turn twenty in four months.

Burke knew she would never see her twentieth birthday.

He knew the six men on the train were riding to their death.

He knew keeping the news from Elizabeth's father and the British government was a mistake, but Turner and Arthur insisted upon total secrecy.

Turner was probably worried his ambassadorship would be recalled.

Arthur was probably worried an international incident would cost him his reelection.

Both men were wrong in their course of action.

Oh, Burke knew they had to try and deliver the ransom and save Elizabeth, but it's what would follow that concerned him.

Arthur and Turner would in all likelihood want to use the army to track down the kidnappers.

Burke's opinion was that the army should never be used for law-enforcement purposes. The men weren't trained for it, and it wasn't their job to do so. To Burke, the army enforcing the law was too similar to a dictatorship.

Burke also knew he needed a backup plan for when the six agents failed in their mission.

He opened a desk drawer, removed the schedule for Grant's speaking tour, and read the dates.

Kai and Julia Grant sat in the dining car in the private train charted for Grant's speaking tour. There were just three more stops before the final engagement in San Francisco.

Each woman had a cup of tea.

"Hiram is very pleased you and Murphy are to be married," Julia said. "Murphy is like a son to Hiram. They share the bonds

71

of battle, and there is no stronger bond than that."

"We are both very happy that you and the general will be attending the wedding," Kai said.

Julia took a sip of tea and delicately set the cup down. "Something is troubling you, Kai. What is it?"

Kai sighed softly. "This business in Washington," she said. "Mr. Burke will show up to woo Murphy out of retirement. I feel it. I know it. I don't know what to do about it."

"There is nothing you can do about it, Kai," Julia said. "It is obvious to everyone how much Murphy loves you. But — and this is a very large but — men like Murphy and Hiram have a sense of duty they must and need to answer to. When that need arises, there is nothing you can do about it except support your man as well as possible."

"How did you handle it?" Kai asked.

"You put on a brave face and allow your man to do what he was born to do," Julia said. "In Hiram's case, it was his destiny to lead men into battle and help save the Union, and then later to become its president. In your case, when the need arises for Murphy to be Murphy, let him."

"Damn," Kai said.

Julia smiled. "I've said much worse many times," she said.

As the team of six agents ate lunch, Heaton said, "Tell me something, Hough. What is this canyon like?"

"Well, it's a very strange place, for sure," Hough said. "Strange and beautiful. Peaks as high as a thousand feet, red like clay and dry as an old bone."

"Do you think we are riding into an ambush as Mr. Burke believes?" Nash asked.

"I think President Arthur is correct in his determination," Hough said. "I think this is the first of more demands to follow. We are delivery boys making the delivery."

"Delivery boys with a Gatling gun," Nash said.

The group burst into laughter.

"Yeah, with a Gatling gun," Hough said.

Grant studied the chessboard while he puffed on a cigar. Then he slid his bishop across the board and put Murphy's king in check.

Murphy quietly puffed on his pipe.

"What's on your mind, Murphy?" Grant said. "I know it isn't chess."

Murphy looked up from the board. "This business back in Washington," he said.

"I figured," Grant said. "Well, what about it?"

"Arthur is handling it all wrong," Murphy said. "They will kill the girl and whoever is sent to deliver the ransom. It should be obvious, even to Arthur."

"Arthur is a politician who discovered what all who become president discover," Grant said. "Campaign speeches are one thing, governing is quite another. Rarely do the two overlap. Arthur is doing what he believes is best for the country, and that may not be what's best for the kidnapped girl."

"Kidnapped girls are disposable nowadays?" Murphy said.

"You know better than that," Grant said.

"What would you have done?" Murphy asked.

"I would have dispatched you immediately and told you not to come back until all involved were dead," Grant said.

Murphy slid a pawn to protect his king.

"But I'm not Chester Arthur," Grant said.

"Thank God for that," Murphy said.

Hough awoke in his bunk and sat up. The other five men were sound asleep. A lantern with the flame on low hung from a wax fixture and provided just enough light for him to read his pocket watch.

It was a little past two in the morning.

Hough left the sleeping car and entered the dining car. It was dark and empty, but he lit a match and ignited the wall lantern. There was a large icebox in the cooking area where he found a steel container of cold milk and filled a glass. He took it to a table to drink it and looked out at the blackness of night.

"I'm riding to my death," Hough said aloud. "And taking everyone along with me."

CHAPTER NINE

Hough drove the army wagon. Because of the excessive weight of the gold, Gatling gun, and supplies, the wagon required four horses to pull it. He left his horse with the army at their outpost just north of Blanding.

Vinton rode point about ten yards in front of the wagon. Nash and Walker road to the left and right. Heaton and Edwards rode ten yards to the rear.

The first night in the canyons, the sky was so clear they could see millions of stars overhead. The dry air was tainted with the smell of dust and yet smelled almost sweet at the same time.

Hough fell asleep looking at the stars. When it was his turn to stand guard, he saw three shooting stars, something he never saw in Washington.

Vinton turned his horse around and rode to the wagon.

"Let's noon," Vinton said. "Your horses look beat."

They rested the horses for two hours. Around a fire they ate a hot lunch and studied the maps provided by the army.

"According to the coordinates, we should reach this point in the valley by noon tomorrow," Hough said.

"I'm curious as to why that particular place was chosen as the drop-off point," Heaton said.

"Good cover, probably," Hough said.

"So you know this particular area?" Vinton asked.

"Before I joined the service, I spent five years as a cavalry officer," Hough said. "We had many patrols through the canyons rounding up stray renegades off various reservations. Unless you know the area really well, one canyon looks like another, so there must be a specific reason for these coordinates."

"I guess we'll find out soon enough," Vinton said.

Shortly before noon the following day, the team was riding through flat ground surrounded by majestic peaks that glowed red in the high sun.

Hough called for a brief rest.

"I know this area," he said. "Up ahead are narrow passes through steep canyon walls, some a quarter-mile deep."

"I'll scout ahead and have a look," Vinton said.

"Heaton, go with him," Hough said. "We'll rest our horses until you return."

Vinton and Heaton rode a thousand yards to the entrance of a narrow pass between two high peaks.

They dismounted and walked to a hand-written paper nailed to a wood post.

The sign read *Leave the gold five hundred feet into the pass. Return in 24 hours for the girl.*

"Let's ride in five hundred feet and check it out," Vinton said.

They rode approximately five hundred feet into the pass. It was about twenty feet wide, and the walls of the peaks topped out at close to a thousand feet high.

"They could close the front and back door on us, and we'd be trapped," Heaton said.

"We'd best report back," Vinton said.

Hough stopped the wagon at the entrance to the pass.

"We'll carry it in," he said.

The oversized metal box had four rings, one at each corner. Hough slid a six-foot-long metal bar through two rings on each side, and four men lifted the box from the wagon to the ground.

"Vinton, Heaton, you follow us with your Winchesters," Hough said. "The rest of us will carry the box."

Even with four men carrying the box, it took nearly thirty minutes to haul such a weight five hundred feet.

Once the box was in place, the men retreated to the wagon and horses.

"Our instructions are to return in twenty-four hours to pick up the girl," Hough said. "We'll retrace our path until dark, make camp, and return here for the girl at this time tomorrow."

After dark, around a campfire and a hot meal, the men discussed the plan for the following day.

"And what if there is no girl?" Nash asked. "What do we do then? Return to Washington with our tail between our legs?"

"We'd have no choice," Hough said. "But let's not get ahead of ourselves here. So far, the kidnappers have shown no signs they mean to harm the girl. They could have set a trap and ambushed us and didn't. I believe this is about the gold and nothing more."

"I think I agree with you, but I also believe we should take every precaution to safeguard ourselves," Walker said.

"I've been studying on that," Hough said.

At the pass, the men dismounted with their Winchesters in hand.

Hough removed the canvas cover on the wagon, exposing the Gatling gun.

"There's something in the pass," Nash said.

Hough used binoculars to zoom into the pass. "Why, it's a . . . sofa."

"A sofa?" Vinton said.

"There's someone lying on it," Hough said.

"Is it the girl?" Nash said.

"Her back is to us," Hough said. "Can't see her face."

"Well, let's do this," Heaton said. "We're wasting time talking."

Vinton, Walker, Nash, Heaton, and Edwards climbed aboard the wagon.

Walker took the reins. Hough stood behind the Gatling gun at the ready. Walker drove the wagon to within ten feet of the sofa.

"She's not moving," Walker said.

"I'll check. Keep your eyes open," Hough said.

Hough jumped down from the wagon and approached the sofa. He touched the figure and was surprised to discover it was a women's clothing store mannequin. He turned and looked at the men in the wagon.

"It's a dummy," Hough said.

From almost a thousand feet high, a dozen men with rifles appeared and immediately opened fire at the five men in the wagon.

Hough threw himself on the ground and covered his head with his hands.

The shooting lasted just seconds, but the echo inside the pass made it seem like minutes. When the last echo faded, Hough uncovered his head and slowly looked up. He wasn't shot, but the men in the wagon were all clearly dead.

At the sound of approaching horses, Hough stood up.

Two riders wearing Klan masks approached from each end of the pass.

"Take this to Washington," a rider said, and tossed a sealed envelope at Hough's feet. "Leave your wagon; take a horse and supplies and go."

"My men," Hough said.

"We'll see to them," a hooded rider said. "Now go."

Hough slowly walked past two of the hooded riders and out of the pass, where six additional hooded riders waited. The six riders watched Hough carefully as he mounted the largest horse that belonged to Heaton and rode away.

CHAPTER TEN

Burke and Arthur read the note given to Hough at the conference table in the Oval Office.

The price for the girl has just doubled. Await our next telegram.

"Well, you were right, William," Arthur said. "All I did was send those poor bastards to their death."

"Shall I get Turner?" Burke said.

"Yes, and have Agent Hough wait in the hallway until the ambassador arrives," Arthur said.

"My niece is dead, isn't she?" Turner said after he read the note.

"We don't know that for sure," Arthur said.

"They killed the others, didn't they?" Turner asked Hough.

"Yes," Hough said. "They left me alive to deliver this message."

"And now they want to extort more money in the guise that Elizabeth is still alive," Turner said.

"Ambassador, she may very well be alive. We just don't know," Arthur said.

Turner looked at Burke. "What is your opinion, Mr. Burke?"

"Your niece is dead," Burke said.

"Mr. President?" Turner said.

Arthur slowly nodded.

"I see," Turner said. "Well, I certainly can't abide paying these men any additional money for the privilege of murdering my niece and five brave souls."

"I agree with you, sir," Arthur said.

"Well then, what is to be done now?" Turner asked.

"Mr. Ambassador, allow me some time to think about my options," Arthur said.

Burke entered the private telegraph office in the basement of the White House. During normal business hours, two operators were on duty to handle the heavy traffic, but after eight in the evening, just one operator was all that was needed.

When Burke opened the door, the operator was reading a newspaper, drinking coffee, and eating a roast-beef sandwich.

"Mr. Burke, what brings you down here

so late?" the operator said.

"I need you to send a telegram to Ulysses Grant at this location," Burke said.

"President Grant?"

"Don't let Arthur hear you say that," Burke said. "I'll be waiting in my office for the reply."

The operator nodded. "Yes, sir," he said.

Grant and Julia were dressing for dinner when a hotel clerk knocked on their hotel door.

"Yes?" Grant said when he opened the door.

"Telegram, Mr. Grant," the operator said.

Grant took the sealed envelope. "Thank you."

Julia emerged from the bedroom and joined Grant in the living room of their suite. "What is it, dear?"

"Telegram," Grant said and sat on the sofa. He opened the envelope, removed the folded document, and read it carefully.

"What is it, Hiram?" Julia asked.

Grant handed her the telegram. She read it quickly. "What are you going to tell him?" she asked.

"I'm going to do as Arthur suggests and lie," Grant said.

Julia stared at Grant.

"I don't like it any more than you do," Grant said.

"So, Kai, what do you think of San Francisco?" Grant asked at the dining table in the hotel restaurant.

"It's a beautiful city, but I can't wait to return to the country where I feel more at home," Kai said.

"I have the same feeling myself," Grant said. "Tomorrow we take the morning train east, and we will be back in New York in five days."

"Just five days?" Kai asked.

"Private train," Grant said. "We stop only for water and coal. I would like to make a quick stop in DC, if that's permitted."

"It's your train, General," Murphy said. "May I ask why the stop?"

"Documentation," Grant said. "I've decided to add the incident in Washington to my memoirs, and I'd like to be as up-to-date as possible."

Kai looked at Julia across from her. Julia's face told Kai that Grant was lying to Murphy. Julia nodded ever so slightly to Kai, getting her message across in the way only women could communicate, a way lost on men.

Julia's eyes and tiny nod asked Kai to not

say a word.

Kai's eyes and tiny nod told Julia that she wouldn't.

"How long a layover do you figure?" Murphy asked.

"A couple of hours should do," Grant said.

"Well, that shouldn't hurt anything," Murphy said. "But, I will be glad to get home. My father is too old to be watching his place and mine, and we have a wedding to plan."

Grant picked up the menu. "Let's see what's good for dessert."

In their hotel room, as Murphy removed his jacket and tie, Kai came up behind him and hugged him tight around the waist.

"What brought this on?" Murphy asked.

"Take me to bed," Kai said.

"Who am I to argue?" Murphy said.

As Grant removed his jacket, Julia glared at him.

"What?" Grant asked.

"I would not want to be in your shoes when we reach Washington," Julia said.

"Murphy will be mad, but he will see and do what is necessary for the country," Grant said.

"I'm talking about Kai," Julia said. "Don't think for one second she doesn't know you lied to Murphy tonight, and I have a feeling she is one hornet you don't want to face when she is angry."

"Maybe you could talk to her and soothe —" Grant said.

Julia stormed off to the bedroom and slammed the door.

"Right." Grant sighed.

CHAPTER ELEVEN

A White House carriage met Grant, Murphy, Julia, and Kai at the platform in Washington.

Grant told the conductor to resupply the train for the ride to New York. The carriage driver took them directly to the White House, where they were met by Burke at the front steps.

"Mrs. Grant, Kai, it's nice to see you ladies again," Burke said. "I promise we won't keep the men too long."

"Oh, hell, William," Julia said. "Kai and I are attending this meeting, so you better just be quiet and lead the way."

Burke looked at Grant.

"Better do as she says, William," Grant said. "You ought to know better."

"Yes, sir," Burke said.

"Mrs. Grant, I'm afraid this is a closed meeting," Arthur said after Burke ushered her into the Oval Office.

"Oh, bullshit, Chester," Julia said. "It was my husband who was nearly killed, and now it is Murphy you will ask to clean up the mess you made by not listening to him in the first place, so don't tell me it's a closed meeting."

Arthur looked at Grant.

"Better listen to her, Chester," Grant said.

"Very well," Arthur said. "Does everybody remember Ambassador Turner?"

Murphy read the note brought back by Hough. "Mr. Hough, are you positive they wore Klan hoods and not just hoods make from pillow cases to hide their faces?"

"I'm positive," Hough said.

"And now they want double the amount in gold," Murphy said.

"Which the ambassador and I have agreed not to pay," Arthur said.

"My niece is dead. I realize that," Turner said. "And I haven't told my brother or anyone in England as yet. I'm hoping to avoid an international incident that would be bad for both our governments at all costs, you see."

"He was dying of cancer as you suspected," Burke said. "The sacrificial lamb for his cause."

90

"And what are you asking of me?" Murphy asked.

Arthur looked at Julia and Kai. "Ladies, please, you are making me very uncomfortable. I'll ask you to please wait outside."

"We will go get a cup of tea," Julia said. "But you do realize, Chester, that Hiram will tell me everything and Murphy will do the same with Kai?"

"Understood," Arthur said. "Mr. Hough, would you escort the ladies to the dining hall?"

After Julia and Kai left the Oval Office, Burke went to the conference table and filled cups with coffee and one with tea for Turner.

Murphy lifted a cup and took a sip. "You agreed not to pay the second ransom because the girl is dead. Mr. Ambassador, I don't see how you can keep this from the girl's father and your government any longer."

Burke lit a cigar. "Those men can't be allowed to get away with their crimes," he said. "The British government will demand we take a swift course of action."

"So take it," Murphy said.

"Murphy, what Chester and Burke are so badly trying to say is they want you to handle this," Grant said.

"I know that," Murphy said. "I want to hear them say it."

"God damn it to hell, Murphy," Arthur said. "What do you want me to do, beg you to come to the aid of your country?"

"These men are criminals," Turner said. "Worse, they are Klansmen. My niece demands justice in the name of God."

"God has nothing to do with any of this," Murphy said. "So why don't you just say it plain."

"Find those men," Burke said. "Bring them to justice. Alive, if possible. If not, then dead. But find them. Help two countries avoid a scandal and an international incident."

Murphy sipped from his coffee cup, and then set the cup down onto the table. "General Grant, we have a train waiting to take you home," he said.

"For God's sake, Murphy," Arthur said.

"I'm to be married soon," Murphy said. "And I do not want to be the one to have to tell her I'll be leaving home to ride the saddle for possibly months on end."

"I understand," Arthur said. "Maybe the army could find the men and bring them to justice."

"Good luck with the plan, Mr. President," Murphy said. "General, I'll get the ladies and wait for you at the train."

After Murphy left the Oval Office, Arthur looked at Burke and said, "Well, that didn't go as planned."

"Nothing ever does with Murphy," Burke said.

"That's it then," Turner said. "I shall have to inform my brother and my government of the loss of my niece."

"Before you do anything, wait to hear from me," Burke said. "Oh, I might be gone a while."

"You haven't said six words since we left Washington," Kai said.

"Where is Grant?" Murphy asked.

"In the dining car with Julia," Kai said. "The conductor asked if we wanted dinner, but you weren't listening."

Murphy looked at his pocket watch. "It's three hours to New York, I suppose a bite to eat couldn't hurt."

Murphy stood and took Kai's hand. Together they walked one car back to the dining car. Murphy slid the door open, and he led Kai into the car.

Burke sat at a table with Grant and Julia.

"Wait here," Murphy said.

He walked across the car to the table, reached down, grabbed Burke by his suit jacket, and yanked him out of the chair.

"Give me one good reason I don't open a window and toss you off this train," Murphy said.

"Don't be an ass, Murphy," Julia said. "Put William down this very instant."

Murphy released Burke's jacket.

Kai appeared at Murphy's side. "I somehow feel compelled to say, sit, give me your paw, and reward you with a treat," she said.

Julia, Grant, and Burke looked at Kai, and then all three burst into laughter.

"I'm not that bad," Murphy said.

"You don't think so?" Kai said.

"Sit down, Murphy," Grant said. "I just ordered steaks all around."

"Forget the international mess an incident like this will cause if it goes public here and in Great Britain," Burke said. "We just paid the Klan a quarter of a million in gold that they will use to finance a reconstruction of their vile beliefs. The war hasn't been over twenty years yet, that cannot happen. Those vile beliefs cannot be allowed to reach prominence once again."

"I'm really learning not to like you, Mr. Burke," Kai said. "But I have to agree with what you said. I don't want Murphy leaving me so close to our wedding, but it's his decision and his alone."

Murphy looked at Grant. "What would you do, General?"

"I would ask Julia to forgive me and then go do my duty," Grant said.

Murphy sighed. "Son of a bitch," he said.

"How soon can you return to Washington?" Burke said to Murphy.

"Son of a bitch," Murphy said.

Murphy and Burke sat on the front porch of Grant's home and sipped from glasses of bourbon. Burke smoked a cigar, Murphy his pipe.

"Full reinstatement as top secret service agent to the president," Burke said. "Name your terms and fee."

"No interference from Arthur, is my terms," Murphy said. "I'll take expense money before I leave, and you can wire my fee to Kai later on."

"When?"

"I want to return home for a day to gather what I'll need and then meet you in Washington," Murphy said. "Five days at most."

Burke extended his right hand. Murphy took Burke's hand in his and they shook.

"Would you really have thrown me off the train?" Burke asked.

"What do you think?" Murphy asked.

"I think I will catch the private train back to Washington," Burke said.

Grant and Murphy shook hands on the front porch while Kai and Julia hugged warmly.

"I feel as though I am losing a daughter," Julia said.

"Best get going, Murphy," Grant said. "That private train isn't going to wait all day."

Murphy and Kai descended the steps to Grant's carriage where a driver waited.

As the train left New York, Murphy looked at Kai. "I'm sorry," he said.

"Don't apologize for being yourself," Kai said. "I knew when we met things like this might and would happen."

"Thank you for being so understanding," Murphy said.

"Do you still wish to marry me?" Kai said.

"Yes, of course," Murphy said. "What kind of question is that?"

"My hand comes with a price," Kai said.

"Tell me what it is, and I'll meet the price," Murphy said.

"When the time comes," Kai said.

"But . . ." Murphy said.

Kai stood up. "Let's see if the private dining car is open. I could use some lunch."

Kai stood up. "Let's see if the private dining car is open. I could use some lunch."

CHAPTER TWELVE

In the kitchen at his farmhouse in Tennessee, Murphy field-stripped his Colt revolver, then cleaned and oiled it. Then he loaded it with fresh ammunition and placed two boxes of one hundred rounds per box into his leather saddlebags.

He thought about taking the Sharps rifle, but it was heavy and cumbersome, and he probably wouldn't need it. He settled for his prized Winchester 75. As with the Colt, Murphy field-stripped the Winchester, cleaned, oiled, and loaded it with fresh ammunition.

He packed two boxes of one hundred rounds of ammunition for the Winchester into the saddlebags.

Kai was taking a bath in the room he'd added to the house just for such a purpose. The large tub came from Chicago and boasted an indoor pump and drainage system that fed the used water into a tank underground that slowly leaked the water into the earth.

The last item he chose for the trip was a long, razor-sharp field knife he housed in a leather case attached to his holster.

Satisfied with his gear, Murphy stood and went to the bathroom.

The bathroom didn't have a window for privacy purposes. Kai had several candles burning and the soft, flickering light brought out the natural beauty of her face.

"I could use a bath myself," Murphy said.

"It could use more hot water," Kai said.

There was a small, flat woodstove in the corner where a large basin of hot water rested. Murphy lifted the basin by the handle and carefully added it to the tub.

Then he stripped and slowly lowered himself into the tub opposite Kai.

"I'm still waiting to hear your price," Murphy said.

"I know," Kai said.

"Well?"

"Well, your parents are going to be here for dinner in an hour," Kai said and handed Murphy a bar of soap. "Better get cleaned up."

Murphy and his father, Michael, sat on the porch after dinner. Each held a mug of coffee. Each smoked a pipe.

"Son, I understand your sense of duty, but there comes a time when a man has to have a sense of himself," Michael said. "You got a nice farm here and a nice woman to help you run things. We turn a nice profit in the whiskey business, and none of us is getting any younger. Time slips past us when we're off looking the other way, and in case you haven't realized it by now, time is the most precious commodity anyone had."

"I know all those things, Pa," Murphy said.

"Yeah, I know you do," Michael said. "How does your lady feel about this?"

"Dad, the older I get the less I understand women," Murphy said.

"When you reach my age, you'll realize you know nothing at all about them," Michael said. "Why don't you sweeten this coffee a bit?"

"I'm so sorry, Kai," Aideen said. "My son and his sense of duty. You can stay at our house until he returns."

"Thank you, but I have a plan of my own," Kai said.

"Really? What?" Aideen asked.

When Murphy entered the bedroom, he

found Kai packing a large satchel decorated in a pattern of flower petals.

"For God's sake, Kai, I can't carry a bag looking like that," Murphy said.

"I know," Kai said. "This bag is for me."

"What do you mean for you?" Murphy asked.

"This is my bag. It's for me," Kai said.

"I don't understand. Are you leaving me over this?"

Kai sighed. "You big buffoon, I am not leaving you. I am going with you."

"What the hell are you talking about?" Murphy said.

"The Navajo — and the Sioux, as well — set up a base of operations they always return to when they need to. Much like the army does with outposts," Kai said.

"I know all that," Murphy said. "What does that have to do with . . . ?"

"I still own my boarding house in Fort Smith," Kai said. "I will stay there. When you need a place to rest and resupply, I will be there waiting."

"If that isn't the damnedest thing I ever heard," Murphy said.

"I go to Fort Smith and set up a base for you, or you can find yourself a new woman to marry," Kai said. "Which will it be, Murphy?"

"I'll pack my bag," Murphy said.

Kai grinned to herself as she resumed packing her own bag.

A lone candle burned on the table beside Kai's side of the bed. As she brushed her long dark hair, she looked at Murphy, who was beside her.

"Now I know you love me," Kai said.

"Now you know? How?" Murphy said.

"You gave in to me rather than lose me," Kai said.

"My father is right. I know nothing about women," Murphy said.

Kai set the brush aside and blew out the candle. Then she rolled on top of Murphy.

"There is only one woman you need be concerned about knowing," Kai said in the dark.

After Murphy settled Boyle into the boxcar, he joined Kai in the first riding car. She was reading a newspaper and eating chocolates from a heart-shaped box.

"Where did you get that?" Murphy asked as he sat down next to her.

"At the newsstand in the ticket office," Kai said.

"I meant the chocolates."

"Your father gave them to me."

"My dad? My dad gave you a box of chocolates?"

"Yes, and they are really delicious."

"Can I have one?"

"Sure. Give me your paw first," Kai said.

After Murphy walked Boyle out of the boxcar, he met Kai at the end of the platform. He loaded the two satchels onto the saddle, and they walked off the platform to the wide, dirt street.

Judge Isaac Parker's courthouse loomed large in the background of Fort Smith.

"We'll stable Boyle on the way to your boarding house," Murphy said. "And then I'll drop in and see Judge Parker."

Kai's boarding house was a two-story home located on the fringe of town on a quiet, tree-lined street.

Yellow with pink trim and a large, fenced-in garden of flowers out front, the home usually had a full residence of twelve boarders.

"We should be in time for supper," Kai said as they walked up to the porch.

Mrs. Leary, a widow Kai had hired to run the house, stepped out on the porch and was surprised to see Kai and Murphy.

"Mrs. Leary," Kai said and greeted her

103

with a hug.

"When I got your telegram, I cleaned and made up your room," Mrs. Leary said. "Welcome home."

"When did you send a telegram?" Murphy asked.

"In Washington," Kai said.

"How did you . . . ?" Murphy said.

"We'll talk later," Kai said. "Right now, I thought you wanted to see the judge."

"What brings you back to Fort Smith, Murphy?" Judge Parker asked as he handed Murphy a glass of whiskey.

"Assignment for President Arthur," Murphy said. "At the moment it's classified. While I'm working, Kai will be staying in town at her boarding house."

"It will be good to see her again," Parker said. "How are things going between you two, if you don't mind an old friend asking?"

"Kai will be handwriting you an invitation to the wedding," Murphy said.

"Well, let's drink to that," Parker said.

Parker and Murphy sipped from their glasses.

"I'll be leaving for Washington in the morning, and I'll be back in a day or so," Murphy said. "I might need to poke around

Fort Smith and ask some questions. If that need arises, I'll let you know why."

"Anything I can do to help, just let me know," Parker said.

"I will."

"How does it feel to be back in your bed in your house?" Murphy asked as he removed his pants.

"I miss the farm," Kai said.

"We've only been gone one day," Murphy said.

"If you don't get killed, I will sell this house to Mrs. Leary," Kai said.

"And if I do get killed?" Murphy said as he got into bed beside Kai.

"I will never forgive you," Kai said.

Kai saw Murphy off at the railroad depot.

"I'll be back probably on the late train tomorrow," Murphy said.

Kai nodded.

"Stop by the livery and check on Boyle for me," Murphy said.

Kai nodded again.

She left him with a soft kiss and, as the train rolled away from the station, Kai sat on a bench.

"Do not let yourself get killed," she said aloud.

Burke slid a thick envelope across his desk to Murphy.

"Twenty thousand dollars for expenses," Burke said. "If you need more, ask and I'll wire it to the nearest bank."

"What about Captain Wallace?" Murphy said.

"He should be here within the hour," Burke said.

Murphy reached into the small travel bag he'd brought, removed a sealed bottle of his father's whiskey, and set it on the desk.

"I figured you might be out by now," Murphy said.

Burke opened a drawer and produced two shot glasses. Murphy opened the bottle and filled each shot glass.

"What has Arthur done about the second demand?" Murphy said.

"Exactly as we planned. Nothing."

"Well, here's to nothing then," Murphy said and tossed back his shot.

Three shots later, Wallace arrived at Burke's office with a large satchel.

"Mr. Murphy, I'm surprised to see you again," Wallace said.

Puffing on a long cigar, Burke said, "As of

this moment and going forward, you are never to speak of this visit to my office. Is that clear, Captain Wallace?"

"Something tells me I'm better off not knowing anyway," Wallace said.

"Put the bag down," Murphy said.

Wallace set the satchel on the floor.

"What did you find out about the Remington pistol?" Murphy said.

"Nothing. The man who purchased it died about five years ago," Wallace said. "It's unknown how it fell into the assassin's hands."

"The photograph of the assassin?" Murphy said.

"In my report."

"You can go," Murphy said.

Wallace looked at Murphy.

"I wasn't asking," Murphy said.

Wallace blinked a few times and then left the office.

Burke grinned. "Let's go see the president," he said.

Murphy read the second telegram in the Oval Office.

"They want five hundred thousand in gold this time," Arthur said. "Once I reply and agree, they will telegraph with a new location."

"You realize they will kill whoever you send to deliver the ransom?" Murphy said.

Arthur nodded.

"How can they send telegrams without a location?" Burke asked.

"Ever see a portable railroad telegraph box?" Murphy asked.

Burke shook his head.

"It has a hook," Murphy said. "You hang the hook over any telegraph line. It draws power to the box, and you can send and receive messages from anywhere. In an emergency, a conductor can find a telegraph line and tap into it."

"Where can you buy such a box?" Arthur asked.

"You don't," Murphy said. "You'd have to steal one."

"About a reply?" Chester said.

"Tell them to go to hell," Murphy said. "I see no reason to pay them to commit murder, do you?"

"No, I don't," Arthur said.

"What does Turner say at this point?" Murphy asked.

"He agrees with us on a course of action and has yet to inform his brother or the British government of the incident," Arthur said.

"Do you have my papers ready?" Murphy asked.

Arthur slid open a drawer, produced an envelope, and handed it to Murphy.

"I'll be in touch through Burke," Murphy said.

Arthur sighed loudly and said, "I hope to God we are doing the right thing."

Walking back to Burke's office, Agent Hough caught up to Burke and Murphy.

"Hello, Mr. Burke," Hough said. "Mr. Murphy, I was wondering if I may have a word with you in private."

"I'll be in my office," Burke said.

After Burke walked away, Murphy said, "What is it, Hough?"

"I would like to work with you," Hough said. "I know you will be doing something about the ambassador's niece, and I would like to work with you on that."

"No," Murphy said and turned and walked away.

"Wait. Mr. Murphy, please," Hough said.

Murphy paused and turned.

"Just no?" Hough said. "May I ask why?"

"You're not good enough, and I don't feel like having to bury you somewhere out west in an unmarked grave," Murphy said.

"What are you basing your opinion of me

on?" Hough asked. "We don't even know each other."

"You led your men into a trap you should have been fully aware of," Murphy said. "You might be a decent-enough agent to protect the president, but you're not good enough for the job at hand."

Murphy turned, walked away from Hough, and entered Burke's office.

"I'll be off now," Murphy said.

"Where are you staying the night?" Burke asked.

"The Carter Hotel near the railroad station."

Burke filled the empty shot glasses on his desk with bourbon. "One for the road," he said.

In his hotel room, Murphy inspected the assassin's clothing, shoes, and revolver. He ate a light supper while he read Wallace's report on the weapon.

The .32 caliber revolver was made eight years ago and delivered to a gun store in Dallas, where it was purchased, according to the serial numbers, by a man named Thomas Anderson, a local businessman. He died five years earlier of natural causes.

Murphy took a small notebook out of his traveling bag and made notes in pencil

Remington .32. Dallas.

Clothing. Fort Smith.

Medical records of assassin?

Murphy picked up the photograph taken of the assassin. It was a close-up of his face. In death his eyes were closed, but they'd be recognizable to any who knew the man.

Murphy set the photograph aside and picked up the pencil.

Connection to Klan?

Connection to ambassador's niece and kidnappers?

Murphy closed the notebook and finished his light supper. He reached into the overnight satchel for the bottle of his father's whiskey, broke the seal, and filled a small water glass. Then he lit his pipe and sat and thought for a while.

The niece was dead, of that he had no doubt. Her murder could spark a harsh international incident between two powerful countries that were engaged in economic trade beneficial to all.

He opened the notebook again.

Is the Klan involved or was the assassin acting on his own when he said "The South shall rise again"?

Murphy puffed on his pipe until the last bit of tobacco was spent. Then he lowered the flame on the oil lamp, flipped down the covers on the bed, and settled in for a night's sleep.

Just before he drifted off, Murphy sat up, returned to the desk, and increased the flame on the lamp.

He picked up the pencil, opened the notebook, and wrote, *Kidnappers possible Confederate officers during the war.*

Burke saw Murphy off at the railroad station.

"Agent Hough stopped by my office this morning," Burke said. "He told me you said he wasn't good enough for this mission."

"He isn't," Murphy said.

"He thinks you blame him for the incident at the pass."

"He blames himself," Murphy said. "Look, maybe he'd take a bullet for Arthur, I don't know. But I haven't the time or the inclination to partner with a man I'd have to babysit out of one eye and watch my back out of the other."

"I understand," Burke said. "Wire me with progress reports."

"Let me know what the response is after the kidnappers receive Arthur's rejection," Murphy said.

As Murphy stepped onto the train, Burke said, "He resigned this morning. Hough."

"Too bad, but probably for the best," Murphy said.

CHAPTER THIRTEEN

Kai sipped cold milk from a tall glass as Murphy ate a bowl of beef stew. The rest of the boarding house was dark and quiet, as it was after ten in the evening.

"How long will you be in Fort Smith?" Kai asked.

"A few days at least," Murphy said. "After that I'll head to Dallas. Then I don't know."

"I was thinking maybe we could . . ." Kai said and paused.

Murphy looked at Kai. "What?"

"Nothing," Kai said. "I'll tell you later. I'm tired and want to go to bed."

"Okay, I'll be up as soon as I finish eating," Murphy said.

Kai rolled off Murphy and waited to catch her breath.

"Women believe the best time to ask her man for something is after she makes love to him and he's satisfied," she said.

"Women say that?" Murphy said.

"They say that after lovemaking, a man is at his weakest and is most likely to say yes to what you want," Kai said.

"They say that?"

"Women say a lot of things when men aren't listening."

"I have the feeling you are leading up to something," Murphy said.

"I loved my first husband, but I could bend his will like a soggy noodle," Kai said. "I don't think I could budge you unless you really wanted to be budged."

"Hold that thought a moment," Murphy said. "I'd like to ask you something. As long as we're in Fort Smith, why not ask Judge Parker to marry us before I leave? We can have a church ceremony when we get home later on."

Kai sat up in bed and turned up the flame on the oil lamp. "Did you . . . how did you know what . . . you knew what I was going to say, didn't you?"

"I had an idea," Murphy admitted.

"So you let me butter you up and give you all that good loving knowing I was trying to soften you up and take advantage of you in a moment of weakness?" Kai said.

"I guess it was a bad idea," Murphy said.

"I didn't say that," Kai said.

"Well, what are you saying?" Murphy asked.

Kai sighed. "It's a good idea," she said. "We'll see the judge in the morning."

She reached over and extinguished the lantern.

"I could use a bit more buttering up," Murphy said in the dark.

Kai placed her head on his chest. "Go to sleep," she said. "We have plenty of time for churning butter."

"That's a fine idea, Kai," Parker said. "I'd be pleased to marry you and Murphy. Where is he?"

"He's talking to some shopkeepers in town," Kai said. "He said he would be in to talk to you later today."

"In the meantime, stop by the court clerk's office and pick up the paperwork necessary for me to perform the ceremony," Parker said.

"I will. Thank you."

"I'm very happy for you, Kai," Parker said. "Murphy is a lucky man."

"Thank you, Judge," Kai said.

Murphy found Bryant's Haberdashery on Main Street in the center of town. He carried the small satchel into the store and waited by the counter for a man to finish waiting on a customer.

The customer left, and the man went behind the counter.

"May I help you, sir?"

"I'm looking for the owner or the tailor," Murphy said.

"That would be me, Jeb Bryant."

"The owner or the tailor?" Murphy asked.

"One and the same," Bryant said.

Murphy set the satchel on the counter, opened it, and removed the suit jacket. "Did you make this suit?" he asked.

Bryant looked at the suit and then at Murphy. "I'm not in the habit of revealing personal information to strangers," he said.

Murphy removed his wallet from his jacket pocket and showed his identification to Bryant.

"Secret service?" Bryant said. "Is the president coming to Fort Smith?"

"No. About this suit, did you make it?" Murphy said.

Bryant inspected the jacket carefully. "It's my label and my stitching. It's my work. Why do you ask?"

"Who did you make this suit for?" Murphy said.

"Mr. Murphy, is it? I make a lot of suits for many men in town and far away as

Texas. I have no idea who I made this suit for unless you have a name."

Murphy removed the photograph and set it on the counter. "This man was wearing your suit," he said. "Recognize him?"

Bryant picked up the photograph. "Is he . . . dead?"

"Yes. Do you recognize him?"

Bryant nodded.

"Do you keep records?" Murphy asked.

"Yes. How did he die?"

"That's classified. Get the records please."

"I'll close the shop, and we can go to my office," Bryant said.

Murphy sat behind Bryant's desk and read his logbook.

"Are you sure this is the man you made the suit for?" Murphy asked.

"I'm sure," Bryant said.

"What can you tell me about him?" Murphy said.

"Very little I'm afraid," Bryant said. "As you can see from the entry, I made the suit about a year ago. He said he was in town on business. I fitted him, and he returned two weeks later and picked it up."

"Did he say what his business was in Fort Smith?" Murphy asked.

"No, and I didn't ask," Bryant said. "I

have a policy of minding my own business."

Murphy copied all the information into his notebook and then said, "Do you remember if he was armed?"

"Armed? I don't believe he was," Bryant said. "Is that important?"

"Thank you for your time, Mr. Bryant," Murphy said.

Not far from Bryant's Haberdashery, Murphy entered a small restaurant and ordered a cup of coffee. He sat at a small table beside a window and read his notes.

Jonas Jessup, the assassin Murphy killed, gave his residence as Dallas, Texas. He stood five-foot-eight-inches tall, according to Bryant's precise measurements for the fitted suit.

He wasn't armed, but most men in Fort Smith weren't armed these days. He could have left his firearm in his hotel room.

The Remington .32 was originally shipped and sold in Dallas.

He would go to Dallas as planned.

Murphy left the restaurant and walked to the courthouse.

Judge Parker was in his office when Murphy was escorted in by a deputy.

"Murphy, Kai was just here no more than

an hour ago," Parker said.

"I know," Murphy said. "About getting married."

"Kai is a fine woman," Parker said. "It pleases me to no end to see her so happy."

"Thank you, Judge," Murphy said. "I'm here on another matter at the moment. My business in Fort Smith."

"Oh?"

Murphy reached into the satchel, produced the photograph of Jessup, and handed it to Parker.

"His name is Jonas Jessup, a businessman from Dallas," Murphy said. "Have you ever seen him before?"

"Can't say as I have," Parker said. "What happened to him?"

"I shot him through the heart," Murphy said.

Parker lowered the photograph and looked at Murphy.

"He was attempting to shoot General Grant," Murphy said.

"I see," Parker said.

"He shouted 'The South shall rise again' just as he was about to pull the trigger," Murphy said. "A year ago he had a suit made at Bryant's Haberdashery. That's the suit he wore the day I shot him."

"I see," Parker said.

"Bryant recorded Jessup was from Dallas," Murphy said. "I'll be going there tomorrow."

"What about Kai?"

"She'll stay here in Fort Smith until I return," Murphy said. "Judge, has there been any Klan activity in town at all, recently or during the past few years?"

"Not since Grant gave me my appointment back in seventy-five," Parker said. "I made it a point to drive such scum out of Fort Smith."

"What about underground activity?" Murphy asked.

"There is always the possibility of that, but I'm sure I would have gotten wind of such activities," Parker said.

"About marrying us, when can you do it?"

"As soon as you fill out the court documents and bring them in," Parker said.

Kai and Murphy sat on chairs on the porch and filled out the required documents needed for them to be married by Judge Parker.

The documents needed to be completed in ink. Kai used Murphy's pen and dipped it into a bottle of ink and filled out all appropriate lines.

Kai watched as Murphy filled out his

parts. "You need to put down more than just Murphy," she said.

"Judge Parker won't . . ." Murphy said.

"Marry us without your complete name," Kai said.

Murphy looked at her and saw her sly grin.

"You're enjoying this, aren't you?" he said.

"Blame your parents for your name, not me," Kai said.

Murphy stared at the documents.

"Well, go on," Kai said.

As Murphy wrote his full name, Kai burst out laughing.

"It isn't that funny," he said.

"Yes," Kai said with tears in her eyes. "It is."

The Fort Smith General Store carried a selection of wedding bags. Kai and Murphy looked at the various rings and Kai said, "That plain one for me."

The clerk removed it from a sleeve of rings and Kai tried it on.

"Now you pick yours," Kai said to Murphy.

"Men don't wear rings, Kai," Murphy said.

"My man does. Pick," Kai said.

"Kai . . ."

"Pick."

Murphy looked at the clerk. "What do you have for men's rings?"

"Plain basic gold bands," the clerk said. "You're a rather large man. I'd better measure your finger."

The clerk reached under the counter for a thin board. Holes with numbers printed under each hole represented a ring size. Fourteen was the largest. Murphy's finger wouldn't fit into the size-fourteen hole.

"I've never seen so large a finger," the clerk said. "I'll have to resize a ring to fit you, sir."

"How long will that take?" Kai asked.

"I'd have to send the ring to Little Rock where a jeweler does that kind of work," the clerk said. "It will be at least a week. I'm sorry."

"Send it to Little Rock," Kai said. "I'll pick it up in a week."

"And your ring?" the clerk said.

"I'll take it now, thank you," Kai said.

As they walked to the courthouse, Murphy said, "I'm sorry about the ring, Kai."

"I'll hold it for you," Kai said.

They passed a tobacco store and Kai paused. "Be right back," she said and dashed into the store.

"Kai, women don't go into . . . ." Murphy said.

He stood in front of the window as Kai spoke to a clerk behind the counter. She exited a few moments later and handed Murphy a large cigar. "It came from the island of Cuba," she said and handed Murphy the cigar.

"Is this for after the ceremony?" Murphy said.

"If you wish," Kai said. "But the band around the cigar will come in handy, don't you think?"

Judge Parker read the marriage documents and then looked up from behind his desk at Murphy.

"Is that your real name?" Parker asked with a grin.

"Who would make up a name like that?" Murphy snarled.

"Okay, don't get hot," Parker said. "I'll send for a witness. Have you a ring for Kai?"

"We both have rings," Kai said.

Parker looked at Murphy. "Both, huh?"

Kai placed the small ring box on Parker's desk and removed the lid.

"Kai, one of those is a cigar band," Parker said.

"They didn't have a ring large enough to

fit him," Kai said.

"Oh, well, why the hell not?" Parker said.

With arms linked, Murphy and Kai strolled back to her boarding house.

"I'll be leaving for Dallas in the morning," Murphy said.

"Married one day and already fleeing," Kai said.

"It should only be for a few days," Murphy said.

"We still have the whole afternoon to do something," Kai said.

"What did you have in mind?" Murphy said.

As Murphy spread the blanket, he said, "When you said we had the whole afternoon, I thought you had something else in mind."

"I know what you thought," Kai said as she placed the picnic basket on the blanket.

They were in a field of wildflowers about five miles east of Fort Smith.

Kai sat and opened the basket. "We have fried chicken, fruit, a small pie, a bottle of champagne, and I brought a coffee pot, in case you want some coffee," she said. "Open the bottle and we'll drink a toast."

Murphy removed the wrapper from the

bottle, dug out the cork, and filled the two champagne glasses Kai removed from the basket.

They linked arms.

"To us," Murphy said.

"To us," Kai said.

They sipped and kissed.

"Grant loves this stuff," Murphy said. "I once watched him drink three bottles at a banquet, and he didn't so much as blink."

Kai sipped from her glass and then looked at Murphy. "There is something I want to ask," she said.

"Ask," Murphy said.

"Last year you told me the story of why you went to war," Kai said. "That you hated being a farmer and used the war as a means to escape the plow."

"That was a long time ago," Murphy said. "I was young and foolish."

"After this job, when we return to the farm?"

"Things are different now, Kai," Murphy said. "I have a dozen hands who plant corn and see to the harvest. The corn goes to my father's distillery, of which I'm half-owner. We don't even need to be there."

"Then where do we need to be?" Kai asked.

"I was hoping to bring this up at a later

date," Murphy said. "But I was thinking of taking another shot at being a congress-man."

"In Washington?"

"That's where Congress is," Murphy said.

"And what do I do?"

"Anything you want," Murphy said. "When Congress is not in session, we'll spend time at the farm."

"And will the society women in Washington accept a quarter-Navajo in their little sewing circles?" Kai asked.

"Do you know who John Menard is?" Murphy asked.

"No."

"He was elected to Congress in eighteen sixty-eight," Murphy said. "A black man, just three years after the war. I wouldn't worry about what the hags on the Hill think."

"Hags on the Hill, is it," Kai said. "I see you are just as smooth a talker as a congress-man as you are a lawman."

"Soon to be ex-lawman," Murphy said.

"I will drink to that," Kai said and tossed back her champagne.

"What do you say we take off our clothes and go swimming under this here blanket?" Murphy asked.

"Such a smooth talker, you. How could I

say no?" Kai said.

After loading Boyle on the boxcar, Murphy walked to Kai, who waited on the station platform.

"I'll wire you from Dallas when I'm coming home," Murphy said. "I don't expect to be too long."

Kai nodded. "I told you once before, I'll make you a good wife, but a poor widow."

CHAPTER FOURTEEN

The ride from Fort Smith was long and boring. Murphy tried to occupy his thoughts with the events at hand, but his mind kept slipping back to Kai's words.

It was true he'd hated farming before the war broke out. His father's place wasn't much better, as he just got his start in the whiskey-making business. The work was brutal and endless.

Sunup to sundown behind a plow, clearing the fields of rocks to ready it for planting. He cleared so many large rocks, he built a wall standing four feet high and stretched a hundred yards or more using the rocks.

The war beckoned him, and he answered the call to duty.

The truth was the war was a welcome relief from the farm. Every day in battle, no matter how bloody and gruesome, was better than being behind the plow.

If he survived the war, Murphy planned

to return home and pick up the plow again. He never figured army deserters would attack the farm and murder his wife and child.

For fifteen years since, he'd carried the guilt of deserting his family to escape the farm as if he were carrying a sack of bricks.

The guilt often wore him down right to the bone.

Now he had a second chance at life with Kai, and here he was riding off again and leaving her behind.

Murphy took out his pipe, filled the bowl with fresh tobacco, struck a match, and puffed smoke.

A conductor punching tickets entered the car. Murphy handed him his ticket.

"What time is the restaurant car open?" Murphy asked.

"Ten minutes," the conductor said.

Murphy nursed a third cup of coffee and second bowl on his pipe as he sat at a window table in the dining car.

Scenery raced by at fifty-five miles an hour, a dizzying speed.

He opened his notebook and removed a pencil from a pocket.

He knew who the assassin was now. He knew Jonas Jessup had been dying of cancer. What he didn't know was Jessup's connection to the kidnapping and his connection to the Klan, if any at all.

What did Jessup do for a living?

He is too old to have served in the war as a soldier. Did he serve in another capacity for the South?

How did Jessup gain possession of the Remington .32?

Knowing he was dying of cancer, did Jessup plan on being killed after he shot Grant?

Murphy set the pencil aside and finished his coffee. Several tables in the car were occupied with diners. He waved to the server behind the counter.

"What have you got in the way of food?" Murphy asked.

"Beef stew, steak, baked chicken, and chuck-wagon stew," the server said.

"I'll have a bowl of the chuck-wagon stew with bread and another cup of coffee," Murphy said.

"Right away," the server said.

Murphy opened his notebook and jotted another note.

If not the Klan, who?

Late in the afternoon, Murphy led Boyle from the boxcar to the dusty street at the railroad depot.

Dallas was a sprawling town of about

fifteen thousand people that relied heavily upon the railroad and trade for its livelihood.

As he walked Boyle from the depot into town, few horses with riders were visible. There were mostly wagons and carriages.

Men on the streets wore fine suits. Women dressed in fashionable gowns and skirts. Few, if any, cowboys were visible.

Firearms weren't banned in Dallas, but Murphy didn't spot one man sporting a holster and gun.

As they neared Main Street, Murphy patted Boyle's neck and said, "Don't worry, boy, we'll go for a run soon enough."

Murphy walked Boyle along Main Street until he reached the office of the United States Marshal. He tied Boyle to the post on the street, stepped up onto the wood sidewalk, and opened the office door.

Marshal Rourke sat behind his desk, writing in a logbook. He looked up when the door opened.

"Murphy," Rourke said. "What brings you back to Dallas?"

"Is Sheriff McCoy in town?" Murphy asked.

"In his office, last I saw of him," Rourke said.

"Maybe you could join me for dinner at

the Hotel Dallas in about an hour?" Murphy said.

"Official or just for the company?" Rourke asked.

"Both," Murphy said.

The Hotel Dallas had its own livery. After Murphy set Boyle up for the night, he went to his room to wash up and change his shirt.

He met Rourke and McCoy in the dining room shortly after seven p.m.

"Good to see you again, Murphy," McCoy said.

"As I recall, they serve a real Texas steak here," Murphy said as he took a chair. "Don't be shy in ordering. I'm on expense account."

After steaks were ordered, Rourke said, "Well, let's get to it."

"Ever hear of a man named Jonas Jessup?" Murphy asked.

"I expect most people in town know of him," McCoy said.

"What can you tell me about him?" Murphy asked.

"Before the war he was a prosperous businessman in town," McCoy said. "Came here before the war and opened a hardware store. I wasn't yet a deputy then, but as I recall, he sold a lot of merchandise to the

Confederate Army. After the war, he lost everything."

"Where did he live?" Murphy said.

"A small spread about ten miles east of town," McCoy said. "It belongs to his son, but he lives there most of the time."

"Did he belong to the Klan?" Murphy asked.

"We didn't see much Klan activity after the war, but it wouldn't surprise me none," McCoy said. "He hated the freed slaves with a passion. Now, what's this about?"

"About a month or so ago, he tried to shoot General Grant at a speaking engagement," Murphy said.

"Jesus," Rourke said. "What happened?"

"I had no choice but to kill him," Murphy said. "He shouted 'The South shall rise again' as he attempted to shoot Grant."

"Like I said, it doesn't surprise me none, given how much he hated freed slaves and blacks in general," McCoy said.

"When was he seen last in town?" Murphy said.

"I can't say," McCoy said. "Dallas isn't exactly a small town anymore."

"His son, Carsten, might be able to give you more information," Rourke said.

"I'll take a ride and see him tomorrow," Murphy said.

"If I have nothing pressing, I'll go with you," Rourke said.

The waiter rolled a cart to the table with three plates.

"How many doctors in town?" Murphy asked.

"Five," McCoy said.

"After we eat, I'd like to make some house calls," Murphy said.

Doctor Hayward, a man in his early sixties, was in bed when Murphy and Rourke knocked on the front door of his home.

Once Hayward lit a lantern and opened the door, he looked at Rourke and said, "Marshal, is somebody ill or hurt?"

"Doc, this is Murphy," Rourke said. "He's a federal agent, and he needs to ask you a few questions."

"Now? It's ten o'clock at night," Hayward said.

"It's important, Doctor," Murphy said. "We've seen three other doctors tonight looking for information about Jonas Jessup."

"Jonas? What of him?" Hayward said.

"So he was your patient?" Murphy said.

"He was."

"Invite us in for a drink," Murphy said.

Hayward looked up at Murphy.

"Doc, I don't think that was a question,"

Rourke said.

Hayward took a small sip of whiskey as he looked at Murphy.

"I can't say as I'm surprised," Hayward said. "Jonas Jessup was a man full of hate and bitterness if I ever saw one."

"You knew he was dying of cancer?" Murphy said.

Hayward nodded. "He had a cancer deep down in his back," he said. "There was nothing anyone could do. He would have to be gutted like a fish."

"How much time did he have?" Murphy asked.

"Six months. Less. More. It's hard to say how fast his cancer would spread," Hayward said.

"Did he ever speak of the Klan or anything like that?" Murphy asked.

"Like I said, he was full of hate," Hayward said. "I know he was involved with the Klan after the war, but not to what extent."

"Thank you, Doctor," Murphy said. "And thank you for the drink."

Murphy sat in a chair opposite Rourke's desk and sipped whiskey from a glass.

"I'll be going with you in the morning to see Jessup's son," Rourke said.

"What is his name again?"

"Carsten."

"Is he like his father?"

"In some ways," Rourke said. "He's not interested in the Klan, I can tell you that much."

"How do you know?"

"He has a hundred and sixty acres and employs just one hand, a black man named Luke," Rourke said.

Murphy tossed back the whiskey and set the glass on the desk.

"What time does the telegraph office open?" Murphy asked.

"Eight sharp."

"I'll see you for breakfast at seven-thirty," Murphy said.

CHAPTER FIFTEEN

After breakfast in the hotel dining room, Murphy and Rourke walked several blocks to the telegraph office.

"Good morning, Wilson," Rourke said as he and Murphy entered the room.

"Morning, Marshal. What can I do for you?"

"This is Mr. Murphy," Rourke said. "He needs to send a wire."

Wilson picked up a pencil and licked the tip. "Go ahead," he said.

"I'll send it myself," Murphy said.

Wilson stared at Murphy. "Company policy forbids . . ."

"Mr. Murphy is a federal agent, Wilson. It's all right," Rourke said. "Let's go outside and have a smoke."

"Do you know how to . . . ?" Wilson asked.

"I'm sure he knows," Rourke said.

Rourke and Wilson left the office and Murphy sat behind the table. The first telegram went to Kai. The second telegram went to Burke at the White House.

Done, Murphy stepped outside where Rourke and Wilson were smoking cigarettes.

"Thank you for the use of your telegraph, Mr. Wilson," Murphy said. "There will be no reply."

Wilson returned to his office.

"Let's get our horses," Rourke said.

Rourke and Murphy rode ten miles east of town to the Jessup farm. As they neared a small farmhouse, fields of wheat blew gently on a soft breeze.

The farmhouse was modest. Beside it stood a small barn with a corral. Carsten Jessup was in the corral, shoeing a team of plow horses when Murphy and Rourke arrived.

Carsten stopped what he was doing and exited the corral as Murphy and Rourke dismounted.

"My father is dead, isn't he?" Carsten said. "I can think of no other reason why you'd ride out here."

"Let's go in the house," Rourke said.

Carsten served coffee at the tiny kitchen table. He listened carefully to Murphy and didn't speak until Murphy was finished.

"I loved my father, but a more hateful man I never did know," Carsten said. "I know you had no choice but to kill him, Mr. Murphy. I knew he was still involved with people from the Klan, but he never spoke of it to me."

"Do you know why he traveled to Fort Smith?" Murphy asked.

"I didn't know he went to Fort Smith," Carsten said. "I knew he was trying to get back into the hardware business, so maybe he knew somebody there?"

"Where did he stay when he was here?" Murphy asked.

"I have two bedrooms," Carsten said. "I'll show you his."

Carsten took Murphy and Rourke to a small bedroom at the rear of the cabin. Except for some clothing, the room was void of anything of use.

"He didn't own much," Murphy said.

"He only stayed here a few nights a month," Carsten said. "Most of the time he stayed with his lady friend."

"Where?" Murphy asked.

"In town."

"Dallas?" Murphy said.

"Yes, Dallas."

"Do you know who she is?" Murphy asked.

"She's a widow," Carsten said. "Woods. Her name is Woods. I believe she had a yellow house on Houston Street near the courthouse."

Murphy looked at Rourke. "Know where that is?"

"I do."

"Mr. Jessup, did you know your father owned a .32 caliber Remington handgun?" Murphy said.

Carsten nodded. "It was mine. I needed a small handgun for snakes and small varmints in the fields," he said. "Carrying a rifle or shotgun seemed impractical behind a plow. He asked me for it because he wanted protection riding into Dallas."

"How did you come by it?" Murphy asked.

"Bought it used in town at Worth's Gun Smith Shop," Carsten said. "Paid twenty-five dollars for it."

"I noticed you plant wheat," Murphy said. "Hard crop to grow."

"It is," Carsten said.

"Next harvest, plant corn," Murphy said. "You can get three rotations and sell it for top dollar in Tennessee to my father."

"Your father?" Carsten said.

"Corn makes the best whiskey," Murphy said. "That's what he makes, and he makes the best. I'll write down the address. He'll be expecting to hear from you."

"Is that true what you said about corn?" Rourke asked as he and Murphy rode back to Dallas.

Murphy removed the thin silver flask from his jacket pocket and passed it to Rourke.

"My father's brand," Murphy said.

Rourke unscrewed the top and took a sip.

"Damn, that's good," Rourke said.

"I got a bottle in my room," Murphy said. "We can have a drink later after dinner."

A block from the courthouse, Murphy and Rourke dismounted in front of a yellow and gray house at the end of the block.

There wasn't a hitching post, so they tied the horses loosely to the picket fence surrounding the home.

Rourke opened the gate and, as he and Murphy walked to the porch, the front door opened and Mrs. Woods stepped out. She was sixty years old, dressed in a plain skirt and blouse, and carried a shotgun.

"That's far enough, you two," she said.

"Mrs. Woods?" Rourke said.

"Who is asking?"

"Marshal Rourke."

"Step closer so I can see your badge. My eyes ain't so good anymore."

Rourke climbed the porch, and Woods looked at his badge.

"Who's the big fellow?" she asked.

"His name is Murphy. He's a federal agent."

"Well, what do you want?"

"Mrs. Woods, could you put the shotgun down?" Rourke said.

"A woman can't be too careful around menfolk, you know," Woods said.

"Oh for —" Murphy said, walked past Rourke, and snatched the shotgun away from Woods.

"That's my property," Woods said.

"Mrs. Woods, sit down and shut up," Murphy said.

Woods looked at Rourke. "Are you going to allow him to speak to an old woman that way?"

"Mrs. Woods, I would do as he said," Rourke said.

Glaring at Murphy, Woods took a seat on a rocking chair. "Now what is it you want?"

"Do you know Jonas Jessup?" Murphy said.

"Why do you want to know?"

"Because I shot and killed him," Murphy said. "In Washington, DC, where he attempted to shoot General Grant."

Woods stared at Murphy. Her face drained

of all color, and for a moment Murphy thought she might faint.

"Poor old Jonas," she said. "He finally went crazy."

"What do you mean by that?" Murphy asked.

"I've known Jonas since fifty-five," Woods said. "He was a prosperous young man back then. During the war he made a small fortune selling goods to the Confederate Army, but after the war, he lost everything to the depression that hit the South. He blamed the freed slaves and the North for everything bad in his life."

"Was he involved with the Klan after the war?" Murphy asked.

Woods nodded.

"And now?" Murphy said.

"The past few years he met with like-minded men who wanted the South returned to its antebellum, but it was mostly the talk of old defeated men," Woods said. "I couldn't tell you who they are by name. It was just the talk of old, worn-out men."

"Do you know why he traveled to Fort Smith?" Murphy asked.

Woods nodded. "He said he was meeting with a man named Charles Weaver about getting back into the hardware business."

"In Fort Smith?" Murphy said.

"Yes."

"Mrs. Woods, did you know Jonas Jessup was dying?" Murphy asked.

"I did. He told me the doctors said he had about six months to live," Woods said. "They gave him laudanum to deaden the pain whenever it struck him too bad. That's why it seemed odd to me he was thinking of going back into business. Maybe he didn't believe the doctors. I don't know."

"He lived here with you most of the time?" Murphy asked.

Woods nodded again.

"Show me all of his possessions," Murphy said.

Jonas Jessup had little in the way of possessions for a man nearly sixty years of age. His clothing was mostly a decade old. There was a small box containing a silver pocket watch, a gold wedding ring, and a few other trinkets.

Before they left, Mrs. Woods served coffee on the porch.

"Mrs. Woods, did Jonas ever speak of his friends or acquaintances?" Murphy asked.

"Just this Weaver fellow in Fort Smith," Woods said. "Otherwise, he had no real friends. Even his son didn't like him much. Jonas wasn't a likable man, you might say."

145

"You again," Wilson said. "Let me guess. You want me to wait outside."

"If you don't mind," Murphy said.

"Would it matter if I did mind?"

"No. Out you go."

Wilson left the telegraph office and stood outside with Rourke.

Murphy sat behind the table and began tapping the key.

As they walked to Rourke's office, Murphy said, "I'm going back to the hotel to freshen up a bit. Why don't you and Sheriff McCoy join me for supper around seven-thirty."

"Sounds good," Rourke said. "Will you be leaving in the morning?"

"Ten o'clock train," Murphy said.

Chester Arthur read the telegram at his desk and then looked up at Burke.

"Murphy's identified the assassin as Jonas Jessup out of Dallas," Arthur said.

"Apparently so," Burke said.

"He'll be back in Washington in a few days with more information," Arthur said.

Arthur set Murphy's telegram aside. "The kidnappers' response that they will kill the niece if we don't pay them. Do you believe them?"

"With all due respect, Mr. President, I believe they have already killed the niece," Burke said.

"Unfortunately, I do too," Arthur said.

Kai sat at the desk in her bedroom, opened the envelope, and removed the telegram.

Home tomorrow night. Murphy.

"Well, aren't you just such a bucket mouth," Kai said.

Judge Parker sat behind his desk and waited for US Marshal Cal Witson to arrive.

There was a soft knock, the door opened, and Witson entered the office.

"You sent for me, Judge?" Witson said.

Parker held out Murphy's telegram. Witson took it and read it quickly.

"Charles Weaver?" Witson said. "Of Weaver's Hardware?"

"Apparently so," Parker said. "Do as Murphy requests."

"Pick him up and hold for questioning," Witson said. "For what, Judge?"

"That's classified at the moment," Parker said. "Best go pick him up."

"It's after hours," Witson said.

"Find out where he lives, and pick him up

147

at home."

"Yes, sir," Witson said.

After dinner, Murphy, Rourke, and McCoy took coffee on the porch of the hotel. Rourke and McCoy rolled cigarettes. Murphy smoked his pipe.

"Is there a store in town that sells fine women's jewelry?" Murphy said.

"Several," McCoy said.

"Which do you recommend?" Murphy asked.

"Simms Women's Fashion Shop on Austin Street," McCoy said. "I believe they open at nine."

"Will you be back this way, Murphy?" Rourke asked.

"Don't yet know where the evidence leads," Murphy said.

"Hard to believe about Jessup," McCoy said. "But some folks just can't accept modern times."

"We had a lot of that in Texas after the war," Rourke said. "Those who fought for the North were branded and rejected by those who fought for the South. Once the carpetbaggers showed up . . . well, it wasn't good for anybody."

"Gentlemen, I'll see you before I leave in the morning," Murphy said and stood up.

CHAPTER SIXTEEN

Charles Weaver sat in a chair before Judge Parker's court and waited. Standing beside Parker, Cal Witson kept an eye on Weaver.

Murphy stood in front of Parker's bench and waited for the judge to speak.

"How long are you going to keep me here?" Weaver said. "I haven't done anything, and I've been here for twelve hours."

"Be quiet in my court until I ask you to speak," Parker said.

"But what am I charged with?" Weaver asked.

Murphy turned and looked at Weaver.

"Conspiracy to commit murder," Murphy said. "Kidnapping, extortion, conspiracy against the government, and treason, just to start."

Weaver jumped to his feet and looked up at Murphy. "You're crazy," he shouted. "I've done no such —"

"Sit down and shut up, or I will shut you

up myself," Murphy said.

Weaver glared at Murphy as he sat.

"Mr. Weaver, do you know why they call me the Hanging Judge?" Parker asked. "It's because I've hanged nearly two hundred men since my appointment as territorial judge."

"Hang? I haven't done anything. You can't hang me," Weaver said.

"Jonas Jessup says differently," Murphy said.

Weaver's face suddenly blanched the color of flour.

"You do know Jonas Jessup, don't you?" Murphy said. "He told me all about you and your involvement with a movement to resurrect the Klan in the South."

"But I . . ." Weaver said.

"Shut up Mr. Weaver," Parker said. "I am about to pronounce sentence."

"But I haven't even been charged yet," Weaver said.

Parker looked at Witson. "Marshal Witson, would you tell the hangman to prepare the gallows."

"Right away, Judge," Witson said.

"Now just you hold on a minute," Weaver yelled as he stood up. "I haven't even had a trial yet. You don't have any evidence I did anything wrong. You can't just hang me."

"This is your trial, and I can hang any damned one I please in my court," Parker said.

"Judge, do you still want me to get the hangman?" Witson asked.

"Yes," Parker said.

"No. Wait. Just listen to me, please," Weaver said.

"Marshal, hold on," Parker said. "I'm listening, Mr. Weaver."

"What . . . what do you want to know?" Weaver said.

Murphy walked to Weaver and towered over him. "Anything and everything you know about Jonas Jessup," he said.

Weaver looked up at Murphy.

"Start with how you know him," Murphy asked. "And talk slow, so I can write everything down."

Murphy, Parker, and Witson had a drink in Parker's office once Murphy was satisfied with Weaver's statement.

"Thanks for going along with all that, Judge," Murphy said. "You, too, Marshal."

"I'm just glad you got what you needed," Parker said.

"It's a start," Murphy said.

"Headed back to Washington?" Witson asked.

"Home first," Murphy said. "Maybe tomorrow."

Well after ten at night, Kai and Mrs. Leary sat in chairs on the porch and sipped tea. The air was hot, the guests were asleep, and neither woman was sleepy.

"I see a man coming in the dark," Mrs. Leary said. "Looks awful big."

"That would be my husband," Kai said.

Mrs. Leary stood and adjusted the flame on the wall-mounted oil lantern. "So it is," she said. "I'll be going to bed now."

Mrs. Leary entered the house as Murphy reached the stairs and walked up to the porch.

"Your letter-writing skills leave much to be desired," Kai said.

"I don't . . . what are you talking about?" Murphy said as he sat next to Kai.

"Four words in a telegram are what I'm talking about," Kai said. "I expected a little more than . . ."

"Hold that thought for a moment," Murphy said.

He opened the satchel and removed a small box. He opened the box and removed the large diamond ring he'd purchased in Dallas, took Kai's left hand, and slipped the ring on in front of her wedding band.

Kai looked at the diamond.

"Okay, what were you saying?" Murphy said.

Kai sighed. "I was saying that if you didn't eat on the train, I can fix you something," she said.

Kai held Murphy's hand as they waited for the train to enter the station.

"I'm not sure how long I'll be gone," Murphy said. "A few days at least, so check on Boyle for me. He gets lonely."

"Your horse gets lonely?" Kai said. "But not your wife?"

"You know what I mean," Murphy said.

"Wire me from Washington," Kai said.

"I will," Murphy said.

The train arrived. They parted with a kiss. Murphy boarded, and Kai took a seat on a bench to watch it leave the station.

After the train was gone, Kai said, "His horse gets lonely," and stood up.

On the ride to Washington, Murphy read his notes.

According to Charles Weaver, he met Jonas Jessup after the war when both were active members of the Klan.

Weaver stated that Jessup became a

member because he blamed the freed slaves for his business troubles. Weaver stated that over time Jessup came to hate the black race and everything connected with the North.

Weaver shared Jessup's views on the North, although not on the black race.

Weaver became aware of a small group of men who wanted to reinstall the Klan to start a new movement in the South.

Weaver named six men Jessup was to have met with during the past year.

Jessup confided in Weaver that they planned to start a movement throughout the South, but first they needed financing.

Jessup never discussed how they planned to raise finances for the movement, and Weaver was never asked for money for the cause.

Weaver did supply Jessup with small amounts of money for living expenses, but out of friendship and not for their cause.

Murphy lit his pipe and closed his notebook.

He looked out the window.

As a native to Tennessee, he had seen firsthand how issues such as slavery and freedom can tear people apart. The state was divided between those who believed the

154

South should secede from the Union and those who were loyal to the Republic.

Murphy's parents were loyal to the Republic, as was Murphy, although he joined the fight for different reasons.

After the war, when reconstruction began, Murphy was away tracking the men responsible for murdering his family. It took two years before he located and executed the six army deserters responsible, and when it was over, Murphy was fully prepared to surrender himself to the law.

General Grant stepped in and recruited Murphy for the pacification detail out west, so the railroad could complete its task of connecting East Coast to West without the natives killing workers and burning tracks.

With the rank of colonel, Murphy headed west and took command of a unit of soldiers assigned to pacify the natives. Most of the railroad workers lived in fear of the Indians, as attacks on them were swift and decisive.

Murphy led entire units against the natives and rounded up thousands and took them to reservations. He allowed no soldier to mistreat a native warrior. He allowed no soldier to openly display bigotry or prejudice toward a native warrior.

The Indians were a proud race of people fighting for their land and way of life, and

Murphy held them in high regard.

Under orders from General Grant, Murphy's unit traveled with the railroad until it completed the connection in Promontory, Utah, in 1869.

What Murphy witnessed was a bond formed between the freed slaves who worked on the railroad and the whites and the Chinese. They were hard men who worked all hours of the day and night to lay track and blast through mountains. Many died along the way.

After the railroad was completed, Murphy returned home to his Tennessee farm, but Grant came calling again. He appointed Murphy to head the newly formed Secret Service Agency that was devoted to protecting the president, a necessity after Lincoln's assassination.

Murphy quickly found that Grant had many other duties in mind for Murphy, including shutting down the Klan as quickly as possible. Because he was from the South, Murphy knew and understood the Klan's thought process. He organized and led a large federal force that raided and disbanded the Klan quickly and efficiently. By 1871, most Klan members had gone into hiding, and little to nothing was heard from them for nearly a decade.

It was about that time Murphy became known as Grant's Regulator in Washington circles, and then simply as the Regulator.

"Washington. The next stop is Washington," the conductor said as he walked from car to car.

Murphy grabbed his satchel, stood up, and waited for the train to roll to a stop.

CHAPTER SEVENTEEN

Murphy and Burke sat at the conference
table in the Oval Office and waited for
President Arthur to take a chair.

Arthur was at the small bar against the
wall. When he turned around he held a tray
with three drinks on it. He carried the tray
to the table and set a small glass of whiskey
in front of Burke and Murphy.

"I'm not shocked that men such as these
still exist nearly twenty years after the war,"
Arthur said as he took a chair. "I am
shocked they would murder an innocent girl
to gain their means."

"Have they contacted you again recently?"
Murphy asked.

"Yesterday another telegram arrived,"
Burke said. "It reads: *last chance to pay the
ransom before the niece dies.*"

"And you replied?" Murphy asked.

"I told them to go to hell," Arthur said.
"And Turner agrees with me. His niece is

158

already dead, so why pay them for their crimes?"

"The six men Weaver named as associates of Jessup, they have to be connected in some way," Murphy said. "They are probably too old to do the dirty work and recruited younger, like-minded men to do the riding and killing."

"They have to be stopped," Arthur said. "We put a quarter of a million in gold in their hands. That money could finance a major Klan movement. The country isn't nearly healed enough to withstand an onslaught of such bigotry and hatred so soon after the war."

Burke lit one of his long cigars and then looked at Murphy. "Time is another factor, Murphy," he said. "Ambassador Turner can't keep his niece's kidnapping hidden from her parents and the British government much longer."

Murphy looked at Burke. "Take the six names over to Defense and find out who served and for which side. Then check land records and see who owned what and who lost what during the war," he said. "And have them check if any of them presently own land and where."

"That could take a week," Burke said.

Murphy nodded. "It could. Better get

started," he said. "Wire me in Fort Smith when you have the results."

Burke puffed on his cigar. "Are you sure you don't want to wait in Washington?"

"I'm sure."

Murphy was on the balcony of his hotel room, sipping a small drink and smoking his pipe. The balcony faced the Washington Monument, which was still years away from completion.

There was a soft knock on the door, and Burke said from the hallway, "It's William Burke."

"Door is open," Murphy said.

The door opened, and Burke entered the room and walked to the balcony.

"Help yourself to a drink," Murphy said.

Burke went to the dresser, picked up the bottle of whiskey, poured two ounces into a water glass, and joined Murphy on the balcony.

Burke took a small sip and said, "Your father is a genius when it comes to making whiskey."

"You came all the way across town to tell me what I already know?" Murphy said.

Burke removed a long cigar from his breast pocket and lit it with a wood match.

"The army clerks at Defense had a fit,"

Burke said.

"That's expected," Murphy said.

"If the press gets wind of this, it not only will create an international incident, but will ruin Arthur's administration and invite others to try the same tactics," Burke said.

"It's refreshing to know a politician cares more about the life of a dead young girl than his own legacy," Murphy said.

"That's horseshit and you know it," Burke said.

"Do I?" Murphy said.

"Arthur wants to know what you're prepared to do," Burke said.

"Why didn't he ask me when we were sitting across the table from each other?"

"For the same reason I am not here in your hotel room," Burke said.

"What does Arthur want?" Murphy asked.

"Justice. He wants justice," Burke said.

"Justice is bringing all the responsible men in for trial," Murphy said. "Arthur wants the problem to disappear, and those two things aren't related."

Murphy looked at Burke.

"Yes, disappear," Burke said. "With extreme prejudice."

Murphy took a sip from his glass and looked at the dark streets below.

"Thanks for the drink," Burke said and

set the empty glass on the balcony railing.

Murphy nodded as Burke turned and walked to the door.

"Wire me in Fort Smith as soon as you have results," Murphy said.

Burke opened the door and left the hotel room.

Kai waited on the bench at the railroad station for the train to arrive. It was after dark, and oil lanterns mounted on posts illuminated the platform.

She looked down track at the approaching train. Two oil lanterns mounted to the engine car grew larger as the train sped closer.

Kai wasn't alone. A man waited at the other end of the platform in the dark. She heard his footsteps as he made his way toward her.

Kai reached into the right pocket of her skirt for Murphy's two-shot, .45 caliber derringer and removed it. She cocked the hammer and waited.

The man slowly emerged from the shadows and stood about six feet from Kai.

"What's a little lady doing all alone in the dark?" he said.

"I'm neither little nor alone," Kai said.

"I don't see nobody else," the man said.

Kai raised the derringer. "I have two friends with me," she said. "Both will blow a hole in your stomach a grapefruit would fit in."

"Lady, I . . ." the man said.

"Are you still here?" Kai said as she stood up. "Maybe you'd like to stick around and meet my husband when he gets off the train? He's about six-four, with a wicked bad temper."

"I'm going, I'm going," the man said.

He walked to the edge of the platform, stepped down, and vanished in the darkness.

Kai de-cocked the derringer and returned it to her pocket. A few minutes later, the train arrived.

Murphy stepped off the platform, along with a handful of others, and was surprised to see Kai waiting for him.

"What are you doing here at this hour?" Murphy asked.

"Besides shooing off a bum, waiting for my husband," Kai said.

"What bum?" Murphy said. "Where?"

Kai saw the look in Murphy's eyes, a look she rarely got a glimpse of, and knew she immediately had to defuse his temper.

"Just a harmless old bum," Kai said and took Murphy's arm. "Let's go home."

As they walked along the quiet streets of Fort Smith, Murphy said, "I'll be home at least a week. I don't know where I'll go next until Burke sends me a telegram."

"Do you want to stay in Fort Smith or return to the farm?" Kai asked.

"Fort Smith," Murphy said.

"Good. I have a plate of fried chicken keeping warm in the oven," Kai said.

The night air was cooler on the porch than in the kitchen, and Murphy ate his late supper in a chair while Kai drank a glass of cold milk.

"I've been rolling something around in my head on the ride down from Washington," Murphy said.

Kai sipped milk. "I'm listening."

"I've come to realize I don't have the temperament for Congress," Murphy said.

"You just realized that?" Kai said. "It's not exactly a Washington secret."

"Let me finish," Murphy said.

Kai took another sip of milk. "Go on," she said.

"I know how much you like it here in Fort Smith," Murphy said. "I was thinking we could spend the summer here and the winter at the farm."

"Living in one room is fine for a few days,

164

but an entire summer?" Kai said.

"Not one room, a house," Murphy said. "There's lot of land outside of town where we could build a home and, come winter, head south to Tennessee."

"And while we are vacationing like a couple of New York society people, what will we be doing with all our free time?" Kai said.

"Whatever we want," Murphy said. "You could run your boarding house. I plan to stay active in my father's whiskey business. And we can travel. Have you ever seen California, San Francisco and the beaches in San Diego?"

"You are serious, aren't you?" Kai said.

"I am," Murphy said.

"You won't miss rubbing elbows with the Washington elite?"

"I despise Washington, especially the elite," Murphy said. "I'm in the mood for some apple pie. Do you have any?"

"Mrs. Leary made peach cobbler."

"That will do," Murphy said.

Kai was on top of Murphy when all of a sudden she burst into tears and rolled off him.

"What is it? Are you hurt, are you sick?" Murphy said.

Kai stood up, crossed the room, filled the washbasin on the dresser with cold water, and splashed some on her face.

"No, I am not sick," she said.

"I don't understand," Murphy said.

Kai dried her face on a small towel and then sat on the bed next to Murphy. "I can't have children," she said.

"I know that," Murphy said.

"I didn't think much about it before you came along," Kai said. "A woman alone doesn't think much about having children, but now it is all different. A woman should be able to give her man children."

Murphy wrapped his arms around Kai's shoulders. "I already knew you couldn't have children," he said.

"Don't you want a son, an heir to carry on your name?"

"What is going through that head of yours?" Murphy asked.

"Nothing. Forget it. Forget I ever mentioned it."

"There's an agency over in Little Rock for orphans," Murphy said. "Maybe we could —"

"Yes!" Kai said and pounced on Murphy and kissed him so hard he thought his lips would bleed. "Oh, God, yes."

All women are crazy, Murphy thought as

166

Kai all but smothered him.

The hall of records in the courthouse opened at ten in the morning. Murphy and Kai were the first customers of the day.

"What can I do for you folks?" the clerk asked.

"We're interested in a piece of land just outside of town," Murphy said.

"Well, let me get the maps, and you can look at what's for sale," the clerk said.

Murphy drove Kai's buggy south out of town to the place on the map that showed three acres of land for sale. Kai had packed a picnic basket for lunch and, while Murphy studied the maps, she spread a large blanket on the grass.

"I can see Fort Smith in the distance," Murphy said. "So it's not too far from town. About an hour in the buggy."

Kai sat and removed her boots.

"That stream comes off the Arkansas River, so the water is good," Murphy said.

Kai stood and removed her riding pants.

"And there's plenty of room for a house, barn, and garden," Murphy said. "And the grass is sweet for Boyle."

Kai unbuttoned her blouse and tossed it on the blanket.

"Maybe we could tap into the stream and have a pump in the kitchen," Murphy said. "What do you think?"

Murphy turned around and Kai was naked on the blanket.

"What are you doing?" Murphy said.

"Getting ready to make love to my husband, what's it look like?" Kai said. "You big dolt."

Murphy dropped the maps and walked to the blanket.

"Just checking," he said.

"Why must you go back?" Kai said as Murphy drove the buggy back to Fort Smith. "Why can't they find someone else to finish this job?"

"Who?" Murphy asked.

"I don't know who. Somebody," Kai said.

"Kai, they kidnapped and killed a nineteen-year-old girl and five secret service agents," Murphy said.

"And they will probably kill you, too," Kai said. "You damn fool."

"Well, don't get mad about it," Murphy said.

"Don't get . . ." Kai said and socked Murphy in the jaw. "I'll give you don't get mad about it."

Murphy stopped the buggy and rubbed

his jaw. "You've a fine color when you're on the scrap, Kai. A mite painful, but fine."

Kai glared at Murphy and then burst out laughing.

"You damn fool," she said.

All women are crazy, Murphy thought as he tugged on the reins.

Burke was at his desk when Colonel Graham was escorted in by an aide.

"Mr. Burke," Graham said.

"What news have you for me, Colonel?" Burke said.

"We've identified three of the six names on your list," Graham said.

"The other three?"

"By the end of the week at the latest."

"Then why are you here? To deliver an incomplete report?" Burke asked.

"No, sir."

Graham stared at Burke.

"Well what is it, man? Spit it out," Burke said.

"Of the three men we've identified, one of them appears to be a distant cousin to a former secret service agent," Graham said.

"Which one?" Burke asked.

"Retired agent named Murphy," Graham said. "From Tennessee. Worked in the Grant administration and . . ."

169

"That's enough, Colonel," Burke said.

"Sir?"

"Exclude the information on Murphy's cousin," Burke said. "It has no merit in this investigation. If it leaks, I will have you busted down to private. Am I clear?"

"Yes, sir," Graham said.

"Make a separate report on the cousin for my eyes only."

"Yes, sir."

"Good night, Colonel."

After Graham left, Burke opened a desk drawer and removed a bottle of whiskey and a glass. He poured an ounce into the glass and sipped as he thought.

"Damn," he said aloud.

"A distant cousin?" Arthur said. "Are you sure?"

"That's what Colonel Graham said," Burke said.

Arthur sighed. "Murphy didn't mention this?"

"No. He's probably not aware he's related," Burke said. "I'm sure we all have relatives we're unaware of."

"Do not mention this to Murphy," Arthur said. "He is not to know. That is a direct order, understood?"

"Yes, sir," Burke said.

"And one more thing," Arthur said. "Have that information erased from the records forever."

"Yes, sir," Burke said. "Forever."

CHAPTER EIGHTEEN

Murphy and Kai sat in chairs opposite the desk of Ella Furnell, the director of the orphanage in Little Rock.

Furnell read the application carefully and made notes in the margins with her pencil.

"Mr. Murphy, you wrote that you retired from the secret service, served in Congress, and presently have a large farm in Tennessee," Furnell said. "What do you grow?"

"Corn. Several thousand acres of it," Murphy said.

Furnell nodded. "Mrs. Murphy, you own a boarding house in Fort Smith?"

"Yes," Kai said. "My first husband was a US Marshal. It was our house, but after he was killed by outlaws, I turned it into a boarding house."

"So you plan to live in Tennessee?" Furnell asked.

"We are going to build a home in Fort Smith and live there in the summer and winter in Tennessee," Murphy said.

"Have you considered the child's education?" Furnell said.

"The . . . I don't see the point to that question," Murphy said. "Of course, the child will go to school and get an education."

"I'm talking about all the going back and forth between two states," Furnell said. "It can have an adverse effect upon a child's education and well-being."

"How so?" Murphy said, his eyes squinting.

Kai looked at Murphy. A vein in his neck had started to pulsate.

"Children need stability to feel secure," Furnell said. "Bouncing between two states can give a child the impression he or she has no real home."

"Is that so?" Murphy said.

Kai looked at the vein on Murphy's neck. It appeared as if at any second it would burst open.

"Mrs. Furnell, the child will attend school in Tennessee and spend time in Fort Smith when school is in recess during the summer," Kai said. "The child will learn about farm life as well as life in a large town. His education will be well rounded on both types of lifestyle, and he or she will have many friends in both places."

"You have a valid point, Mrs. Murphy," Furnell said. "I will process your application to the board for review. They will want to meet you in person."

"How long a wait?" Kai asked.

"Several months at least," Furnell said.

"Several . . ." Murphy said.

Kai squeezed Murphy's knee and said, "Thank you, Mrs. Furnell. We look forward to meeting the board."

As they walked to the rented carriage, Murphy said, "That woman has a stick up her —"

"Murphy, we're in public," Kai said. "Watch your temper."

"Yeah, yeah. What time do we meet with the architect?" Murphy said.

"Two."

Murphy looked at his pocket watch. "We have time for lunch," he said.

Colonel Graham sat quietly in a chair while Burke read his complete report. Graham remained silent as Burke read. After thirty minutes, Burke set the report on his desk.

"Colonel Graham, do you intend to retire from the army any time soon?" Burke asked.

"In a few more years, Mr. Burke," Graham said.

"Retiring as a general would provide a great deal more comfort than as a colonel, wouldn't it?" Burke said.

Graham stared at Burke. "Yes, Mr. Burke, it would," he said.

"Make sure no copies of this report exist and all references to Murphy's cousin are removed permanently," Burke said. "Do we understand each other?"

"Perfectly," Graham said.

"Good afternoon then," Burke said. "General."

Arthur read the complete report, set it aside, and looked at Burke.

"Have you sent Murphy a telegram?" Arthur asked.

"I thought you should read the report first," Burke said.

"I read it. Send the telegram," Arthur said.

"I can do better than send a telegram," Burke said.

"Four bedrooms?" Walter Grillo said.

"That's what we want," Murphy said. "And a complete kitchen with cabinets and a sink with a pump. And a full desk at least ten feet wide. You're supposed to be the best architect in the state; can you design such a

175

home for us?"

"Yes, of course I can," Grillo said. "I'll need more information on size and other details, and I would like to survey the land first before I draw up blueprints."

"When can you come to Fort Smith?" Murphy asked.

"A day or so."

"If I'm out of town on business, my wife will take care of all details," Murphy said.

"Very well," Grillo said.

"We have a train to catch," Murphy said.

"I will see you in a few days," Grillo said.

It was after ten o'clock at night when Murphy and Kai returned to the boarding house. While Kai changed for bed, Murphy warmed a glass of milk for her on the stove in the kitchen.

While Kai sat at her dresser and brushed her long black hair, she took small sips of milk.

Murphy sat on the bed with a shot glass of whiskey and watched Kai.

"That man, Grillo. I can meet with him if you are gone," Kai said.

"I know that," Murphy said. "I have every confidence in you."

Kai set the brush down and sat next to Murphy.

"When we meet with the adoption board, I want you to behave yourself," she said.

"What did I do?" Murphy asked.

"Your temper," Kai said. "The vein in your neck looked like a tributary of the Mississippi River."

"But that woman was . . ."

"Never mind what she was," Kai said. "You be nice to her, or she will reject our application."

Murphy tossed back the shot, stood up, and unbuttoned his shirt.

"It won't kill you to be nice once in a while," Kai said. "It will be good practice for raising our child."

"I'm nice to you," Murphy said. "Doesn't that count?"

"I'm your wife. No, that doesn't count," Kai said.

Murphy tossed his pants over a chair.

Kai patted the bed. "I could use a little nice before we go to sleep."

Every last one of them is nuts, Murphy thought as he got into bed.

Kai helped Mrs. Leary prepare breakfast for the dozen guests that would bring their appetites to the table by seven-thirty.

Firewood was running low, so Murphy was behind the house chopping wood. She could hear the steady rhythm of the ax striking wood through the open window. Kai parted the curtains and glanced out and watched Murphy, shirtless, work the ax. With each blow, his heavy muscles rippled.

Mrs. Leary stopped beside Kai and looked out. "Oh, my," she said.

"Never mind 'oh my,' " Kai said. "The toast is burning."

Mrs. Leary went to the frying pan to flip the slices of bread to brown the other sides in butter.

Kai carried a large bowl of scrambled eggs to the table. Most of the guests had assembled. Seated at the end of the table was the man from Washington, William Burke.

Kai closed her eyes for a few seconds, then opened them and began serving eggs.

As she reached Burke, he said softly, "Is that Murphy chopping wood?"

Kai nodded and moved on.

Murphy and Burke sat in chairs on the porch. Each sipped from a cup of coffee as Murphy scanned the documents Burke brought from Washington.

When Murphy finished reading, he set the documents on the small table between them and picked up his pipe.

"You could have sent this by mail," Murphy said.

"I needed to get out of the office and stretch my legs," Burke said. "Besides, I want to give you additional expense money."

"I've hardly touched what I have," Murphy said.

Burke lit one of his long cigars with a wood match. "It's always best to have more than you need," he said. "When do you figure to leave?"

"Tomorrow morning, maybe," Murphy said.

"I'll be headed back to Washington on the noon train," Burke said. "Wire me whenever you can about any progress."

Murphy nodded as he puffed on his pipe.

"Kai is none too happy with me," Burke said.

"I expect not," Murphy said.

"So don't get yourself killed," Burke said. "I'd hate to face that woman alone at night someday."

"Makes two of us," Murphy said.

"I best grab my bag," Burke said. "Walk with me to the train."

Murphy and Burke shook hands on the platform moments before Burke boarded the train.

"Fort Smith has grown quite a bit," Burke

said. "I didn't see one armed man during the entire walk here."

"Modern times, Burke," Murphy said.

"Not so modern you couldn't get yourself killed," Burke said. "You watch yourself."

"Washington is more dangerous than where I'm going," Murphy said.

Burke stepped onto the platform. "I can't say as I disagree with you," he said.

Murphy chopped wood until dark. When he was done and walked to the front porch, he found Kai seated in a chair with a coffee pot and two cups on the small table.

Murphy took a chair. Kai filled the cups and gave him one.

"That should last you for a while," Murphy said. "At least two cords."

"Twice in my life I have married a lawman," Kai said. "Let's hope I didn't make the same mistake twice."

Murphy took a sip of coffee.

"I have a hot bath ready for you in the barn," Kai said.

"Come in with me," Murphy said. "I can't reach my lower back."

A little while later, as they sat in the tub of hot, soapy water and Kai washed Murphy's broad back, she suddenly wrapped her arms around him and started to cry.

Murphy turned around. "What is it?"

"Nothing. I'm being foolish."

"Don't worry," Murphy said. "I'm pretty hard to kill, and I won't be gone that long."

"I'll be fine," Kai said. "I'll keep busy with Mr. Grillo."

"Do you think my ring has arrived?" Murphy asked.

"We can check in the morning," Kai said. "Would you wear it?"

"With pride," Murphy said.

Kai burst into tears again.

"Now what did I say?" Murphy said.

"Nothing. Just hold me for a bit," Kai said.

Murphy held Kai tightly until she stopped crying.

"All men are crazy," Kai said.

"Is it too tight?" Kai asked.

"No, it's fine," Murphy said.

Kai took Murphy's left hand. The ring finger was swelling where the too tight ring was cutting off circulation.

"Take it off, if you can, before your finger rots," Kai said. "I'll have it resized."

Murphy slowly worked the ring off his finger and handed it to Kai. "I guess it could be a mite larger," he said.

"All aboard," the train conductor shouted.

"I'll wire you later today," Murphy said.

"More than four words would be nice," Kai said. "Maybe an 'I love you' tossed in if it's not too painful."

Murphy kissed her and said, "I love you. Right down to my socks."

Murphy boarded the train and Kai sat to watch it leave the station.

"His socks are better than nothing," she said aloud.

Chapter Nineteen

The ride to Austin from Fort Smith was a long one, scheduled at twelve hours, if the train ran on time.

Murphy booked a sleeping car that had a small desk. He took lunch in the car and read Burke's reports for the second time.

Jason Cobb, a wealthy rancher south of Austin, Texas, before the war, was not a slave owner but he did sympathize with the cause and wholly supported the South's decision to secede from the Union. At the time war broke out, Cobb, forty-three years old at the time, sent his two sons to join the Confederate Army. Both were killed in action.

The war not only took his sons, but his wife as well, as she suffered a heart attack at learning she'd lost her only sons in combat. By the end of the war, Cobb's ranch was all but destroyed, and he was bankrupt.

As many did, Cobb blamed everyone but

himself for his troubles and publicly stated blacks and Yankees caused the ruination of the South.

In 1867, Cobb joined the local chapter of the Klan. He was an active supporter, holding meetings at his ranch house, and was instrumental in recruiting new members.

When the Klan was broken in 1871, Cobb returned to ranching with moderate success. He was well known in Austin politics and even served on the city council. Burke's research people dug up old newspaper accounts of Cobb protesting the Fifteenth Amendment allowing freed slaves the right to vote.

How he connected to Jessup was unknown, but he was named by Weaver as one of six men known to associate with Jessup shortly before the kidnapping.

Murphy closed the file and lit his pipe.

Jessup from Dallas, Cobb in Austin. Not too far for a connection between the two men to exist, especially like-minded men.

Murphy checked the coffee pot the waiter brought in with lunch. There was one cup remaining and he filled the coffee mug, then dug out his bottle of whiskey and added an ounce.

He switched gears and thought about Kai. Murphy freely admitted he understood very little about the way women thought in general. They laughed at things that should make them angry, and turned into mad hornets at things they should find funny.

Years ago, after a particularly trying evening in the White House when arrangements for a state dinner went awry, Grant expected Julia to be furious. Instead, she was delighted at how many things went wrong.

In confidence, Grant told Murphy his view on marriage. "A man will feel truly married when he starts to understand the things his wife doesn't say," Grant told him.

At the time that statement made little sense.

It made more sense now.

Murphy finished his coffee and left the tray outside the door for the waiter to take away later.

He sprawled out on the narrow bed and dumped the spent tobacco from his pipe into the spittoon on the floor, refilled the bowl, and struck a match.

Men like Jessup and Cobb were particularly dangerous to the country. Not physically, because they were grains of sand in the desert, but because their beliefs and ideals kept alive the worst in mankind.

They were hornets stirring up a nest to

gain followers for their ideas.

Ideas dangerous to freedom.

Too many good men died to preserve the Union and end those ideas to allow them to resurface like a cancer that rotted flesh off the bone.

Murphy checked his pocket watch. Eight hours remained of the trip. He set his pipe on the stand beside the bed and closed his eyes for a nap.

The train arrived in Austin just a few minutes late. After retrieving Boyle from the boxcar, Murphy walked along dark streets on the outskirts of town to the livelier center, where saloons were alive with music and laughter.

As he walked to the hotel at which he'd wired a reservation, Murphy noticed that what few men were on the street were unarmed. Austin, like many larger towns these days, had ordinances against openly carrying firearms in public.

The Hotel Austin on Main Street boasted four floors of rooms with balconies on every room above the first floor. It also had a large stable in the rear manned twenty-four hours a day.

Murphy took Boyle to the stable before he checked in and removed the saddle and blanket himself. "He won't allow anyone but me to remove his saddle," Murphy told the stable manager. "Or brush him, so don't try. Give him a bag of oats and water, and he'll settle down to sleep."

Murphy carried his saddlebags, Winchester, and bedroll with him into the lobby to check into his fourth-floor room.

Once inside his room, he dug out the bottle of whiskey from the saddlebags, splashed an ounce into a water glass, lit his pipe, and stood on the balcony.

There was a soft knock on the door.

Without turning around, Murphy said, "Who is it?"

"Texas Rangers, Mr. Murphy," a voice said from the hall.

"Door is open, come in," Murphy said.

The door opened and two young Texas Rangers, each with a Winchester rifle, entered the room.

"There is a bottle of some pretty damned expensive whiskey on the table," Murphy said. "Pour yourself a drink."

"There is a city ordinance about carrying firearms," a Ranger said.

"My jacket on the bed," Murphy said. "Check my wallet."

Murphy heard one of the Rangers lift his jacket and check his wallet.

"US Secret Service? Is the president coming for a visit?" one of the Rangers said.

"No. I'm here on a classified assignment," Murphy said. "I'll stop by your headquarters office in the morning. The offer for a drink still stands."

The two Rangers poured small drinks and joined Murphy on the balcony.

"Classified assignment?" one of the Rangers said.

"I'll explain what I can in the morning," Murphy said. "Who is in command?"

"Colonel Richardson, but he's out of town," a Ranger said. "Captain Reid is in charge until the colonel returns."

"Will you see the captain before morning?" Murphy asked.

"We'll be asleep come morning," a Ranger said.

"Can you leave a note for him to join me for breakfast?" Murphy said. "Say, around seven-thirty."

"We can do that," a Ranger said. "Thanks for the drink. It was as you said, really good stuff."

After the Rangers left, Murphy had another drink and then stripped down and got under the covers.

Captain Reid was a slender man of about

188

thirty-five, with brown hair and a clean-shaven face. He met Murphy in the hotel dining room at exactly seven-thirty.

"My men left me a note you're on some kind of secret assignment here in Austin," Reid said after he took a seat at Murphy's table.

"Classified, not secret," Murphy said.

"What's the difference?" Reid asked.

"If you tell a secret, you don't go to prison for five years," Murphy said.

Reid grinned. "I can't fault you on that," he said.

"Order a full breakfast," Murphy said. "I'm on expense account. We have some riding to do, and that's easier to do on a full stomach."

"Where?"

"Rancher named Jason Cobb. Know him?"

"I don't believe so. Who is he?"

"That's the classified part," Murphy said. "I'll tell you what I can on the ride."

"How far?"

"Twenty miles as the crow flies."

After ten miles, Murphy and Reid took a thirty-minute break to rest the horses. The Texas morning was hot. Murphy estimated the temperature was close to ninety degrees.

It wasn't yet eleven in the morning, and he didn't want the horses to overheat.

Murphy had supplies and made a small pot of coffee. He smoked his pipe while he and Reid drank a cup.

"After the war, we had some problems with the Klan, but not as many as we had with the Comanche," Reid said. "I was a kid when the war broke out, and by the time it ended I was a junior officer with the Rangers."

"You had your hands full with the Comanches," Murphy said.

"Up until ten years or so ago," Reid said.

"Had you enlisted, which side would you have fought on?" Murphy asked.

"My leaning would have been toward the North," Reid said. "We didn't have many slave owners in Texas, but my issue would have been to keep the country together."

"I fought for the North for the very same reason," Murphy said. "Although my position wasn't very popular back home in Tennessee."

"This Cobb, he belonged to the Klan after the war?" Reid said.

"And probably still does in some circles," Murphy said. "Well, let's mount up. We have another ten miles ahead of us."

■ ■ ■ ■

The Cobb ranch had seen far better days. When Murphy and Reid arrived and rode through a broken fence that had at one time encircled a house, barn, and corral, a young man was digging a well. He was in a pit deeper than he was tall. A young woman stood over the pit and pulled buckets of mud up with a rope.

"Company," the woman said.

The man climbed out of the pit and stood beside the woman. Both were covered in wet mud.

"That's a Texas Ranger's badge you're wearing," the man said.

Murphy and Reid dismounted.

"Are you relatives of Jason Cobb?" Murphy asked.

"Hardly," the man said. "My name is William Blair and this is my wife, Collie. We bought the place from Mr. Cobb about three months ago."

"Any idea where Mr. Cobb went?" Murphy asked.

"No, sir, just that he mentioned he'd like to try his hand out west," Blair said.

"His hand at what?" Murphy said.

"He didn't say. I assumed ranching," Blair said.

"Did he leave anything behind?" Murphy said.

"No, including water. The well went dry about a week ago," Blair said. "Say, what's this about anyway?"

"Are you sure he didn't leave anything behind?" Murphy asked.

"My husband said so, didn't he?" Collie said. "So state your business or leave."

"I guess we'll leave," Murphy said.

"Wait," Blair said. "You came all this way about Mr. Cobb, and you're leaving just like that?"

"I'm interested in Cobb, not you or your wife," Murphy said. "And you're far enough down that if you drove a pipe two feet into the mud, you'd hit water."

"You've dug a well before?" Blair asked.

"Many times," Murphy said.

"Two feet you say?" Blair said.

"Drive your pipe and then cap it," Murphy said. "Make sure your silt screen is fastened tight, and then fill in your pit with rocks and dirt and attach the pump. I'd build a wall around the pump with cement and bricks and then install a trough, but you do what you want."

Murphy was about to mount the saddle

192

when Collie said, "Wait. There is an old trunk in the barn. We've been meaning to get rid of it but haven't had the time."

"Show me," Murphy said.

Blair and Collie took Murphy and Reid to the barn where an old trunk sat against the back wall.

A rusty padlock sat in the hasp of the trunk. Murphy took a sledgehammer off a workbench, broke the lock in two, and opened the trunk.

It was filled with old newspaper clippings and pamphlets pertaining to the Klan.

"What is all this?" Blair asked.

"Something I'll need to go through," Murphy said.

"Maybe I should make us all some lunch?" Collie said.

"I'll pay you for your trouble," Murphy said.

Murphy and Reid spent two hours riffling through newspaper articles as old as twenty years or more. Most of them centered on the issue of slavery and the South's desire to keep it, while the North opposed it.

Much of the literature pertained to the Klan. Newspaper articles and recruitment posters and pamphlets for the Klan.

There were hundreds of articles about Lincoln and Grant. Often Grant was depicted as Satan by newspaper cartoonists.

The earliest newspaper story was from six years ago. It detailed local Klansmen in the South who were defiant to the laws against discrimination.

Several names were mentioned in the story, including Jonas Jessup's.

Murphy kept that article, then he and Reid carried the trunk out of the barn to a patch of dry ground on the side of the house.

"Mr. Blair, do you have any lantern oil?" Murphy asked.

"In the house and some in the barn."

"Would you get some?"

Blair went into the barn and returned with a container of lantern oil. He handed it to Murphy.

Murphy poured some oil onto the open trunk, then struck a match and tossed it inside. Immediately flames erupted.

"Don't put it out until everything is burned," Murphy said.

"What was the one newspaper clipping you kept?" Reid asked as they rode down Main Street in Austin.

"A connection," Murphy said. "Where's the telegraph office?"

"Near the courthouse."

"Ride over with me," Murphy said.

"What do you mean, I have to step out?" the telegraph operator said. "This is my telegraph office."

Murphy looked at Reid. "Captain Reid, would you escort him outside until I am through in here."

"He can't do that," the operator said. "Can he do that?"

"Afraid so," Reid said. "Wait outside with me."

Alone, Murphy sat behind the desk and tapped in the special code for the operator in the White House. Then he sent a telegram to Burke.

A second telegram went to Kai, telling her he would be home tomorrow morning for a brief stopover.

Done, Murphy stepped outside.

"Where is the post office?" Murphy asked Reid.

"There is one two blocks from here," Reid said.

"Where to next?" Reid said.

"Not sure just yet," Murphy said. "I might be back in Austin before this is over."

"Look me up if you do," Reid said. "The Rangers are always happy to help whenever we can."

Murphy and Reid shook hands, and Murphy boarded the six o'clock train bound for Fort Smith.

Burke handed the telegram to Arthur, who read it quickly.

"What connection? What's he talking about?" Arthur said.

"Between Jessup and Cobb," Burke said.

"I can read," Arthur said. "He neglects to mention the connection."

"I assume that when he said to watch the mail, he mailed it," Burke said.

Arthur glared at Burke.

"Let me know when it arrives," he said.

Burke nodded, turned, and grinned as he walked to the door.

Kai read the telegram on the front porch. She was having afternoon tea with Mrs. Leary when the delivery boy from the telegraph office delivered the telegram.

Kai tore open the envelope and read quickly.

"What does it say?" Mrs. Leary asked.

"He'll be home in the morning," Kai said.

"We best go to the general store first thing," Mrs. Leary said. "We're low on food supplies."

"I'll do it now," Kai said. "I'll place the order and have it delivered in the morning."

"It will be dark soon," Mrs. Leary said.

"I'll be fine," Kai said. "I won't be long."

Kai grabbed her wrap, tucked Murphy's derringer into the pocket of her skirt, and walked to the center of town.

At the general store she placed the order for the week, including ice, and bought a candy stick for the walk back to the house.

The sun was down; the streets on the edge of town were deserted. As she passed a dark alleyway, the man who had accosted her on the railroad platform reached out and grabbed Kai by the arm.

"Let's see what we got here?" he said.

Kai reached into her pocket for the derringer.

"Why, you're that snotty bitch from the railroad," the man said.

He held a long knife in his right hand and he waved it at Kai.

"I'm gonna slice you open like a day-old fish," he said.

Kai cocked the derringer in her pocket, brought it out, and stuck it against the man's stomach.

"I don't think so," she said.

"You stinking bitch," the man said.

He shoved the knife at Kai. It sliced into

her left arm. Kai pulled the trigger and shot the man in the stomach.

The man dropped the knife as he staggered backward. "You shot me," he said.

"I told you I would," Kai said.

The man fell to his knees, slumped over, and looked up at Kai.

"Shot by a snotty bitch," he said.

"Call me that again and I'll shoot you a second time," Kai said.

Moments later, several town deputies arrived in the alleyway.

"Judge, please don't tell my husband about this," Kai said.

She and Judge Parker were in his office. Kai's left arm was bandaged, and she held a small glass of whiskey in her right hand.

"You have a dozen stitches in your arm, Kai," Parker said. "And half the town is already talking about it. I doubt you'll be able to keep this from him."

"The man will live?" Kai asked.

"Yes. He's in the hospital under guard," Parker said. "As soon as he's able, he'll stand trial for his crime."

"I'm afraid of how Murphy will react," Kai said. "He can be a very dangerous man when provoked."

"I see your point," Parker said. "When is

he due back?"

"The morning train."

"I'll have a marshal take you home," Parker said. "Leave Murphy to me."

"What are you going to do?"

"Meet him at the train," Parker said.

"Bring deputies," Kai said. "Lots of deputies."

CHAPTER TWENTY

"It takes six of us to talk to one man," Marshal Witson said.

Parker looked at his pocket watch.

"Would you like to tell Murphy alone about Kai?" Parker asked.

"No, Judge, I would not," Witson said.

"I see the train down track," Parker said.

Parker waited for Murphy to retrieve Boyle from the boxcar before he met him on the platform.

Murphy looked at Parker and the six marshals with him.

"Something's happened to Kai," Murphy said.

"She's alright," Parker said. "She's home and —"

"Who? Where?" Murphy said.

"A vagrant and —"

"The bum she told me about," Murphy said. "Where is he?"

Parker saw the look in Murphy's eyes. It was a look Parker didn't like.

"He's in custody," Parker said. "And he'll stand trial for —"

Murphy glared at Parker. "Where is he?"

"I told you, in my custody," Parker said. "Kai is at home. That is where you should go before anything else."

Murphy tossed his satchel over the saddle horn, mounted up, and raced Boyle past Parker and the marshals to the street.

"I would not like to scrap with him," Witson said. "No, sir."

"Double the guards at the hospital," Parker said. "Two men wouldn't stand a chance against him if he decides to push it."

"Okay, Judge," Witson said.

"On second thought, triple the guards," Parker said.

Murphy slid out of the saddle before Boyle came to a complete stop and raced up to the porch, where Kai was having tea with Mrs. Leary.

"I'm all right," Kai said. "Barely a scratch."

"Do they usually cover an entire arm in bandages for just a scratch?" Murphy said.

"To keep it clean," Mrs. Leary said.

Murphy glared at her.

"I have some things to tend to," Mrs. Leary said and went inside.

Murphy sat next to Kai. "The harmless bum from the railroad station?" he said.

"I went for groceries," Kai said. "He attacked me in the dark. He cut me with a knife. I had your derringer and shot him once in the stomach."

"It holds two bullets," Murphy said.

"One did the job," Kai said. "I didn't see the need to kill him."

Murphy looked at Kai's arm. "How bad?"

"Twelve stitches. It could have been much worse," Kai said.

"You're a quarter Navajo. You should have finished him," Murphy said.

"I'm only a quarter Navajo. I used a quarter of the bullets," Kai said.

"Wait for me inside. I won't be long," Murphy said and stood up.

"No," Kai said. "He will be punished in Judge Parker's courtroom according to the law and not by you."

"Kai, a man doesn't —" Murphy said.

"Step off this porch, and you can have your ring back," Kai said.

"You don't mean that."

"I'm part Navajo," Kai said. "I never say what I don't mean."

"You don't leave a man much room, Kai,"

Murphy said.

"In this case, none," Kai said. "Make your choice."

Murphy sighed. "Can I put Boyle away?"

"Put your holster on the railing first," Kai said.

Murphy removed his holster and slung it over the railing. "Satisfied?"

"I saved some supper for you," Kai said. "Beef stew and fresh bread."

"Can you mix some of the powders the doctor gave me with a glass of water?" Kai said.

"Is it hurting?" Murphy said.

"Some. A bit."

Murphy went to the dresser where a small box of pain medication sat beside a pitcher of fresh water. The box contained six envelopes of powder. Murphy opened one small envelope, shook the powder into a glass, and added water.

Kai, already in bed, took the glass and drank the entire contents in several long swallows.

"Get in beside me," Kai said.

Murphy got into bed and held Kai close.

"I knew that man was going to stab me when he recognized me from the railroad platform," Kai said. "I shot him because I had no choice."

"I know that," Murphy said. "You did what any woman would do, faced with that situation."

"What went through my mind was not seeing my husband again," Kai said.

"I understand your concern for me," Murphy said.

"I don't think you do," Kai said.

"What do you mean?" Murphy asked.

"The story you told me about your wife and child and how you found the men responsible," Kai said. "If not for General Grant, you'd be rotting in some prison somewhere. Then with the woman Orr, you would have killed the man who raped her if he hadn't gotten away."

"Any man would do the same," Murphy said.

"You are not any man," Kai said. "You are a man of the law, and that makes you different. A man of the law who betrays the law is worse than any common criminal. Think about that while I sleep."

Murphy held Kai as she drifted off to sleep and then got out of bed and covered her with a blanket.

He went downstairs to the dark kitchen and lit a wood match to ignite the lantern on the table. He opened the icebox and filled a glass with cold milk, then extinguished the lantern and returned to the room.

He placed the milk on the small table beside the bed, then poured a small drink of his father's whiskey and sat in a chair with his pipe.

The guilt in his heart from blaming himself for the loss of his family was something Kai could never understand. He joined the Union Army not out of patriotism or because he believed in preserving the Union, but because he hated being a farmer and saw the war as a means of escaping the plow.

He was young at the time and full of juice, but that was no excuse for deserting the family that needed him.

His father had told him many times that had he stayed behind, when the deserters invaded the farm, they would have killed him along with his wife and child.

That was probably true.

That he lived and his family didn't made Murphy's guilt even greater.

The years had dulled the wounds.

The incident with Sally Orr had opened them and brought them back to life again.

Kai rekindled the feelings he'd felt for his wife and Sally, and the hole in his chest slowly closed.

Murphy wanted the hole to stay closed

forever, but he would kill any man who laid a hand on her, no matter what the circumstances.

He heard movement and in the dim light of the lantern on the table, he saw Kai sit up in bed and look at him.

"There is a glass of milk beside the bed," Murphy said.

Kai took a few sips. "Thank you. Now come to bed and keep me warm."

Murphy set down his pipe, tossed back his drink, and did as instructed.

CHAPTER TWENTY-ONE

Kai opened the letter from Mrs. Furnell and read it quickly.

She and Murphy were having coffee after breakfast on the front porch.

"She says our case will be reviewed within two months," Kai said.

"What about Grillo?" Murphy asked.

"He will be here sometime this afternoon," Kai said.

"I'll be back tomorrow late afternoon," Murphy said.

"He'll be here more than one day," Kai said. "Come on, I'll walk you to the railroad."

"Your arm . . ." Murphy said.

"I don't walk on my arm," Kai said. "The train is scheduled to leave in thirty minutes; let's go."

After Kai saw Murphy onto the train, she walked to the courthouse and asked a deputy if she could see Judge Parker.

"Kai, what are you doing here?" Parker said when Kai entered his office. "You should be in bed."

"I heal quickly," Kai said. "I just saw Murphy off on the train to Washington."

"I'll have a marshal walk you home," Parker said.

"Not necessary. Judge, how is the man I shot?"

"Out of danger," Parker said. "He'll be fit for trial in a few weeks."

"That's what I wanted to talk to you about," Kai said. "If possible, can you hold his trial when Murphy is away on business?"

"That's a fine idea, Kai," Parker said. "No sense tempting fate."

"I'm not worried about tempting fate," Kai said. "Tempting Murphy is another matter."

"You're a smart woman, Kai," Parker said. "We'll hold the trial when Murphy is away."

Kai took a nap after taking her pain medication. When she awoke, it was midafternoon and Grillo was having coffee with Mrs. Leary in the kitchen.

"Mrs. Murphy, Mrs. Leary told me what happened," Grillo said. "I can come back when you're feeling better."

"I feel fine and you're here," Kai said. "We might as well get started."

"Very well," Grillo said. "I have a portfolio of blueprints and sketches for you to review, and then we can take a buggy ride to the site you've chosen to build."

"Mrs. Leary, can you make a fresh pot of coffee?" Kai asked.

President Arthur sat at his desk and looked at Murphy, Burke, and Ambassador Turner, who sat in chairs opposite him.

Murphy unfolded the old newspaper clipping and handed it to Arthur.

"A direct connection between Jonas Jessup of Dallas and Jason Cobb in Austin," Murphy said. "I found this newspaper clipping at Cobb's ranch. Both members of the Klan. My guess is they both still are, as are the others on the list."

"May I see that?" Turner asked.

Arthur passed Turner the clipping.

Turner read it quickly and sighed. "There is no doubt my niece is dead, is there?" he said.

"It appears so," Murphy said.

"I'm afraid I can't hold off any longer and must contact her parents and my government," Turner said.

Arthur looked at Murphy. "What do you

209

say, Murphy?"

"What Ambassador Turner does is his business," Murphy said. "I intend to find the men responsible and see that justice is done."

"Ambassador Turner, can you wait a while longer before you make those contacts?" Arthur said.

Turner looked at Murphy. "How much time do you need to finish the job?"

"I can't answer that with a set date," Murphy said. "All I can give you is my word I will find the men, and they will answer for their crimes."

"One month, Ambassador," Burke said. "Give Murphy one month before you make any contacts home."

"Is that suitable to you, Ambassador?" Arthur asked.

"One month," Turner said. "You have my word."

"This is a fine location for a home, Mrs. Murphy," Grillo said. "Excellent water, an hour's ride to town, good sun in the morning, excellent sunset in the evening. How much land did you purchase?"

"Ten acres," Kai said. "Enough room for the house, barn, a small corral, and a vegetable garden."

"The plans call for an indoor water pump," Grillo said. "Would you consider two? One for the tub in the bathroom?"

"Can you do that?" Kai asked.

"This close to an active stream, I'm sure water runs underneath our feet right where we are standing," Grillo said. "It's just a matter of digging the well and running pipe, and then building the house around it."

"My husband would like that," Kai said.

"Let me get my survey equipment from the buggy and do some rough estimates," Grillo said.

"Where to next, Murphy?" Arthur asked.

Murphy, Burke, and Arthur were having dinner in the smaller dining room in the private quarters of the White House.

"Fort Smith for a day or two, and then I'll start tracking the other five men," Murphy said. "Nobody can disappear forever without leaving some kind of trail. I suspect they recruited younger men to do the dirty work, and they are more likely to talk in the face of a prison stretch."

"Do you think you can deal with such men?" Arthur asked.

"If we want to find out what happened to the niece, we'll have to deal with them," Murphy said.

"Are you talking about pardons?" Arthur asked.

"That's getting ahead of ourselves," Murphy said. "I won't know the situation until I've tracked these men first."

"And you're sure you can?" Arthur said.

Murphy looked at Arthur.

"I suppose you know best in such matters," Arthur said.

Grillo reserved a room at the hotel on Main Street, but had dinner with Kai and the other guests at the boarding house.

"That was an elegant dinner, Mrs. Leary," Grillo said.

Kai and Grillo took coffee on the porch.

"I'll return home in the morning and begin work on blueprints," Grillo said. "I'll wire when they're completed, and we can make arrangements to show them to you and Mr. Murphy."

"He might still be away," Kai said.

"May I ask what your husband does?" Grillo said.

"He is a federal lawman," Kai said.

Grillo nodded. "Yes, he certainly has that look about him," he said.

Murphy and Burke had a drink in Burke's office after dinner.

212

"We've known each other for a long time, Murphy," Burke said. "Save the rhetoric for Arthur and Turner and tell me what you really plan to do."

"Stop an international incident from happening before it gets the chance," Murphy said. "Do you really want to know more?"

Burke sipped his drink. "No, I suppose I don't," he said.

"Let's have another nightcap," Murphy suggested.

Burke nodded. "Good idea."

CHAPTER TWENTY-TWO

Kai met Murphy at the railroad station, and they held hands as they walked to the boarding house.

Along the way, Kai told him about her meeting with Grillo.

"Did you ask about price?" Murphy said.

"House, barn, corral, indoor plumbing, blueprints, he estimated ten thousand," Kai said.

Murphy nodded.

"That's a fair amount of money," Kai said.

"It is," Murphy said. "But I have a fair amount of money saved and a good income from the farm in Tennessee. When this job is over, I'll even be available to help with construction."

"When will it be over?" Kai asked.

"Soon," Murphy said. "I hope."

"What month does 'I hope' fall in?" Kai asked.

"It won't be that long," Murphy said.

"When will you be going again?" Kai asked.

"Day after tomorrow, probably," Murphy said. "I need to study things for a bit before I decide."

While Kai helped Mrs. Leary prepare dinner for the guests, Murphy studied his notes in the bedroom.

The man closest to Fort Smith was Benjamin Cabble in Mississippi, a tobacco farmer before the war. He had eight hundred acres of prime land suitable for growing tobacco and once owned six slaves.

The war had devastated Cabble's farm, and he became an active member of the Klan after the war ended. He had a wife and two sons, but little was known about Cabble's family life after the war.

Murphy closed his notebook when Kai entered the room with a large tray of food.

"I thought we might eat in our room tonight," she said.

Kai set the tray on the table.

Murphy stood and slid out a chair for Kai.

"I frighten the guests, don't I?" he said as Kai sat.

"No. Maybe. Just a few of them," Kai said.

Murphy sat and looked at Kai. Together they broke out into laughter.

"Maybe if you shaved your beard and trimmed your hair, you wouldn't look so intimidating?" Kai said.

"Are you volunteering?" Murphy asked.

"I'm a fair hand with a scissors and razor," Kai said.

"How is the arm?"

"It doesn't hurt anymore and, as you can see, I can use it."

"Then we'll take a bath tomorrow, and you can trim me up a bit," Murphy said.

Kai nodded. "Eat your supper before it gets cold."

"Yes, ma'am," Murphy said.

Seated beside the stream on their newly purchased property, Kai clipped Murphy's hair using a scissors and comb.

"When you said a bath, I wrongfully assumed a tub full of hot, scented water," Kai said.

"A little cold water never hurt anybody," Murphy said. "How does my beard look?"

"Neat as a pin. Now stop talking so I can finish your hair."

"Two pumps, you said," Murphy said. "One in the kitchen and one for the indoor bathroom?"

"Yes, now hold still. I'm just about finished."

"We'll need a drainage system like I have on the farm."

"Mr. Grillo knows those things," Kai said. "There, finished. And quite handsome, I might say."

"Well, let's break out a bar of soap so we can eat our picnic lunch with clean hands," Murphy said.

Burke sighed as he walked from his office to the Oval Office, telegram in hand.

When he reached Arthur's office, he knocked softly, then opened the door and entered.

At his desk, Arthur looked up at Burke.

"You'll want to read this right away," Burke said.

Burke walked to the desk and handed the telegram to Arthur.

As he read the telegram, Arthur's face drained of color.

"I've already wired Murphy in Fort Smith," Burke said.

Arthur nodded.

Kai entered the boarding house while Murphy put the buggy and horse in the livery stable.

As she passed the small table in the hallway, she stopped and looked at the sealed telegram that stood out with the mail. She picked up the telegram. It was addressed to Murphy.

She took it to the porch and waited for Murphy to return from the livery.

When he arrived and walked up to the porch, Kai handed him the envelope.

"I'll get some coffee," she said and entered the house.

Murphy took a chair and used his small penknife to open the envelope. He read the telegram twice, then tucked it back into the envelope and took out his pipe.

Kai returned with two cups of coffee, handed one to Murphy, and then took a chair.

"Is it bad?" she asked.

"They are threatening to kidnap and murder one prominent figure from Washington every week unless they receive one million in gold," Murphy said. "Arthur has two weeks to raise the money."

"You'll leave in the morning?" Kai said.

"Yes."

Kai sipped coffee as she looked at Murphy. "Should I pack your bags for a long trip?"

"A week at least," Murphy said.

Kai nodded, stood, and entered the house. Murphy sat with his coffee and smoked his pipe.

Murphy sat in a chair and watched Kai brush her hair at her dressing table. In the light of the oil lantern, her black hair appeared as if made of silk.

Even when she did so simple a thing as brushing her hair, she stirred his blood.

Satisfied with her hair, Kai stood and removed her robe to reveal her naked body. She turned down the bed and Murphy noticed a purple bruise on her left cheek.

"Where did you get that bruise?" Murphy asked.

Kai reached around and touched the bruise.

"This afternoon, after our bath in the creek," Kai said. "I was lying on top of a stone under the blanket."

"Why didn't you say something?"

"It pleases me that my husband desires me so," Kai said. She slipped into bed and patted Murphy's side. "Now it is my turn to be pleased," she said.

Murphy read the actual telegram as he sat in a chair opposite President Arthur. Burke sat beside him and waited for Murphy to finish. Done, Murphy set the telegram on Arthur's desk.

"Burke, can you do something for me?" Murphy said.

"If I can," Burke said.

"They must be using a railroad telegraph machine to send these telegrams without a location," Murphy said. "Contact the railroad managers and find out if any were stolen in the last year."

"That's a tall order," Burke said.

"I know it is," Murphy said.

"Do you believe them; do you think their threat is viable?" Arthur asked.

"Yes," Murphy said.

"What are we supposed to do?" Arthur said. "I can't very well quarantine Congress and every diplomat in Washington, now can I?"

"Have you spoken with Ambassador Turner recently?" Murphy asked.

"That last meeting we held in my office about . . ." Arthur said. "Oh, Jesus Christ."

"Burke, do you know where Turner lives?" Murphy said.

"No, but give me ten minutes and I'll find out," Burke said.

After Burke left the Oval Office, Arthur looked at Murphy. "Do you have any idea the scandal this will cause, not to mention it will destroy diplomatic relations with Great Britain?"

"If you're worried they will seek military action, they won't," Murphy said.

"I know. But they can cause us serious economic decline through sanctions and damage our relations with other governments," Arthur said. "We aren't their equal economically at this point, and they can ruin us for a generation if they see fit."

"Don't get ahead of yourself," Murphy said. "I'm sure Turner is fine and at home."

Burke returned with Turner's address.

"He lives about a half mile from the British Embassy," Burke said.

"Is your buggy outside?" Murphy asked.

"It is," Burke said.

"Let's take a ride," Murphy said.

Burke stared at Murphy.

"The fresh air will do you good," Murphy said.

"I'll need to stop by my office first," Burke said.

As Murphy drove Burke's buggy, he glanced at the revolver in Burke's waistband and grinned.

"Back in the war, I knew a wagon master who always took his Colt out of the flap holster and tucked it in his pants just like you're doing now," Murphy said. "He figured it would save time drawing if he needed it. I warned him a hundred times not to do it, but he wouldn't listen."

"Why are you telling me this?" Burke asked.

"Covering some rocky terrain in Virginia I believe, he hit a bump and the Colt went off in his pants and blew his privates clean off," Murphy said.

"You're joking?" Burke said.

"No, I'm not," Murphy said. "Clean off."

In the dark, Burke discretely removed the Colt from his pants and set it on the seat.

"I think we have arrived," Murphy said.

Murphy stopped the buggy in front of an expensive town house. Light glowed from several windows.

"At least he's not asleep," Murphy said, and he hopped down from the buggy. "Coming?"

Murphy and Burke walked to the porch and Murphy knocked on the door. After several seconds, Turner came to the door.

"Who is there?" Turner asked from behind the door.

"Mr. Burke and Mr. Murphy, Ambassador," Burke said.

Several locks turned behind the door and it opened.

"Has something happened?" Turner asked.

"Ambassador, do you have any whiskey?" Burke asked.

Turner sat on the sofa in the living room and sipped whiskey from an expensive glass.

"My God, whatever can we do with these people?" Turner said.

"Do you have living quarters at the embassy?" Murphy asked.

"Yes, of course," Turner said. "I prefer this house, however."

"Understood, but it's safer in the embassy," Murphy said.

"I'm no coward, Mr. Murphy," Turner said.

"No one said you are," Murphy said. "But we're dealing with bushwhackers and backstabbers who ambush their victims. Go pack. We'll wait."

Turner stood up from the sofa.

"Excellent whiskey by the way," Burke said.

Murphy sat in a chair opposite Burke's desk and smoked his pipe.

"I'll be leaving in the morning for Virginia," Murphy said. "The man, Arnold Farris, on the list of six is closest. I might as well see him first."

Burke nodded. "If he's even still around."

223

"I'd like to use the White House telegraph to send a wire to Kai," Murphy said.

"Go ahead," Burke said. "And stay the night in one of the guest bedrooms. I'll see you for breakfast."

CHAPTER TWENTY-THREE

It was early afternoon by the time the train delivered Murphy to Richmond, Virginia.

Richmond wasn't New York or Chicago in size and scope, but it was a massive town of sixty thousand residents. Many were freed slaves held over from the war who decided to stay. As he walked Boyle from the railroad station into town, Murphy became aware of the many stares he drew from people on the street.

Carriages and buggies were the order of the day, and a man walking a horse through town had become an unusual sight. Especially if the man was armed with a sidearm and rifle.

As he crossed a wide street, two deputies approached Murphy.

"Open firearms are prohibited here in Richmond," a deputy said.

"Even for lawmen?" Murphy said.

"I don't see a badge," a deputy said.

"I don't carry a badge," Murphy said. "But I can show you my identification."

One deputy looked at the other.

"Get his gun first," a deputy said.

"Son, reach for my Colt, and you won't have any front teeth to smile with," Murphy said. "Now I'm going to hand you my wallet, and then we'll go see your boss."

Sheriff Plummer ran a department consisting of eighteen deputies and one full-time clerk. He was in his fifties and was first elected sheriff before the war. His reputation was as a smart, tough, and fair lawman.

Behind his desk, Plummer read Murphy's identification. "Is the president coming to town?" he asked.

"No," Murphy said. "I missed lunch on the train. What say you and I grab a bite?"

"I can't say as I'm familiar with the Farris family," Plummer said. "But if their farm is twenty miles west of Richmond, they probably don't get to town much."

"I'm not sure the Farris family is even still there," Murphy said. "But they probably do their local business with a town closer to their farm."

They were having lunch in the dining

room of the Richmond Hotel.

"What is your business with them anyway?" Plummer asked.

"That's classified information," Murphy said. "Truth is, if the railroad could get me closer than Richmond, I wouldn't have stopped here."

"Maybe it's classified, but does it have anything to do with my town?" Plummer asked.

"No."

"Fair enough," Plummer said. "Let's enjoy our lunch then."

Kai and Mrs. Leary were washing linen in a tub of boiling water behind the house when the delivery boy from the telegraph office arrived with a telegram.

Kai took the telegram and tipped the boy with a dime.

She sat on the bench behind the house to read the telegram.

Murphy wrote that he was headed to Virginia and would telegram again in a few days. He added that he loved her.

Kai lowered the telegram. "Well, that must have hurt to say," she said aloud.

Murphy and Plummer spent the afternoon visiting shops and stores in town. Murphy made polite inquiries concerning the Farris family, but most businesses had opened after the war, and the owners had little knowledge of old Virginia, as they called it.

Murphy bedded Boyle down at the Richmond Hotel livery and went directly to his fourth-floor room.

He studied his maps while having a small glass of whiskey. He needed to leave right after breakfast to make the twenty-mile ride to the location of the Farris farm by early afternoon.

As he removed his shirt to ready for bed, a soft knock at the door sounded.

He had removed his holster and placed it on the chair beside the bed and grabbed the Colt and walked to the door.

"Yes?" Murphy said.

"Are you the lawman asking questions about Farris?" a male voice asked.

Murphy cocked the Colt, unlocked the door, yanked it open, and stuck the Colt in the face of the man at the door.

"Who wants to know who I am?" Murphy asked.

The man was sixty or older, dressed in a tattered, dirty suit. His face was unshaven, and his hands hadn't seen soap in a while. He looked up at Murphy.

"I'm unarmed, and even if I was, I get the

feeling it would do me no good," he said.

"What is your name?" Murphy said.

"Stevens."

"Well, Mr. Stevens, what do you want?"

"A drink and a meal."

"Does my room look like a saloon to you?" Murphy said.

"You been asking all over town about old Arnold Farris," Stevens said.

"Come in, sit down, move one inch, and I'll shoot you," Murphy said.

Stevens entered the room and Murphy closed the door.

"On the bed," Murphy said.

Stevens sat on the bed. Murphy took a chair and held the Colt on his lap.

"Say, you wouldn't happen to have a drink around here?" Stevens said. "My whistle is god-awful dry."

"On the table beside the bed. Pour yourself a drink."

Stevens reached for the bottle and filled a water glass with six ounces of whiskey and took a long swallow.

"That's mighty fine whiskey, mister."

"Now tell me why you're here," Murphy said.

Stevens smacked his lips. "I was old Arnold's foreman before the war," he said. "Sixteen hundred acres of prime tobacco and twenty darkies to work the land."

"I don't think they're called darkies anymore," Murphy said.

"No? What do you call them then?"

"People."

"Suit yourself."

"Mr. Stevens, I'm a man of little patience," Murphy said.

Stevens took another sip from the glass and smacked his lips. "Well, the war took its toll on old Arnold for sure," he said. "Lost most everything. His two sons still work the place, but only three hundred acres a year. Without the darkies . . . I mean, people, to work the fields, that's about the best they can do."

"When did you see him last?" Murphy said.

"Maybe two months ago," Stevens said. "I work cleaning out the livery stables over on High Street, and he came in to board his horse overnight. I was in the loft fixing hay and he didn't see me, but I heard him tell the manager he was catching a train in the morning."

"Did you hear for where?"

"No, he didn't say."

"His sons still live on the farm?"

"As far as I know," Stevens said. "Last I seen them was the last time they came to town to ship tobacco to market. That must have been four months ago."

"What do you know about Farris?" Murphy said.

"In what capacity?"

"Did he hate black people?"

"Of course he hated them," Stevens said. "To him they were no better than a plow mule."

"After the war, did he join the Klan?" Murphy said.

"Him and most other slave owners in these parts," Stevens said.

Murphy took a ten-dollar gold piece from a pocket and tossed it to Stevens.

"Get yourself something to eat," Murphy said.

Stevens stood up. "You're some kind of lawman, ain't you?"

"Good night, Mr. Stevens," Murphy said.

CHAPTER TWENTY-FOUR

After breakfast, Murphy rode Boyle twenty miles west of town to the Farris farm. As he rode onto the farm, most of the acres were bare. About four hundred acres were covered with tobacco plants.

He rode to a large house that, in its heyday, must have been a grandiose sight. Today it was in disrepair and desperately needed fresh paint and a new roof.

Murphy stopped in front of the house and dismounted. "Hello in the house," he shouted.

Murphy's greeting went unanswered.

He tied Boyle to the hitching post, went up to the porch, and took a chair. He lit his pipe and looked at his watch.

Late in the afternoon, as Murphy sat on the porch chair and sipped coffee from the pot he took the liberty of making, a wagon arrived with three men in it. Two of the men were white, the third was black.

The man driving the wagon stood up. "Who are you, mister? What do you want?" he said.

"My name is Murphy. I'm with the US Secret Service," Murphy said. "I've been waiting quite a while. I hope you don't mind that I made a pot of coffee."

"You made a . . ."

"Who are you?" Murphy asked.

"Albert Farris. This is my brother, Arnold, and our friend, Hoke."

"Pleased to meet you all," Murphy said.

"So, what is it you want?" Albert said.

"Let's start with another cup of coffee," Murphy said.

"My pa left about three months ago when Hoke came to work for us," Albert said. "When the war broke out, I was just twelve. My brother Arnold, who was named after Pa, was all but ten. Hoke was the son of one of Pa's slaves and about the only friend we had in the world. After the war, Hoke moved north to Boston."

"We lost just about everything," Arnold said. "Crops, money, seed, everything."

"Is that when your father joined the Klan?" Murphy said.

Albert nodded.

"And now?" Murphy said.

"He left three months ago after Hoke came to work for us," Albert said. "It took some doing to find him up north, but with Hoke working for us, we plan to make a go at this place."

"Left for where?" Murphy said.

"We don't know," Arnold said. "He was in a rage over Hoke working here, packed and left. We haven't heard from him since."

"With Hoke, we've upped our working acres from three hundred to five," Albert said. "We plan to hire on Hoke's cousin next year and up it to a thousand acres split four ways."

"Do you plan to market the crop in Richmond?" Murphy said.

"Yes, sir," Albert said.

"Before he left, do you know what your father was involved in?" Murphy said.

"What do you mean?" Albert said.

"Was he active in local politics? Did he ever talk about the Klan? Things like that," Murphy said.

"Our father is a very bitter man, Mr. Murphy," Albert said. "He blamed the North and the freed slaves for all his troubles. In eighteen sixty he was a prosperous tobacco farmer. By eighteen sixty-five, he was all but penniless."

234

"He joined the Klan in hopes of rising the South, but it went nowhere," Arnold said. "The last few years he spent sitting on the porch with a jug and talking about the grand days before the war."

"Do you have any idea where he went?" Murphy said.

"Sure don't," Arnold said.

"I do," Hoke said.

Arnold and Albert looked at Hoke.

"What are you talking about, Hoke?" Arnold asked.

Murphy looked at Hoke. "Best tell me what you know," he said.

"When we was kids, I never knew I was Mr. Farris's property," Hoke said. "Me and Arnie and Albert would play in the open field behind the house. We had us a big paper kite we'd fly all day long. Remember?"

"We remember," Arnold said.

"The day I turned twelve, that son of a bitch Stevens dragged me out to the fields and put me to work," Hoke said. "I found out pretty quick I was nothing but a piece of property like a pair of Mr. Farris's plow mules. I still wear scars on my back from his whip and walking stick."

"We didn't even realize what happened ourselves, Hoke," Arnold said. "It was never our doing."

"I know that," Hoke said. "I wouldn't be here if I thought otherwise."

Murphy looked at Hoke. "You said you knew where he went."

Hoke nodded. "The day he left, I was plowing the south field," he said. "He was riding his horse, and he stops and gets down. He had his old Colt Dragoon and aimed it at me. He said, 'Nigger, when I return from Fort Smith, there won't be one darkie left in the South.' Then he got back on his horse and rode away."

"My pa said all that?" Arnold said.

"Are you sure he said Fort Smith?" Murphy asked.

"I'm sure," Hoke said.

"Do you know what my pa meant by that?" Arnold asked Murphy.

"I'm afraid I do, but it's classified information," Murphy said. "Well, I guess I'll head on out. Thanks for the coffee."

"It's a day's ride to Richmond and the same west to the next town," Arnold said. "You're welcome to stay for supper and make use of our extra room."

"It's Hoke's night to cook supper, and he makes a mean beef stew," Albert said.

"That was a fine supper, Hoke," Murphy said.

They were on the porch with cups of coffee. Murphy smoked his pipe and blew lazy clouds of smoke that vanished in the dark.

"Sorry we don't have any whiskey to offer you a drink, Mr. Murphy," Arnold said. "We don't get to town more than twice a month."

"Hold on," Murphy said. He stood, entered the house, went to the room his gear was in, removed a bottle of his father's whiskey from a saddlebag, and returned to the porch.

He added an ounce to each coffee cup and then sat.

"Give that a taste," Murphy said.

After taking a sip, Arnold said, "That's fine whiskey, Mr. Murphy."

"My father has been making whiskey for nearly forty years," Murphy said. "He makes it from corn. Grow a couple hundred acres of corn next season, and my father will buy it. I'll give you the address in the morning."

"Corn, huh?" Albert said.

Murphy nodded. "Whose turn is it to make breakfast?"

Late in the afternoon, Murphy walked Boyle through the streets of Richmond to the railroad depot.

"Murphy, what are you doing back in town?" Sheriff Plummer said when he spot-

237

ted Murphy in the street.

"About to catch a train," Murphy said.

"Did you find the Farris place all right?"

"I did."

"I won't ask if you had a satisfactory outcome," Plummer said. "Do you have time for a cup of coffee?"

"Let me check the schedule and buy a ticket first," Murphy said.

They walked together to the ticket office. The next train to Fort Smith was scheduled to leave in two hours.

"Take a walk with me to the livery before we have coffee," Murphy said.

"Which one?"

"High Street."

"That's ten blocks from here."

The walk took about ten minutes. The High Street Livery was large, with stalls for forty horses and rented carriages. A manager was on duty in an office and stepped out to greet Murphy and Plummer.

"Sheriff, what can I do for you?" he asked.

"Do you have a man in your employ named Stevens?" Murphy said.

"Who are you?" the manager said.

"A man with very little patience," Murphy said.

Plummer looked at the manager. "Better get him out here," he said.

238

The manager poked his head into the stables. "Stevens, get out here," he shouted.

A few seconds later, Stevens appeared. "Did you need . . . ?" he said and looked at Murphy.

"Hoke says hello," Murphy said and punched Stevens in the jaw.

Flat on his rear end, Stevens looked up at Murphy.

"If you weren't an old drunk, I'd beat you to a frazzle," Murphy said.

"I was just doing my job," Stevens said.

Murphy took the reins and walked Boyle away from the livery.

"Well, I was," Stevens said.

"I didn't know about that sorry son of a bitch," Plummer said.

"Men like Hoke wear the scars for a lifetime because of men like Stevens," Murphy said.

"He's working for the sons of the man who once owned him," Plummer said. "I don't know if I could do that without wanting to kill them."

"They're making a go of it," Murphy said. "That's what counts now. Well, I'd best catch my train."

CHAPTER TWENTY-FIVE

The streets of Fort Smith weren't yet light when Murphy led Boyle from the railroad depot to the boarding house. Shops and homes were dark and quiet, but not everybody was still in bed.

A wagon from the creamery was delivering bottles of milk and pounds of butter. A coal wagon was delivering coal. The sanitation people were cleaning the streets of horse manure.

As he passed a bakery, Murphy caught the scent of fresh-baked bread.

He reached the boarding house and tied Boyle to the hitching post. "I'll be back in a few minutes," he said.

The front door was open. Mrs. Leary was in the kitchen preparing breakfast for the guests.

"Mr. Murphy, you startled me," Mrs. Leary said.

"Is Kai still in bed?" Murphy said.

"Yes, but I expect her down soon."

Murphy pointed to the coffee pot on the stove. "Is that ready?"

"Yes."

Murphy filled two cups with coffee. "Thank you," he said.

He carried the cups up to the second floor, set one cup down for a moment to open the bedroom door, and then picked it up. The first hint of light filtered through the window, but the room was still dark. He set the cups on the small table beside the bed and lit the oil lantern.

The slight movement and noise was all Kai needed to wake up. She looked up at Murphy.

"I brought you fresh coffee," he said.

Kai sat up, then stood up and hugged Murphy around the waist.

"Take off your gun belt," she said. "And anything else you've a mind to."

Murphy and Kai sat on the porch with cups of coffee and the morning sun on their faces.

"How long are you home for?" Kai asked.

"At least a day, maybe a bit longer."

"We got a letter from Mr. Grillo," Kai said. "He will be here in two days with some sketches and blueprints."

"The checkbook I use for expenses for the

241

farm is in my bag in the closet," Murphy said. "Write him a check for what he requires."

"Maybe you will be here to write it yourself?" Kai said.

"Maybe," Murphy said. He looked at his pocket watch. "Parker should be in his office by now. Can you walk to his office and tell him I'll be stopping by directly?"

Kai stood. "Let me get my wrap," she said.

"He didn't say why?" Parker said.

"No, and I've learned not to ask," Kai said. "He just said he'd be along directly."

"Well, directly isn't exactly a specific time," Parker said. "The courthouse cafeteria is open; let's have ourselves a cup of coffee while we wait."

When Murphy entered Weaver's shop shortly after it opened, Weaver was sweeping the floor. He took one look at Murphy and immediately stepped behind the counter.

"I remember you," Weaver said. "Mr. Murphy, isn't it?"

"Close your shop, Mr. Weaver. You're taking the day off," Murphy said.

"See here, I just opened," Weaver said.

242

"And I've already told you everything I know."

"Mr. Weaver, I wasn't asking," Murphy said.

"I have rights," Weaver said.

"Either you walk with me to see Judge Parker, or I will kick you the entire way on Main Street for the entire town to see," Murphy said. "Which will it be?"

Weaver sat at the conference table in Parker's office and stared at Parker.

"I have rights, Judge. You can't do this," Weaver said.

"Be quiet, Mr. Weaver," Parker said. "This is my courtroom, not yours."

"This isn't the courtroom, Judge. It's your office," Weaver said.

"I'm a presidential appointee, Mr. Weaver. My courtroom is wherever I happen to be," Parker said. "Now don't say another word until I tell you otherwise."

Several minutes passed before the door opened, Murphy entered the office and closed the door behind him. He held several documents in his hand and tossed them on the table in front of Weaver.

"Your statement from our last meeting. Do you remember?" Murphy said.

"Of course, I remember," Weaver said.

"And I already told you everything I know about Jessup and his associates."

"Put your hands on the table, palms up," Murphy said.

"Why?"

"Because I told you to," Murphy said.

Reluctantly, Weaver placed his hands on the table, palms up.

"Last time you told me you knew of Jessup's desire to rekindle the Klan and he met with the six men you named, but you had nothing to do with it except to loan Jessup some money," Murphy said. "Is that correct?"

"That's what I said," Weaver said.

Murphy placed two fingers on each of Weaver's wrists.

"What the hell are you doing?" Weaver said.

"Taking your pulse," Murphy said.

"What the hell's a pulse?" Weaver said.

"Your heartbeat, Mr. Weaver," Murphy said. "It registers as a pulse on your wrists. If you're sitting or sleeping it registers a nice even beat. But if you're working hard or exercising, it will increase to a rapid beat. You can't help it; that's the function of the heart."

"What the hell does that have to do with me?" Weaver said.

"The other remarkable thing is that, when a person lies, the body feels stress. That stress registers as a rapid heartbeat," Murphy said. "Right now your heartbeat is racing."

Parker looked at Murphy's fingers on Weaver's wrists.

"Either you tell me what I want to know, or I'll ask the judge to toss you in jail to await trial," Murphy said. "And with his backlog, that could take a year or longer."

"A year? I have rights. What charges?" Weaver said.

"Withholding evidence, obstruction of justice, conspiring to assassinate a former president, blackmail, kidnapping, extortion, murder, and illegal membership in the Klan," Murphy said. "And if your heart beats any faster, I believe you will have a stroke."

"God damn you! Let me go," Weaver said.

Murphy released Weaver's wrists and said, "Judge, have a deputy toss him into a holding cell in the basement."

"Just hold on. Just wait a minute," Weaver said. "I'm a business owner and an upstanding member of this community, and I have rights."

"You're a member of the Klan, Mr. Weaver," Murphy said. "An organization created to basically undermine the American government. That's treason, an offense where usually the offender is hanged. Right, Judge?"

"In my court, that's a definite," Parker said.

Weaver closed his eyes.

"Mr. Weaver?" Parker said.

"I'd have to leave Fort Smith," Weaver said. "Sell my shop and move to where nobody knows me."

"Or you could rot in jail or be hanged," Murphy said.

Weaver opened his eyes and looked at Murphy. "You are one son of a bitch," he said.

"Maybe so, but I'm not the one looking at a rope," Murphy said.

"Judge, I want your word I'll walk out of here a free man, and no one will stop me from leaving Fort Smith," Weaver said.

"That is up to Murphy here," Parker said.

Weaver looked at Murphy. "Well?"

Murphy nodded.

"What do you want to know?" Weaver said.

"All that stuff you said about pulse rate and heartbeats, was that for real?" Parker said.

Parker and Murphy were having a small

drink after Weaver was taken away by a court deputy.

"It's real," Murphy said.

"How long do you want me to hold him?" Parker asked.

"Until his story checks out," Murphy said.

"I can't hold him forever," Parker said.

"Hold him just long enough," Murphy said. "If he complains, tell him he's in protective custody of the court for his own welfare."

Parker sipped his drink. "Murphy, seeing as how you and Kai are building a home here in Fort Smith, why not let me appoint you senior marshal to the court? You'd still travel a bit, but not outside of Arkansas."

"Judge, I made a promise to Kai that my days as a lawman would end when this job does," Murphy said. "It's a promise I'd like to keep."

Parker nodded. "I understand," he said.

"And speaking of Kai, I'd best get home," Murphy said.

Murphy was surprised to see Kai sitting on the courthouse steps talking to Marshal Cal Witson.

"Murphy, I hope you don't mind me stealing your wife for a few minutes," Witson said.

"How have you been, Marshal?" Murphy asked.

"Fine. Kai was just telling me your plans to build a house. I hope it goes well," Witson said.

"When it's done, we'll have a barbecue to christen the occasion and invite half the town," Murphy said.

"Sounds good," Witson said. "Well, the judge is waiting on me."

After Witson left, Kai stood and took Murphy's arm.

"I thought you might like to buy your wife lunch at Delmonico's," she said.

CHAPTER TWENTY-SIX

Murphy sat on the porch and read his notes as dictated by Weaver.

Kai sat beside him with a pair of knitting needles and a ball of yarn.

Each had a cup of coffee.

Murphy smoked his pipe.

Weaver admitted he had allowed Jessup and the others from his list of names to use his storage room for Klan meetings during the past year. The idea of kidnapping a Washington bigwig to finance their Klan membership was Jessup's, but the victim was selected by committee. How they selected the victim came after the group relocated to a small town called Durango in Colorado.

The purpose of relocating was unknown to Weaver, but he assumed it was to plot the kidnapping from a safe distance, so no locals would be suspected.

Murphy thought the location was chosen

due to its close proximity to the canyons, where the money was delivered by the team of secret service agents.

Weaver's role, besides funding the start of the operation and providing a meeting place, was to recruit new members from the South to join the cause.

Weaver claimed no knowledge of what became of the kidnapping victim.

When Murphy asked, Weaver stated he believed in the Klan because he held in his heart that the freed slaves were inferior to white men and would only serve to ruin the country.

Murphy lowered the reports.

"I have to go to Washington in the morning," he said. "Probably just overnight. Want to come and have dinner with the president?"

In mid-stitch, Kai said, "Again?"

"The latest telegram claims one member of Congress will be kidnapped every week until one million in gold is paid," Burke said.

"We need to stall them to give me time to go to Colorado and look around," Murphy said.

"Do you believe this man Stevens?" Arthur asked.

"Yes."

"Then what do you suggest?" Arthur said.

"Did they leave contact instructions?" Murphy asked.

"They will send delivery instructions in two days," Burke said. "We are to respond immediately if we comply. If not, members of Congress will start to disappear shortly thereafter."

"When they make contact, tell them we comply, but we will need time to raise the one million in gold," Murphy said. "Ten days, at least."

"And if they refuse to grant the time?" Arthur said.

"We're no worse off than we are now," Murphy said. "These men want the money to fund their ambitions. They will grant the time if they believe we will pay."

"This town, Durango, what do we know about it?" Arthur asked.

"It sits close to the border of Utah," Murphy said. "A couple of days' ride to the area where the agents delivered the first ransom demand. I doubt they will use the same location for a drop point, but in the general area, where they can see for miles without being seen."

"I suppose if I contacted the army post at Tonopah, it would just alert them and send

251

them into hiding," Arthur said.

"They are already in hiding," Murphy said. "In Durango."

"And you're willing to go in alone?" Arthur said.

"It's not just these six old men," Murphy said. "They've recruited younger men to do the riding and killing. We're after all of them, and there is something else you need to focus on."

"And that is?" Arthur said.

"For this to have happened the way that it has, those six men had to have recruited someone who knows Washington very well," Murphy said. "It's the only way they could have known how to get to Turner's niece."

"An insider, of course," Arthur said. "That makes their threat to kidnap one congressman for every week we delay even more viable."

"There are still a great many people in Washington who still believe in the old South," Murphy said. "Maybe enough to partner with the six? I've given it a lot of thought and don't see any other way but an insider."

Arthur sighed heavily. "When will you leave for Durango?"

"As soon as the next demand comes in," Murphy said.

"Well, we're back to the waiting game then," Arthur said.

"We can't allow them to kidnap another victim," Arthur said. "That victim, gold or not, won't be returned alive."

Murphy stood up from his chair. "Kai is waiting for me," he said. "We'll see you at dinner."

As Murphy and Kai walked through the lobby of the fashionable Washington hotel, Murphy glanced at the four men seated in chairs around a table. They whispered to each other as they looked at Kai.

One of the men whispered loud enough for Murphy and Kai to hear, "I guess they let anybody in here these days, even a squaw."

Kai took hold of Murphy's arm and immediately felt it tighten.

"Don't bother with it," she said and guided him to the desk.

As they reached the desk, the men snickered.

Murphy set his satchel down and turned.

"No trouble, please," Kai said. "It isn't important."

Murphy walked directly to the four men. They silenced as he towered over them.

"My wife is part Navajo and part Irish,"

Murphy said. "Either side of her would put you four in your grave."

"See here," one of the four men said.

"Say another word and it will be your last," Murphy said. "Unless it's to apologize to my wife."

The four men stared at Murphy.

"I wasn't asking," Murphy said.

The four men continued to stare at Murphy. Then they stood and meekly approached the desk where Kai waited.

As Kai and Murphy soaked in a large tub, she said, "What did you say to those men in the lobby?"

"I told them you're part Navajo, and if they didn't apologize, you would find their rooms and take their scalps in their sleep," Murphy said.

"And they believed that nonsense?" Kai said.

"They apologized, didn't they?"

"I am beginning to realize that my husband is a little bit crazy," Kai said.

"This water is getting cold," Murphy said.

"We need to get dressed for dinner, anyway," Kai said.

"I was thinking of some other way to warm things up," Murphy said.

"I know what you were thinking," Kai

said. "Now come on, or we'll be late."

"You look lovely Mrs. Murphy," President Arthur said when she and Murphy arrived at the dining room in the White House.

"Thank you, Mr. President," Kai said.

Murphy pulled out a chair for Kai to sit next to Burke, and then took the chair to Kai's left.

"Mrs. Murphy, how do you like Washington?" Arthur asked. "I believe the last time you were here, the circumstances weren't conducive to good conversation."

"There is nothing wrong with Washington, just with some of the people in it," Kai said. "But I suppose you can say that about any city or town."

"May I ask what languages you speak?" Arthur said.

"Navajo, Sioux, Apache, and some Cheyenne," Kai said. "A bit of French, a touch of the old Irish, and, of course, English."

"Have you ever thought of becoming a teacher?" Arthur asked.

"What do you think about President Arthur's offer to teach school on the reservation in Fort Smith?" Kai asked as she slipped out of her evening dress.

"I'm surprised Judge Parker didn't think

of it himself," Murphy said.

"It would be a big commitment," Kai said. "Four hours a day, three days a week."

"You were wondering what to do after I retired," Murphy said. "Besides, it's only for the summer months. It wouldn't interfere with spending the winter in Tennessee."

"So you're not upset?"

"Since we've been married, I've been home one day out of seven, I don't have the right to be upset," Murphy said. "Besides, I think you'd be really good at it."

"What about our adoption application?"

"The child will need an education. Who better than his mother to teach him at school?"

"President Arthur told me he will have a letter to take to Judge Parker," Kai said. "When will you be coming home?"

"Day after tomorrow," Murphy said. "Hopefully Mr. Grillo will still be in town."

"Ask him to stay an extra day," Murphy said. "He'll agree."

"Let's go to bed," Kai said.

"Are you tired?"

"I said let's go to bed," Kai said. "I said nothing about being tired."

"I will ask Mr. Grillo to stay a few extra

256

days if he can," Kai said.

"If he can't, you can handle things," Murphy said.

Kai nodded.

"The train is boarding," she said. "And the boys in the schoolyard are waiting to play with you."

"What are you looking for?" Burke asked.

He and Murphy were in the congressional library, where Murphy was studying maps.

"Most telegraph lines out west follow the railroad tracks, because the land is already cleared," Murphy said.

"So?"

"So Durango doesn't have a telegraph office yet," Murphy said. "How far are you willing to ride to find a telegraph line to use a railroad box?"

Burke looked at the path Murphy had traced using a red pencil. The Southern Pacific line was twenty miles to the north of Durango.

"Twenty miles north to send a telegram, and sixty miles west to the desert," Burke said. "All an easy riding distance."

"They planned well in Weaver's storeroom," Murphy said. "We're going to need those ten days to stall them, Burke."

"Are we done here?" Burke asked.

"For now."

"Let's go to my office and have a drink," Burke said. "All this waiting makes me thirsty."

CHAPTER TWENTY-SEVEN

After he read Arthur's letter, Parker set it down and said, "How does Murphy feel about this?"

"He said he's surprised you didn't think of it first," Kai said.

"Frankly, so am I," Parker said.

"I'd like to do this, Judge," Kai said.

"I'll draw up the papers and we can take a ride out to the Indian Nation," Parker said.

Burke was dozing at his desk when the telegraph operator knocked on the door and came storming in.

"It's here," the operator said and handed Burke the telegraph.

"Where is Murphy?" Burke said.

"Last I saw him, he was chopping wood behind the White House."

"It's eight o'clock at night. Get him. Tell

him to report to the telegraph office right away."

Shirt unbuttoned, sweat dripping down his chest, Murphy entered the White House telegraph office to find Arthur, Burke, and the operator waiting for him.

"They want to know if we comply," Burke said.

"Tell them yes, and ask for ten days to get the gold together," Murphy said.

The operator looked at Arthur, and the president nodded yes.

The operator tapped the keys.

Three minutes passed before the reply came. The operator wrote the message on a piece of paper and handed it to Arthur, who read it aloud.

"We agree to the terms. Await delivery instructions in ten days."

Arthur looked at Murphy. "I hope you know what you are doing," he said.

Murphy and Burke ate a late supper in the dining room of Murphy's hotel.

"Do you?" Burke asked.

Cutting into a steak, Murphy paused. "Do I what?"

"Know what you're doing."

"If I knew what I was doing, I'd be home

in my warm bed with my even warmer wife instead of sitting here with you," Murphy said.

"When will you leave?"

"In the morning," Murphy said. "For Fort Smith to pick up Boyle and my gear. I'll need you to do something for me before I leave."

"What's that?"

Murphy removed a folded paper from a pocket and handed it to Burke.

"Have Arthur sign this for me."

Burke unfolded the paper, read it quickly, and nodded.

"Thank you," Murphy said.

Marshal Bass Reeves drove Parker's buggy to the boarding house. Kai and Judge Parker rode in the back. Reeves stopped the buggy beside the steps and jumped down to extend a hand to Kai.

"Would you like to come in?" Kai said. "I'm sure Mrs. Leary has plenty of leftovers keeping warm on the stove."

"Thank you, no," Reeves said. "My wife is waiting on me, and I know the judge has things to do at the courtroom."

"Then I'll say good night to you both," Kai said. "And thank you again, Judge."

"Thank you, Kai," Parker said. "I'm sure

261

you'll make a fine teacher for the kids on the reservation."

Once Kai was safely in the house, Parker moved to the front and Reeves moved the buggy back to the street.

"Judge, it's all over town that Weaver is in your jail," Reeves said. "What is going on around here?"

"It's a federal matter, Bass, and classified," Parker said.

"Aren't you a federal judge and me a federal marshal?" Reeves said.

"Yes, that's true, but . . ." Parker said.

"But what?" Reeves said.

Parker sighed. "If you tell a living soul, I'll have you jailed, marshal or not," he said.

"Do you really think someone in Washington is behind this?" Burke asked.

"Not behind, but definitely recruited to help," Murphy said.

They were on the front porch of Murphy's hotel. Each had a cup of coffee. Murphy smoked his pipe, Burke a long cigar.

Murphy removed a silver flask from his jacket pocket and splashed a bit of whiskey into each coffee cup.

"The six men from Weaver's list are behind the plot, but they need help, and a lot of it, to make their scheme work," Murphy said. "Money can buy a lot of things, including a traitor."

Burke finished his coffee and stood. "I'll see you off in the morning and give you the signed letter," he said.

"It ain't right, Judge," Reeves said. "It just ain't right."

"Before you go to bellowing all over town, Bass, this was told to me in strict confidence," Parker said.

"It sticks in my craw, Judge," Reeves said.

"You're not alone on that matter," Parker said. "Look, Bass, you've been a top marshal for a number of years now. Not just that, but a fine man and member of this community as well. Let's wait and see what Murphy says before we go off half-cocked."

Reeves nodded. "Okay, Judge. Good night."

"Good night, Bass," Parker said.

Burke handed the letter signed by President Arthur to Murphy, who in turn handed it to the railroad depot manager.

The depot manager read the letter and then looked at Murphy.

"I might have one in a storeroom," he said.

A few minutes later, Murphy held the railroad telegraph box in his left hand as he shook hands with Burke.

"I'll be in touch," Murphy said.

CHAPTER TWENTY-EIGHT

Murphy and Kai were having coffee on the porch of the boarding house after supper when Parker and Reeves arrived in Parker's buggy.

"Judge, Marshal Reeves, what brings you out after dark?" Murphy asked.

Parker and Reeves stepped down from the buggy and approached the porch.

"Kai, with your permission, I'd like a few private words with Murphy," Parker said.

"He's only been home for an hour," Kai said.

"This won't take long, I promise," Parker said.

Kai stood. "I'll be in the kitchen with Mrs. Leary."

Parker and Reeves took chairs on the porch.

"What little I know of your classified assignment I confided in Marshal Reeves," Parker said. "And before you chide me on that breach of trust, I would say that Marshal Reeves had earned that privilege."

"I wouldn't disagree with that, Judge," Murphy said. "But had you stayed silent, there would be no reason for this visit."

"I'm volunteering my services to help you," Reeves said. "That's the reason for this visit."

Murphy looked at Reeves.

"To go after the Klan?" Murphy said.

"There's no better marshal than Bass Reeves," Parker said.

"No doubt, Judge, but where I'm going, they'll likely shoot a black man on sight," Murphy said.

"I was born a slave," Reeves said. "My name, Reeves, was my master's name. My whole race of people has been freed, but we ain't really free, not as long as men who want the Klan still exist."

Murphy looked at Parker.

"Having backup can't hurt, Murphy," Parker said.

"How are you with a long gun, Marshal?"

"I can hit a bird flying with my Henry rifle."

Murphy nodded. "We leave in two days."

"I'll be ready," Reeves said.

"But I run the show," Murphy said. "The chain of command is me, then you.

Agreed?"

"I never saw it otherwise," Reeves said.

"Then I'll meet you at the train at eight in the morning, day after tomorrow," Murphy said.

Parker looked at Reeves. "Can I go home now?" he said.

"Damn fool men," Kai said. "Always in such a hurry to get yourselves killed."

"I'm not in a hurry to . . ." Murphy said.

"We have a new house about to be built, the farm in Tennessee, the possible adoption of a child, I'm going to be teaching school on the reservation, and you can't wait to go off and get yourself killed," Kai said.

Murphy was learning that when Kai was in a tirade, it was best to just leave her alone until it passed.

She sat at her dressing table and started to brush her hair. "And now you're going to get Marshal Reeves killed along with you," she said.

Murphy stuffed his pipe with fresh tobacco.

"I've known Marshal Reeves for ten years or more," Kai said. "He's a fine man with a wife and six children, but do you care? No. Just bring him along after a group of dangerous Klan members. Sure, why not?"

Murphy struck a match and lit the pipe.

"I have an idea," Kai said. "Why don't I go with you? I can do the cooking while you go off and track these murderers. When you get killed I can sing the Navajo death song over your grave so your spirit will go to heaven."

Murphy blew a smoke ring at the ceiling.

Kai set the brush aside, turned, and looked at Murphy. "None of this makes any sense," she said.

"I know it doesn't," Murphy said.

"Why can't you turn it over to the secret service? They have dozens of men," Kai said.

"I like to finish what I start," Murphy said. "And when it's done, that's it."

"Can you make that promise?" Kai said.

"I can," Murphy said.

Kai nodded. "I'll hold you to it," she said.

"I know."

"Men are all fools," Kai said.

"I won't argue that point," Murphy said.

"At last we agree on something. Put out the lantern, and let's go to bed," Kai said.

Grillo had brought a portable drafting table with him and set it up in the field so that Murphy and Kai could study his blueprints and sketches.

"It's a fine piece of work you've done here," Murphy said as he studied the blueprints. "When can you get started?"

"I can have materials shipped in ten days and have a crew in place in two weeks," Grillo said.

"How long to completion?" Murphy asked.

"One month, if the well and plumbing don't give us any problems," Grillo said.

Murphy looked at Kai, and she nodded.

"My wife will write you a check," Murphy said. "And when we get back to town, we'll have lunch at Delmonico's."

After lunch, in front of Delmonico's, Murphy said, "Mr. Grillo, I need to see Judge Parker for a few minutes. Would you escort my wife back to the boarding house?"

"Certainly," Grillo said.

Kai looked at Murphy, but he turned away and walked toward the courthouse.

Parker read Murphy's one-page long last will and testament. It stated that, in the event of his death, Kai will take sole possession of all his property and liquid assets. It also stated that if Marshal Bass Reeves was to be killed along with him, ten percent of the yearly profits from his farm in Tennes-

269

see be given to Reeves's widow and children.

Parker lowered the document.

"This is quite a will," Parker said.

"It's only fair," Murphy said. "Will you sign it and make it binding?"

"With pleasure," Parker said.

Kai was on the porch with a cup of coffee and her knitting needles when Murphy returned.

"The coffee is keeping warm in the kitchen," she said.

Murphy went inside and returned a minute later with a mug, then sat next to Kai.

"What was that about after lunch?" Kai asked.

"Nothing," Murphy said. "I've never asked you what you're knitting there."

"A top cover for our bed in the new home," Kai said.

Murphy looked at Kai, and he could see the fear in her eyes.

"Don't worry," he said. "I'm not so easy to kill."

"My first husband used to say that to me every time he left home to go after some outlaw," Kai said. "And when he came home, he would say 'See, I'm still alive.' Until one day he didn't come home and one

270

day he was no longer alive."

Murphy sipped some coffee as he looked at Kai. "We need a proper honeymoon," he said.

"What?" Kai said.

"A honeymoon. We need a proper one," Murphy said. "When I get back and the house is still being built, we should take a proper honeymoon."

Kai looked at Murphy.

"Where would you like to go? What would you like to see that you've never seen before?" Murphy said.

"You're serious?"

"Of course, I'm serious," Murphy said. "So what's your pleasure? What would you like to see most?"

"Anywhere?"

"Name it."

"There is a place far to the north called Alaska," Kai said. "I've read about it and have seen pictures in books of the great ice walls. I would like to see that."

"It's cold that far north, even in the summer months," Murphy said.

"I will knit us warm sweaters," Kai said.

"Alaska it is," Murphy said.

Kai nodded. "Would you be a dear and get me some more coffee?"

Murphy stood and took Kai's mug. "Be

right back."

The moment Murphy was inside the house, Kai set the knitting aside and burst into tears.

Murphy walked Boyle to the boarding house where Kai stood on the porch.

"No need to walk with me to the railroad," Murphy said. "We can say goodbye here."

"I'll walk with you," Kai said.

Kai stepped down from the porch and took Murphy's arm.

"Do you have all your gear?" she asked.

"Everything I need," Murphy said. "Anything extra, I can always buy."

As they walked through the center of town, Kai noticed the citizens of Fort Smith stare at Murphy. She knew that with his towering height, black trail clothes, and custom-made Colt around his waist, Murphy was a sight, but this was something different.

She could see in their eyes they understood what they were looking at was a man born to be a lawman.

It was the moment Kai stopped being afraid.

They reached the depot.

"I'll wire when I can," Murphy said.

"I will take care of things with Mr. Grillo,"

Kai said.

"I believe we will have to travel to Seattle to take a ship to Alaska," Murphy said. "Maybe you can do some research on that while I'm gone."

"I will get started knitting us sweaters," Kai said.

Murphy stared at Kai.

"I haven't got the words," he said.

"I know," she said. "Go do your job."

CHAPTER TWENTY-NINE

Bass Reeves rolled a cigarette as he looked out the window and watched the Arkansas scenery roll by at fifty miles an hour.

Seated opposite Reeves, Murphy smoked his pipe as he read a newspaper.

Reeves struck a match and lit the cigarette.

"How sure are we these men are hiding in Durango?" he asked.

"Close to positive," Murphy said. "They may have relocated to a new site, but it won't be far from the desert and canyons."

"How do you plan to smoke them out?" Reeves said.

"How do you get angry bees out of a hive?"

"With smoke."

"We'll do the same," Murphy said.

"You've been with the secret service a long time," Reeves said.

"Since Grant started it in seventy," Murphy said. "Before that, they used mostly

Pinkerton's. I did take a few years off to run for Congress. I can't say as I enjoyed that very much."

"The gossip is you're going to settle in Fort Smith after this assignment," Reeves said.

"Part time," Murphy said. "Kai likes it in Fort Smith, but we'll winter in Tennessee."

"So it's true what I heard. This is your last assignment?" Reeves said.

"It is."

"What do you plan to do after?"

"My father has been in the whiskey-making business nearly forty years," Murphy said. "It's time I took over."

"Me, I don't know anything else but being a marshal," Reeves said. "All I knew before that was being a slave and farming, and I was terrible at being a farmer. I expect I'll die wearing a badge."

"How does your wife feel about it?" Murphy said.

"We got six kids with number seven on the way the end of the month," Reeves said. "She can't wait for me to hit the road after some outlaw."

Murphy grinned. "We'll see if we can get you home for the delivery."

"No hurry," Reeves said. "My wife will just cuss me for causing her so much pain

275

and throw me out of the house."

"Marshal Reeves, I do believe the dining car is open and serving lunch," Murphy said.

"Murphy left for Durango this morning," Burke said. "He sent a wire before boarding the train."

"He has seven days before they make contact again," President Arthur said. "Is that enough time?"

"It will have to be," Burke said.

Arthur sighed. "I hope you're right, William," he said. "I hope to God you are right."

Kai was boiling linen behind the house when Judge Parker arrived in his buggy. Mrs. Leary told him Kai was out back, and he walked around the side of the house.

"Hello, Judge," Kai said. "Is something wrong?"

"No, but the man who attacked you is fit for trial," Parker said. "I'd like to hold the trial tomorrow morning at ten, if that's all right with you."

"It is," Kai said. "Come in the house for a cup of coffee."

■ ■ ■ ■

"That was a fine steak," Reeves told the waiter.

"Care for more coffee, Marshal?" the waiter asked.

"Touch us both up," Reeves said.

After the waiter filled the cups, Reeves said, "There was a time not so long ago I would have had to ride in the boxcar with the horses."

"Times change," Murphy said.

"You know, when the war broke out, I ran away and lived with the Cherokee," Reeves said. "What's been done to the Indians is as bad as what was done to my people."

"Like I said, times change, and people change along with them," Murphy said.

"Maybe so, but there's still a whole lot of wrong left over," Reeves said.

"When we get to Durango, we'll put a dent in the wrong," Murphy said.

Reeves nodded. "If they don't put a dent in us first."

In his sleeping car, Murphy carefully broke down his Colt revolver and cleaned and oiled each piece of the working mechanism. The ritual of cleaning his weapons was more than just a way to pass the time when there was nothing else to do. It assured Murphy he wouldn't have a misfire. When in the thick of things, a misfire could cost you your life.

The last time Murphy had a misfire was in sixty-four when he was using an eighteen-sixty, cap-and-ball revolver. The misfire nearly cost him his life, and he made sure never to have another one.

With the widespread use of the contained cartridge after the war, misfires were rarer, but could still prove fatal in the right circumstances.

Once the Colt was thoroughly clean, oiled, and assembled, Murphy inspected each of the six bullets he loaded into the wheel for defects. He did the same for the eighteen rounds he loaded into the slots on his holster.

He did the same with his Winchester rifle. To Murphy, his weapons were a valuable tool of his trade and necessary to staying alive.

After the Winchester was cleaned, assembled, and loaded, Murphy stretched out on the bed.

The train was scheduled to arrive in Alamosa at ten in the morning. From there, it was a two-day ride to Durango. That didn't leave much time to smoke out the list of six from their hideout.

The train slowed to a stop. They needed to take on water. Murphy got up from the bed and left the sleeping car.

Reeves was in his sleeping car and opened the door when Murphy knocked.

"How are you with a Winchester?" Murphy said.

"I once hit a turkey at four hundred yards," Reeves said.

"Let's grab some dinner, then crack open a bottle of my father's whiskey and discuss your marksmanship skills," Murphy said.

Murphy awoke at seven in the morning and met Reeves for breakfast at eight.

"I'll be damn glad to get shed of this train," Reeves said.

"When we reach Alamosa, ride south a few miles and wait for me," Murphy said. "I'll pick up supplies and meet up with you. And don't forget to remove your badge."

"This ain't the first time I rode under-cover," Reeves said.

"Maybe not, but how many other times have you gone after the Klan?" Murphy said.

Murphy rode south out of Alamosa with

fifty pounds of supplies tied to Boyle's saddle. Away from town, the Colorado scenery was lush and green. The sort of country a man could lose himself in very quickly.

He found Reeves waiting on some rocks about five miles south of Alamosa.

"We'll ride north a bit to the railroad tracks and pick up the telegraph lines," Murphy said.

They rode north for about a mile, found the railroad tracks, and, just past them, the long stretch of telegraph lines.

Murphy dismounted and removed the railroad telegraph box from his saddlebags, along with a set of lumberjack cleats. The cleats attached on the inside of each boot. Once the cleats were in place, Murphy tied his rope to the hook on the telegraph box and looped the end of the rope to his belt.

"I learned to do this when I was scouting for Grant," Murphy said.

Reeves watched as Murphy dug the cleats into the telegraph pole and shimmied to the top near the lines.

Once he reached the top, Murphy pulled up the box, removed the rope, and hung the hook over the electrified lines. On contact, small sparks flew.

Then Murphy tapped in the special code

for the White House telegraph operator and sent the following message: *Arrived in Alamosa. Riding west to Durango. Will contact again before delivery date. Murphy.*

Murphy removed the box from the lines and tossed it down to Reeves, then climbed down from the pole.

"Let's go, Marshal," he said. "We'll ride until dark."

Burke read the telegram and then took it to Arthur.

"How long will it take him to reach Durango?" Arthur asked.

"Two days."

"He'll have four days to work with before they contact us again," Arthur said.

"I believe Murphy is counting on the fact that there will be at least a week for delivery time," Burke said.

"Yes, you're quite right, William," Arthur said. "Let me know if Murphy telegraphs again."

Murphy and Reeves rode until dark and made camp near a small stream that was a vein of the Rio Grande River.

After building a fire and tending to the horses, Murphy tossed two massive steaks onto the fry pan and filled a second pan

281

with beans and some water.

"Alamosa had a fairly decent general store," Murphy said.

Stirring the beans, Reeves said, "We got a thirty-mile ride tomorrow to reach Durango by nightfall."

"I'll go in alone," Murphy said. "You camp a safe distance from town."

"Alone with no backup? I don't like it," Reeves said.

"It's too late to worry about that now," Murphy said. "Besides, if you show your face in town, it's likely to get us both killed."

"Just don't yourself get killed," Reeves said. "I'd hate to be the one to bring such news to your wife."

"As long as neither of us is dead at the moment, what do you say to a drink before supper?" Murphy said.

"I'd say yes," Reeves said.

CHAPTER THIRTY

"Stand and face the bench," Parker said.

The man who attacked Kai and stabbed her stood and looked at Parker.

"You have been found guilty of attempted murder. I hereby sentence you to five years' hard labor," Parker said. "Sentence to commence immediately."

"For what?" the man yelled. "She's nothing but a squaw bitch. You can't give me five years for a squaw! It ain't right."

"Shut your mouth," Parker said. "Marshal, take him away, he disgusts me."

Marshal Cal Witson took the man's arm to guide him out of the courtroom. The man turned and looked back at the front row where Kai was seated.

"You stinking squaw bitch, when I get out I'll come for you," he shouted. "I'll kill you in the night. You hear me? I'll kill you in the night."

Witson shoved the man through a door

and out of the courtroom.

"Say another word, and it will be your last," Witson said as he closed the door.

Parker looked at Kai.

"Sorry you had to hear that, Kai," Parker said.

At sunset, Murphy and Reeves stopped so Reeves could make camp. Murphy left Reeves most of the supplies.

"I should reach Durango in two hours," Murphy said. "Stay put until I return. I should be back around midnight."

Murphy rode in darkness, something Boyle was used to and skilled at, until the moon rose and provided enough light to guide by.

Durango wasn't really a town in the traditional sense. It was a stagecoach relay station for travelers bound for the railroad. About twenty buildings had sprung up around the station, including a small hotel and saloon.

As Murphy rode in, he didn't see a jail and figured the coach people handled all infractions of the law.

The stagecoach way station was a large log cabin with a corral that held a dozen horses. It was closed for the night and dark.

Centered in the clump of buildings was a saloon.

Murphy dismounted in front of the saloon and tied Boyle to the post, then entered through the swinging doors.

About twenty men occupied tables and places at the bar. A bearded bartender stood behind the bar.

"What will you have?" the bartender asked.

"Whiskey and one of those cigars you have there on the shelf," Murphy said.

The bartender poured a shot of whiskey and grabbed a cigar off the shelf. "That will be one dollar," he said.

Murphy dipped one end of the cigar into the whiskey and then lit it with a wood match. He took a sip of the whiskey and said, "I'm looking for six men who recently moved here or close by."

"Are you a lawman or bounty hunter?" the bartender said.

"Neither," Murphy said. "I'm looking to join their cause."

"And what cause is that?" the bartender said.

Murphy turned and faced the tables where men were watching him closely.

"I'm looking for six men who recently moved here or close by," he said loudly.

"I'm not the law, and I'm no bounty hunter. I'm interested in joining their cause and I will pay five hundred dollars to any man who takes my message to them. That's five hundred dollars to any man who delivers my message. Tell them to meet me here at sunup for breakfast."

Murphy tossed back the shot of whiskey and walked out of the saloon. He took Boyle by the reins and walked to the way station cabin and tied him to the hitching post. Then he took a chair on the porch where he was completely hidden in the dark.

It didn't take long for a lone man to exit the saloon and cross the street to the livery stable. A few minutes later, he emerged on a horse and rode north out of Durango.

Murphy gave him a decent head start and then returned to Boyle and mounted the saddle.

He followed the rider from a safe distance, using the moonlight to track his shadow. After about three miles, Murphy could see the lights of a cabin. He rode closer and watched the shadow of the man dismount and enter the cabin.

Satisfied, Murphy turned Boyle around and rode back to Reeves.

Murphy rode into Reeves's camp around

ten in the evening. Beans and bacon were keeping warm in a pan as was a pot of coffee.

As he scooped beans and bacon into a tin plate, Murphy said, "They're staying at a cabin about three miles north of Durango."

"All of them?" Reeves asked.

"If not, then most. The others have to be close by," Murphy said. "My guess is they'll all vacate at dawn. It shouldn't be too difficult to track six old men across the plains."

"To where?"

"Hopefully to the men they hired to do their dirty work," Murphy said. "Any biscuits to go with these beans?"

"In the sack by my saddlebags," Reeves said.

"They lit out, all right. Three hours ago before dawn. West," Reeves said. "I count seven horses."

"The fellow who rode out to warn them last night must have gone with them," Murphy said.

Reeves mounted the saddle, and he and Murphy followed the tracks at a slow but steady pace.

"Give them room to breathe," Murphy said.

"Where do you figure they're headed?"

Reeves asked.

"They must have at least six men or more hired to do their killing," Murphy said. "My guess is those men are camped near the site where they want the gold dropped."

"There's just two of us, you know," Reeves said.

"Two with the element of surprise is worth a small army, Marshal," Murphy said.

They rode west for a while and stopped at noon for a quick lunch and to rest the horses.

"I've tracked many a man, but never to allow them to gain ground on me," Reeves said.

"We just need to keep them six hours ahead of us," Murphy said.

As he rolled a cigarette, Reeves said, "Mind a personal question?"

"Go ahead," Murphy said.

"Any of your people ever own slaves?"

"Not as far as I know," Murphy said. "My dad came over in eighteen thirty when he was about sixteen. He learned the whiskey trade from his father in Ireland. He came over with some relatives, but I have no notion of where they are."

"You went against the grain when you fought for the North," Reeves said.

"Tennessee was on the fence. I wasn't,"

Murphy said. "I worked my farm sunup to sundown and without the help of any man, free or slave. When the war broke out, the only choice for me was the North."

"Well, let's get moving if we're going to keep them six hours ahead of us," Reeves said.

As Kai walked out of the general store, she bumped into Judge Parker and Marshal Witson.

"We were just walking over to your place," Parker said.

"Is something wrong?" Kai asked.

"No. I just wanted to let you know your attacker was sent to prison today," Parker said. "I hope that puts your mind at ease some."

"For his sake, I hope he stays away when he gets out," Kai said. "Murphy would kill him on sight."

"I expect that's true," Parker said.

"Judge, why don't you and Marshal Witson come to dinner tonight?" Kai said. "There is plenty of room at the table for company."

"Thank you, Kai. What time?" Parker said.

"Six-thirty."

"We'll be there," Parker said.

Murphy inspected the tracks carefully, then stood up and looked at Reeves. "One rider went on ahead. It must be that man who warned them," he said.

"Making tracks for that camp you spoke about," Reeves said.

Murphy mounted the saddle. "We have an hour of daylight left," he said. "Then we'll make camp."

"If they send a rider ahead to warn the others, their camp can't be too far ahead," Reeves said.

"We'll be in Utah come morning," Murphy said. "My guess is they're camped in those canyons where the first drop was made. I figure that's at least three days' ride from here."

Reeves looked at Murphy. "What are you saying?"

"They won't reach their destination," Murphy said.

Reeves nodded.

"We probably will have to kill some of them," Murphy said.

"I got no problem with killing," Reeves said. "As long as I'm on the right side of it when the shooting starts."

■ ■ ■ ■

Kai, Parker, and Witson took after-dinner coffee on the porch of the boarding house.

"That was a fine dinner, Kai," Parker said.

"Elegant, ma'am," Witson said.

"Thank you both," Kai said.

"Have you heard from Murphy?" Parker asked.

"Not yet," Kai said. "I expect he's busy."

"I see the worry in your face, Kai," Parker said. "I doubt you could hurt him with an ax. He'll be fine and home in no time, I'm sure."

Kai sipped her coffee and looked at Parker.

"Judge, I hate to cut this short, but we have two cases on the night docket," Witson said.

"Kai, we'll need to be running along," Parker said.

"I understand," Kai said. "We enjoyed having your company at the table."

After Parker and Witson left, Kai sat on the porch and finished her coffee. Mrs. Leary came out with the pot and a cup, filled Kai's cup, and then sat next to her.

"The judge is a very entertaining man," Mrs. Leary said.

"He is that," Kai agreed.

"I can see you are troubled," Mrs. Leary said. "I'm sure Mr. Murphy will be fine."

"I know," Kai said.

"Well, I'd best finish cleaning the kitchen," Mrs. Leary said.

Kai sat alone with her thoughts until the second cup of coffee was empty. She realized her worry wasn't that Murphy was off on the trail of outlaws. She had come to understand that as a lawman, there was no one better than he.

She also understood that men get an itch and when it struck, it needed to be scratched. Kai wasn't concerned about another woman. Murphy's itch was being a lawman, a Regulator. She figured, sooner or later, that itch would incite and need to be scratched.

"That was a fine supper," Murphy said.

"We needed to use those steaks," Reeves said. "They wouldn't have lasted another day in the saddlebags."

Murphy took out his pocket watch and held it to the fire. "Let's grab two hours' sleep before we ride," he said.

"I'll make some coffee and keep it warm," Reeves said.

"Any more of those biscuits?" Murphy said.

"A good dozen."

"Keep them handy," Murphy said.

CHAPTER THIRTY-ONE

"An hour to daybreak. How long do you
want to wait?" Reeves said.

"Grab your Winchester and rope, and let's
go while there's still enough moonlight to
see by," Murphy said.

They were a half mile from the campsite
of the six men.

"You get behind them and wait for my
signal," Murphy said.

A hundred yards from the campsite,
Reeves veered to the left and went behind
the six sleeping men.

Murphy stopped twenty feet in front of
them and waited.

Dawn broke slowly.

Minutes drew out like a long blade.

Finally, the dark sky gave way to twilight,
with the first hint of a new day on the
horizon.

Murphy drew his Colt and kept it by his
side.

The sun showed itself, and the ground was suddenly a bright yellow.

Murphy looked at Reeves, and Reeves fired a shot into the ground.

The six men bolted awake in the bedrolls.

Murphy cocked the Colt and said, "One twitch out of any of you, and you're dead where you lie."

Arnold Farris grabbed his revolver. Before he could cock it, Murphy shot him in the chest.

"Are you hard of hearing?" Murphy said. "Or are you just stupid?"

"You shot me," Farris said as he held his chest.

"I didn't kill you. Move again and I will," Murphy said. "Now, the lot of you, stand up and toss your weapons. Keep in mind there's a Winchester at your back."

The six men stood and tossed their side-arms.

"I need a doctor," Farris said.

"Open your mouth again, and you'll need a gravedigger," Murphy said.

"Who are you, and why are you harassing us?" James Westbrook said.

"Murphy, United States Secret Service, and I'm not harassing you. I'm arresting you," Murphy said.

"What charge?" Westbrook said.

"Attempted assassination of former President Grant, kidnapping, extortion, conspiracy, and murder, just to name a few," Murphy said.

"We're businessmen on a trip," Lawrence Cain said.

"To where?" Murphy said. "The desert canyons of Utah on horseback?"

"Do you have warrants?" Cain said.

Murphy smacked Cain in the face with the barrel of the Colt, knocking him to the ground. "Consider that your warrant," he said.

"I'm shot. I need a doctor," Farris said.

"Did those five secret service agents you had killed have a doctor?" Murphy said. "Did the young girl you had kidnapped get a doctor? Five good men are dead along with a young girl with her entire life ahead of her, and for what? Your ambition to relive your antebellum. Consider yourselves lucky I don't kill you all where you stand."

Cain stood up with his mouth and nose bleeding. "You can't do this. We have rights under the law and —"

Murphy smacked Cain a second time, knocking him to the ground again. "Those men and that young girl, they had rights too," Murphy said. "Did you care about their rights when you had them killed?

Marshal Reeves, bring your rope and tie their hands. If one of you so much as moves, you won't draw another breath, so help me God."

"I been studying you," Cain said. "You remind me of a man I knew long ago when I first came over from the old country. My cousin, Michael Murphy. You're the image of him if I ever saw one. Bigger, more stout, but the spitting image."

"Marshal Reeves, tie these men up," Murphy said.

"You wouldn't happen to be his son, would you?" Cain said. "You look exactly like him as I remember."

"Open your mouth one more time, and I will close it for you permanently," Murphy said.

As Reeves took hold of Westbrook's wrists, Westbrook said, "This man is a nigger."

Murphy reached out, grabbed Westbrook by the shirt, lifted him off the ground, and tossed him several feet into the air. As Westbrook hit the ground, Murphy kicked him in the jaw.

"Anybody else take offense to the color of the marshal's skin, speak up," Murphy said. "Otherwise, the matter is closed."

Once all six men were tied in a circle,

Reeves and Murphy walked away from the circle.

"What now?" Reeves asked.

"If I'm not back by dawn, ride these six into Gunnison and turn them over to the sheriff. Then telegraph for the army to transport them to Washington in care of William Burke at the White house," Murphy said. "Got that?"

"I got it, but where are you going?" Reeves said.

Murphy walked to the six men.

"You sent your man ahead to warn your hired killers," Murphy said. "I expect they won't make a move without you."

Murphy mounted Boyle and looked at Reeves. "Remember, if I'm not back by dawn, Gunnison is just a day's ride," he said.

"You can't win," Westbrook said. "There are more of us who feel the way we do than you. You maybe can stop us, but others will rise up to take our place."

Murphy drew his Colt and shot Westbrook in the left arm.

"That will give you something to think about on the ride to Gunnison," he said and yanked on the reins and rode away north.

Around two in the afternoon, Murphy

298

rested Boyle for an hour. He fed him grain while he brushed his thick black coat.

Then, as Murphy waited for a pot of coffee to heat on a fire, he walked ahead a bit to check the rider's tracks.

The man's horse had a cracked right front shoe, and it was slowing them down to barely more than a walk.

The coffee was boiling over on the fire when Murphy returned to it and carefully filled a cup. He fished out two biscuits and sat beside Boyle to eat them.

"We could catch him by midnight, the pace his horse is keeping," Murphy said.

Boyle looked at Murphy and snorted.

"I know, boy," Murphy said. "I'd rather be home with Kai, too. But right now we're working and there's no room for thoughts of fancy."

Boyle snorted.

"Because a man thinking about his woman while he's after outlaws is a man waiting to get killed, that's why," Murphy said.

Boyle whinnied.

"Just as soon as I finish my biscuits and coffee," Murphy said. "You're not the only one around here with a stomach, you know."

"Marshal, you got two men here that will be dead by morning if they don't get to a doctor," Cain said.

"I can't tell you how little I care," Reeves said.

"What's the matter, Marshal?" Westbrook said. "Do you hate the white man so much, you'd let him die like some animal on the plains?"

"Mister, I don't hate anybody, not even the man who once owned me and had me whipped on more than one occasion," Reeves said.

"That's because your race is too damn stupid to know better," Westbrook said.

"No, it's because hating is a waste of time that does no man any good," Reeves said. "Now if I was you, I'd worry more about bleeding to death than about my feelings."

Late in the afternoon, Murphy heard a shot sound in the distance. It echoed several times and then faded.

He dismounted and inspected the tracks carefully.

"Right about here he went lame," Murphy said aloud.

He mounted the saddle and rode until dark, dismounted, and made a cold camp to give Boyle a rest.

After about an hour, Murphy spotted a red dot on the dark horizon. He looked at

Boyle. "That's our lighthouse," he said. "Let's give him time to get more comfortable."

Reeves sat in front of the fire, drank coffee, and held the Winchester by his side as he watched the six roped men.

"Hey, Marshal, I think Farris is dead," Cain said.

"You best hope not," Reeves said. " 'Cause you'll be the ones burying him come morning."

"How about some whiskey to deaden the pain of my arm," Westbrook said.

"I don't have any whiskey," Reeves said.

"We do. In our saddlebags," Westbrook said.

"My saddlebags. There's a bottle in my saddlebags. The bay with the white star on her nose," Cain said. "The bags by her legs."

Reeves stood and went to the bay's saddlebags and fished out a bottle of rye whiskey. He walked to the six men, opened the bottle, and poured some on Westbrook's wound on his left arm to wash away the blood.

Westbrook winced in pain. "How about you let me drink some?" he said.

The men were roped around the waist and looped to each other. They were also tied around the ankles and wrists with their arms in front of them. Reeves handed the bottle to Westbrook who took it with both hands.

Reeves returned to his seat beside his saddle and cradled the Winchester.

"It's going to be a long night, Marshal," Cain said. "Best not fall asleep."

"Best not die on me," Reeves said.

The rider had built up the fire and was sound asleep beside it. His horse was nowhere in sight. Murphy figured the shot he heard earlier was the man shooting his horse after the broken shoe caused it to go lame.

The fire was bright enough for Murphy to clearly see the man's outline inside his bedroll. Beside the fire was some cookware and a bottle of whiskey.

Murphy held his Winchester rifle, cocked it, and fired a shot close to the sleeping man. He bolted awake and grabbed for the rifle beside his head.

"Do it, so I have reason to shoot you," Murphy said.

"I got no horse, if that's what you're after," the man said.

"Toss back your blanket and stand up real slow, and your life might not end in the next ten seconds," Murphy said.

The man peeled back the blanket and

rolled to his right as if to stand up. Suddenly he grabbed the gun in his holster. As he drew the weapon, Murphy shot him in the right hand.

The man dropped the gun, grabbed his hand, and screamed. "You shot me. You shot my damned hand, goddamn you," he yelled.

"You're lucky I didn't kill you," Murphy said. "Now stand the hell up."

Holding his bloody right hand in his left, the man slowly stood up.

"What do you want?" he asked.

"What I want is to kill you where you stand," Murphy said. "What I'll settle for is some information."

"Information," the man said. "About what? I'm just trying to get through the territory to a town."

"The men you're going to meet up with, where are they?"

"What men? My horse died. I'm just trying to get through the territory, like I said," the man said.

"I've been tracking you and the six you left behind since Durango," Murphy said. "I'll ask again. Each time you don't answer, I'll put a bullet in you."

"I told you, I'm just a cowboy afoot trying to get through the territory," the man said. "You'd shoot a man for that?"

Murphy cocked his Colt and put a bullet through the man's left thigh. "No, but I will for lying," he said.

The man folded and fell to the ground.

"Sweet Jesus, you shot me again," he cried.

"I'll shoot you four more times and then go to work on you with my Winchester," Murphy said. "I'll make sure you stay alive until you bleed out so you can watch yourself die. I won't even bury you; I'll leave you for the buzzards. Know what they eat first? Your eyes."

"Don't shoot no more. Please, mister, don't shoot no more," the man said.

"I'll ask one more time. Keep in mind I can only burn in hell once for the men I've killed, so killing you is free," Murphy said. "Where are you supposed to meet the men you were riding to?"

"Another full day's ride north into the canyons," the man said. "A day's ride past that there's a notch in the southwest passage. Six men are camped out waiting for the word to move."

"And you were bringing them what message?" Murphy asked.

"I don't know," the man said. "I went ahead, because the old men couldn't keep up. I was supposed to tell those in the canyon the old men were coming and everything was on schedule. That's all I know, I swear."

"And what's your part in this?" Murphy asked.

"Money," the man said. "What else?"

"You're just a paid messenger boy, is that it?" Murphy said. "A clerk in a store without guilt."

The man looked at the Colt in Murphy's right hand as Murphy cocked the hammer.

"All right, okay. Jesus, you don't give a man no room," the man said. "Cain is my Pa. We was rich once, when I was a boy. He wants us to be rich again. Is that such a bad thing, to be rich?"

Murphy stared at the man. If Cain was telling the truth and he was a cousin to Murphy's father, the man in front of him was a distant second or third cousin.

"The bullet go through your hand?" Murphy said.

"Clean through. The leg also," the man said.

"Let's get the bleeding stopped, and I'll take you back to your pa," Murphy said.

Reeves drank coffee and smoked a rolled cigarette as he kept an eye on the six men tied up near the fire.

"Hey, Marshal, best have a look at Farris," Cain said. "I believe he's dead."

"I'll look at him in the morning," Reeves said.

"I don't want a dead man tied to me all night," Cain said.

"Did you care about all the dead slaves you put in their graves when you owned them?" Reeves said.

Cain chuckled. "You're free, all right, because the government says so," he said. "But we both know you're not really free, don't we, boy?"

"I'm freer than you at the moment," Reeves said.

"If you weren't wearing that badge, they wouldn't even let you into a saloon," Cain said.

"Mister, there's nothing can come out of your mouth that rattles me, so why don't you save your breath," Reeves said. "You'll need it to bury your partner come morning."

After cleaning Cain's wounds with whiskey, Murphy bandaged them with a clean bandana. He made a pot of coffee, filled two cups, and added some whiskey to them.

Murphy smoked his pipe as he and Cain drank their coffee.

"How old were you when the war broke

306

out?" Murphy asked.

"About six, I guess," Cain said.

"What do you remember before that?" Murphy said.

Cain sipped some coffee. "You mean about the farm?"

"About anything."

"Pop had a big cotton farm," Cain said. "A plantation, they called it. He had many darkies working the fields, and I used to play with their kids. We'd play roll the hoop and sometimes this game called hide and seek. I didn't even realize they was Pop's property until much later."

"What happened to the plantation after the war?" Murphy asked.

"The house burned. Ma died before the war ended from pneumonia," Cain said. "Pa said it was too much to work without his darkies, so he took to sharecropping the land for half the profits."

"Did you know your father was a member of the Klan?" Murphy asked.

"Not then," Cain said. "By the time I was full-growed, the Klan had busted."

"Son, what do you think this is all about?" Murphy said.

"I went west in seventy-five to work as a cowboy," Cain said. "I worked ranches from Colorado to Texas to Utah and back again.

307

Six, seven months ago I get this letter from Pa saying he needs my help."

"Your pa is trying to resurrect the Klan," Murphy said. "He and the others kidnapped the niece of a British ambassador, murdered five secret service agents, extorted gold from the government, and probably murdered the niece because she's a witness. That is what you are helping with."

"All I do is deliver messages back and forth," Cain said. "I got no part of anything else, and that's the truth."

"But you know what they're up to?"

Cain nodded. "Some, but not the murdering part."

"And you went along with it?"

"He's my pa," Cain said.

"Your pa is looking at the end of a rope," Murphy said.

"Me?"

Murphy shook his head. "Ten years in Yuma maybe," he said. "Maybe more."

"I can't do no ten years, mister," Cain said.

"I can buy you some time off, maybe even get you a pardon if you help me," Murphy said.

"Help you hang my pa?" Cain said.

"Your pa is already in custody, son. He's going to hang, no matter what. Why spend years in prison you don't have to? You going to prison's not going to help him either way. Long after he's dead, you'll still be rotting in a cell somewhere. When you get out, if you get out, you'll be a middle-aged man with no future to look forward to except for cleaning stables."

"Can you really help me?" Cain asked.

"Yes."

"What do you want to know? I don't know much, but I'll say what I can."

"How many men are waiting in that canyon?" Murphy asked.

"Seven."

"Hired gunmen?"

Cain nodded. "A bad bunch, for sure. They have a Gatling gun, although I have no notion where they got it."

"How do your pa and the others send their telegrams?"

"They have this telegraph box they got a hold of somehow. They ride to the nearest telegraph lines and put the box over the lines and send a message. I never seen it done, but Pa told me how they do it."

"When I picked up your pa and the others, they were headed to the canyon?"

"First they was going to send a telegram using the lines near Gunnison," Cain said. "I was to ride ahead to tell the others to

309

expect the gold delivery."

"Who are the men in the canyon?" Murphy asked. "Friends of your pa?"

"Men who think like-minded," Cain said. "That's all I know about them. That and they don't mind killing."

Murphy nodded. "I'm going to tie your hands to my saddle horn," he said. "We have a long ride back to my camp. Don't try to escape. If my horse doesn't kill you, I will."

"Don't worry, mister," Cain said. "I don't want to die or rot in prison for my pa's cause or his crimes."

Se——— Saddle.

CHAPTER THIRTY-TWO

"Well, Marshal, the sun is up and Farris is dead and Westbrook is damn near," Cain said. "What are you going to do now?"

Reeves tossed some wood he'd gathered onto the fire.

"I'll tell you what I'm going to do. I'm going to fix some breakfast," he said.

"For all of us?" Cain said.

"Do you have supplies?" Reeves said.

"We all have supplies in our saddlebags," Smoak said. "We brought enough for the ride to . . ."

"Shut up, Smoak, you damn fool," Cain said.

Reeves looked at Smoak. "Ride to where?" he said.

"Don't tell that nigger a goddamn thing, Smoak," Cain said. "Or I'll kill you myself."

"I don't think you're killing anybody," Reeves said. "Now if you want breakfast, I'll make enough for all. That is, if you ain't too insulted to have a nigger handle your food for you."

"Were you there the day those men killed the secret service agents delivering the ransom?" Murphy asked.

Seated in front of Murphy on the saddle, Cain said, "No, I wasn't. Neither was my pa. We was at the ranch house north of Durango until the gold was delivered."

"How are they recruiting men for their cause?"

"It ain't hard to find those in the South that hates the freed slaves and the North," Cain said.

"I expect not," Murphy said. "In the North, too, I suppose. What's your first name?"

"Josh. Joshua," Cain said. "Ma named me after someone in the Bible."

"Well, Josh, from what you've told me, I have the feeling you don't have any real hatred toward the freed slaves," Murphy said.

"Some of the best cowboys on the ranches are freed slaves," Cain said. "We share the same bunkhouses and eat at the same tables and no one has a problem. Those who do are kicked off the ranch pretty damn quick."

"You see your father is wrong, don't you?"

Murphy said.

Cain sighed. "I know it," he said. "I only went along with him 'cause he's my pa."

"I know this is difficult for you, but you'll have to testify against him in court if asked," Murphy said.

"I figured."

"How are your wounds?"

"Hurt some. Both went clean through. Neither are bleeding. I suppose I'm grateful for you not killing me."

"I would have had you pushed it," Murphy said. "I'm glad you didn't."

"Me, too."

"Westbrook's unconscious," Cain said.

"I can see that," Reeves said.

"You just going to allow him to die?" Smoak said.

"That isn't up to me," Reeves said.

"That son of a bitch shouldn't have shot him," Cain said.

Reeves stood up from where he was seated against his saddle. "Here he comes now. You can tell him yourself," he said.

Murphy rode into camp, dismounted beside the fire, and helped Joshua Cain off the saddle.

"My son," Cain shouted "You shot my son, you murderous son of a bitch."

313

"Be quiet," Murphy said. "Marshal Reeves, can you dish up a plate of that grub for Cain's son here?"

Reeves looked at Joshua Cain. "His son, huh?"

"Save a plate for me, too," Murphy said as he removed the saddle from Boyle.

Burke sat in a chair opposite President Arthur's desk in the Oval Office and puffed on a long cigar. "Tomorrow is the day the next telegram with demands is supposed to arrive," he said.

"I'm aware of that," Arthur said. "Have we heard from Murphy?"

"Not since his last telegram."

"And there has been no word of additional kidnappings?"

"None, but since we agreed to their demands, there shouldn't be any," Burke said.

"And after they realize we called a bluff?"

"That's at least a week from now," Burke said. "By then Murphy will have played his hand."

"Which is what, Burke? Exactly what is Murphy's hand?" Arthur said.

Burke inhaled on his cigar and then blew a large cloud of gray smoke. "It was Grant who recruited Murphy to head his secret service team," he said. "It was Grant who first called Murphy a 'Regulator.' "

"I'm aware of that, William," Arthur said. "Do you have some point to make?"

"A Regulator is a killer of men," Burke said. "You can call it what you will: lawman, secret service agent, or Regulator, but it still means a killer of men. No one wears that mantle better than Murphy."

"Is that your way of telling me to have faith?" Arthur asked.

"Faith can move mountains, Mr. President," Burke said.

"So can dynamite."

"With Murphy, faith and dynamite are sometimes one and the same," Burke said.

Kai sat on the porch and cracked a pot of beans for the evening's supper. She hadn't heard from Murphy since his last telegram. She wasn't worried, not yet. With her first husband, a US Marshal, she worried every time he left home until she got used to the idea that it was his job.

Once the idea took root, she didn't worry so much as feel concern.

Until the day he was killed by an outlaw he went to serve a warrant on.

She awoke with a sick feeling in her stomach that reminded her of morning sickness. The morning sickness usually faded as the morning wore on, but this feeling stayed with her and grew worse.

She learned later it was the day her husband was shot and killed by the outlaw he served papers on.

Kai didn't have that feeling this morning as she cracked beans, not that feeling of impending death.

It was more of a subtle anxiousness building inside her.

An anxiousness to start building a new and eventful life with Murphy. Just a few years ago, Kai's life had been stagnant and bleak, with little to look forward to except dirty crockery in the sink and linen to wash.

And an empty heart.

Now she had a new husband she loved and who loved her, a new home under construction, a teaching job on the reservation, the possibility of adopting a child, and the farm in Tennessee where she was welcomed by Murphy's parents as if she was one of their own.

It could all end in the blink of an eye.

Mrs. Leary stepped onto the porch with two mugs of coffee. She gave one to Kai and then took the chair next to her.

"If worry was gold, you'd be up to your ears in twenty-dollar pieces," Mrs. Leary said.

"I am a bit melancholy, I suppose," Kai admitted.

"I wouldn't worry too much about that man of yours," Mrs. Leary said. "If you must worry, worry about the men he's after."

Kai sipped some coffee and smiled at Mrs. Leary. "Let's make ice cream for our guests for dessert," she said.

Murphy wrote a long note, folded it carefully, and handed it to Reeves.

"When you get to Gunnison, send this telegram to William Burke at the White House," Murphy said. "Wait until the army arrives and then hitch a ride back to Fort Smith."

"That ain't right, Mr. Murphy," Reeves said. "We'll take the prisoners together and . . ."

"Bass Reeves, you're a United States Marshal, and you have a duty to perform," Murphy said. "That duty is to take these federal prisoners into custody to the army outpost near Gunnison."

"All right, I'll do as you ask, but then I'm riding to join you," Reeves said.

"I'll need you to ride with the prisoners to Washington and tell Burke all that's happened," Murphy said. "I'll see you back in

Fort Smith."

Reeves looked up at Murphy. Reeves, no small man himself, felt small in Murphy's presence. But, as Reeves learned a long time ago, a bullet didn't care how big you were.

"I'll be all right," Murphy said.

Reeves nodded.

"Best get the prisoners moving," Murphy said. "I'll bury Farris. When you get to Washington, have Burke notify his family."

Joshua Cain rode Farris's horse. Reeves didn't tie his hands to the saddle horn as he did his father and the others. He rode next to Reeves and behind the others after he gave his word he wouldn't try to escape.

Even if he wanted to escape, where would he go with two holes in him?

"Murphy told me how you cooperated with him," Reeves said. "If you testify, there's a good chance at a pardon like he said."

"I love my pa, but he's wrong in what he's doing, and I don't want to spend twenty years in prison for his crimes," Joshua said.

Cain turned his head and shouted, "Joshua, quit talking to that nigger. Remember your family."

"You shut up or I'll gag you," Reeves said.

"Don't it bother you, being called that

318

word?" Joshua asked.

"It did," Reeves said. "For a long time. When the war broke out, I ran away from my master, Colonel Reeves, and lived with the Cherokee Nation in Arkansas. I hated, you bet I did. But when Judge Parker appointed me a marshal, I learned something about people. Those who hate are generally the most ignorant. Men like Parker and the other marshals showed me men don't need to care about the color of a man's skin, just his character."

"Before Pa wrote me for help, I was cowboying for several ranches. Many of the drovers are former slaves and such," Joshua said. "Some of them are the best cowboys I ever seen. Those that won't ride with them are usually fired. I never had no problems with any cowboy I rode with, black or white."

"White, black, yellow, or red, in my forty-two years of living, I've discovered one thing about people," Reeves said.

"What's that?" Joshua asked.

"We all like to feel that we count for something," Reeves said. "It's the only real measure to say we've been here, counting for something."

Joshua nodded. "That lawman, Murphy, he could have killed me like I was a child."

Reeves grinned. "He's got the hardest bark on him of any man I ever met," he said. "But that bark has a streak of fairness in it, or you wouldn't be alive."

"He counts for something, doesn't he?" Joshua said.

"Oh, yeah," Reeves said. "He counts for something."

Murphy stood over the freshly dug grave of Farris and wiped sweat off his face with his neckerchief.

"I stuck you in the ground, but don't expect me to waste any words over the likes of you, you son of a bitch," he said.

Murphy walked to Boyle and tossed the blanket and then saddle over his massive back. "If you've had enough rest, we have some riding to do," he said.

CHAPTER THIRTY-THREE

Murphy rode north until thirty minutes before sunset. He built a fire, put beans and bacon in a pan, added a splash of whiskey for flavor, and put on a pot of coffee to boil.

While his supper cooked, Murphy groomed Boyle and brushed his coat until it glistened. Then he fed Boyle a bag of grain.

When supper was ready, Murphy dug out two hard biscuits from the sack, filled a plate, and ate with his back against the saddle.

"It's not Kai's home cooking, but it will have to do for now," Murphy said to Boyle.

Already half asleep, Boyle whinnied softly.

"Right," Murphy said.

He added a splash of whiskey to a cup of coffee and then lit his pipe. "Tomorrow we'll be in Utah and then the canyons," he said. "Keep your eyes open for that notch the kid spoke about."

Eyes still closed, Boyle responded to

Murphy's voice with a soft snort.

"Kai's probably serving up a roast beef supper with gravy and all the fixings," Murphy said. "And hot apple pie for dessert."

Asleep, Boyle responded to Murphy's voice by wiggling his ears, but stayed silent.

"I agree with you, boy," Murphy said. "I'm as dumb as a post."

The army outpost just north of the town of Gunnison was large enough to house two hundred soldiers, six officers, and one commanding officer. The sixteen-foot-high walls were patrolled by armed sentries.

Torches were placed every twenty feet on the interior catwalk of the walls where the soldiers patrolled. On the ground, torches were spaced evenly around the fort's perimeter, giving the soldiers a view of the immediate grounds even on the darkest nights.

The corporal of the guard on the catwalk above the front gates stared in disbelief as a train of riders emerged from the dark and stopped beside a torch.

"Hello inside the fort," Reeves shouted.

"Identify yourself," the corporal said.

"United States Marshal Bass Reeves out of Fort Smith, Arkansas," Reeves said. "These men are my prisoners."

The corporal looked down at the runner

on duty. "Private, better get the captain."

"You're a long way from home, Marshal Reeves," Post Commander Captain Jenner said.

They were in the mess hall at the outpost where the cook prepared a steak for Reeves.

"Yes, sir. Captain, did you read my reports?" Reeves asked.

"I have, and my operator has sent your telegrams."

"That kid, Joshua Cain?" Reeves said.

"In the infirmary, and our doctor says he will be just fine."

"The other man, Westbrook?"

"Fifty percent chance of surviving."

"I need to ask the doctor when Joshua Cain will be fit to travel," Reeves said.

"No time like the present," Jenner said.

Doctor Saget, a civilian doctor attached to the army, approached the table. "Captain, Marshal Reeves," he said.

"Doctor, the Cain boy, when can he travel?" Reeves said.

Saget took a chair next to Jenner. The cook brought him a cup of coffee. "Thank you, Sergeant," Saget said. "Now, Marshal, to answer your question, how will you be traveling, by horse or railroad?"

"Railroad," Reeves said.

"In that case, I'd say he'll be fit to travel in three days."

"Westbrook?"

"That's another story," Saget said. "A month, if he lives."

Reeves looked at Jenner. "Captain, I guess I'm your guest for a few days," he said.

"You can use our guest quarters, Marshal," Saget said. "I'll have a hot bath drawn for you after you finish your supper."

Although Burke owned a home a few miles from the White House, he kept a room in the guest quarters for nights when he worked late.

He was sound asleep when the telegraph operator knocked on the bedroom door.

"Mr. Burke, I have a telegram you need to see right away," the operator said.

Burke opened his eyes and sat up on the bed. "Hold on a moment," he said.

Minutes later, wearing a robe, Burke met Arthur in the president's private residence.

By lantern, Arthur sat at his desk and read the telegram from Reeves.

"That son of a bitch Murphy pulled it off," Arthur said. "Who is this Bass Reeves?"

"It says he's a US Marshal out of Arkansas," Burke said.

"Yes, yes, I read that, but who is he?"

"I don't know, but I'll find out," Burke said. "I'll wire Judge Parker in Fort Smith in the morning."

"And where the hell is Murphy? Reeves says he's bringing the prisoners to Washington by railroad," Arthur said.

"Since he doesn't say, we'll have to wait for Reeves to arrive to ask him," Burke said.

"You don't suppose he went and got himself killed?" Arthur said.

"Hardly," Burke said.

"In the morning, contact Ambassador Turner with the news," Arthur said.

Burke nodded. "Good night, Mr. President."

"You want me to send a telegram now?" the operator said.

"I'm awake, you're awake, and I'm sure someone in the army is awake," Burke said. "Send it."

The operator nodded. "Write out what you want to send."

Reeves, after a hot bath, settled into a comfortable bed in a room at the outpost's guest quarters and was nearly asleep when there was a knock on the door.

"Marshal Reeves, it's Captain Jenner. You have a telegram," Jenner said.

Reeves got out of bed, quickly lit the lantern on the table, and walked to the door and opened it. "Telegram?" he said.

"From Special Assistant to President Arthur, William Burke," Jenner said.

Reeves read the telegram. "He wants to know where Murphy is."

Burke was sitting in a chair in his room at the White House, cigar in one hand, a glass of whiskey in the other, when the telegraph operator knocked on the door.

"Come," Burke said.

The door opened and the operator entered and handed the telegram to Burke.

"Should I wait for a reply?" the operator asked.

Burke read the telegram. *Murphy is in pursuit of the remaining outlaws somewhere in the Utah canyons. Location unknown. Marshal Bass Reeves.*

Burke lowered the telegram and looked at the operator. "No, no reply," he said.

After sending the reply, Reeves and Jenner stopped by Jenner's quarters, where Jenner opened a bottle of Irish whiskey and poured two drinks.

"I'll need authorization from the president to dispatch a patrol into Utah," Jenner said.

"I know," Reeves said. "But from what little I know of Murphy's mission, you won't get it."

"Even if it means his life?"

Reeves nodded.

"Politics," Jenner said. "Is a lot like stepping in horseshit."

Reeves lifted his glass. "I'll drink to that, Captain," he said.

CHAPTER THIRTY-FOUR

"You sent for me, Judge?" Marshal Cal Witson said when he entered Judge Parker's office.

"At the request of the president, I have to go to Washington for a few days," Parker said. "I've cleared the court docket until I return. Any new business will just have to wait."

"Yes, Judge," Witson said. "Any word from Bass?"

"No, but I expect this request from Arthur has to do with our missing marshal," Parker said.

After breakfast, Kai walked to town to the courthouse. She was about to climb the stairs when Judge Parker appeared in the doorway, carrying a suitcase.

"Kai," he said as he descended the stairs.

"I was just on my way to see you, Judge," Kai said.

"I expect you want to know if I've heard from Murphy," Parker said. "I haven't. But, I've been called to Washington by the president, so I expect it has something to do with Murphy."

"What time does your train leave?" Kai asked.

"One hour."

"I'm going with you."

"Kai, I don't think . . ." Parker said.

"I'll meet you at the station in one hour," Kai said and turned away.

Parker watched Kai walk back to her house, shook his head, and walked to the station.

"How do you feel?" Reeves said.

"Well enough to travel," Joshua Cain said.

"If the doctor says so, we'll leave today and catch the railroad in Gunnison," Reeves said.

Wearing a blue skirt and white blouse, Kai placed her satchel on the floor beside her and looked at Judge Parker in the seat across from her. They were the only two in the first-class riding car.

"Kai, this isn't a good idea," Parker said. "A person just doesn't pop in on the president of the United States."

329

"I'm not, you are," Kai said.

Parker sighed. "I understand you're anxious for news about Murphy, but . . ."

"They sent him away, the least they can do is tell me what's happened to him," Kai said.

"You wait in the hotel," Parker said. "Any news, and I'll bring it to you directly."

Kai smiled. "They serve lunch on this trip, don't they?" she said.

"I'm assigning two men to escort you to Washington, Marshal," Captain Jenner said. "On a long trip, it's best to have an extra set of hands to keep things neat."

"I appreciate all you've done, Captain," Reeves said. "And the loan of your wrist irons."

Jenner extended his right hand to Reeves. "Good luck, Marshal," he said.

Burke carried the latest telegram to Arthur, who was having lunch at his desk.

"Marshal Reeves has left Gunnison and will be in Washington by tomorrow morning," Burke said.

"Any news of Murphy?" Arthur asked.

"Not yet," Burke said.

"I'll be most anxious to speak with this Marshal Reeves."

"Judge Parker will be here by four o'clock," Burke said.

"I want to see him the moment he arrives," Arthur said.

"I'll take care of it," Burke said.

The train rolled to a gentle stop in the Washington railroad depot. A hundred or more passengers exited the train, and Burke had to weed through them to spot Parker and Kai as they walked along the platform.

"Mr. Burke, what are you doing here?" Kai asked.

"I could ask you the same question," Burke said. "Judge Parker, President Arthur asked me to meet you with a carriage."

"Can we drop Kai off at the hotel?" Parker asked. "The Washington Arms."

Burke looked at Kai. "You could wait in my office instead if you'd like," he said.

"I could," Kai said.

"Judge Parker, by whose authority did you assign Marshal Reeves to assist Murphy in this classified mission?" Arthur said.

"My own," Parker said.

"You're a presidential appointee, Judge," Arthur said.

"Go ahead and remove me then," Parker said. "But before you do, know this. Those

331

men conspiring against the government started in Fort Smith. That makes it my territory and my jurisdiction. Marshal Reeves volunteered to go with Murphy of his own accord. He was born a slave, you see, and has become the best marshal in my court."

"Reeves is black?" Arthur said.

"Were there any other kinds of slaves in this country?" Parker said.

Arthur sighed. "He'll be here in the morning with the prisoners."

"And Murphy?" Parker asked.

"Maybe Reeves can shed some light on that," Burke said.

Kai stood when Burke and Parker entered Burke's office.

"We'll know more in the morning on Murphy's whereabouts," Burke said.

"Reeves is bringing in the prisoners by train. It's scheduled for a ten o'clock arrival," Parker said. "Maybe he can tell us a bit more on where Murphy is."

"Kai, why don't you and the judge be my guest for dinner tonight?" Burke said.

CHAPTER THIRTY-FIVE

Three hundred yards above the encampment the seven men had made for themselves inside the notch, Murphy squatted behind a rock and watched them.

The sun was low and at his back, and the encampment was shrouded in shadow.

Murphy counted seven men seated around a large campfire. They were drinking whiskey from two jugs. A large open wagon with a mounted Gatling gun sat beside their penned horses.

They weren't drunk, but they were well on their way to it.

Sound traveled long distances in the open, thin air, and Murphy could hear most of their conversations.

"What the hell is taking them so long?" a man said. "They should have been here by now."

"Maybe they stopped off at a whorehouse," another man said. "I know I would."

"They're old men. They wouldn't be going to no whorehouse," a man said.

"If they ain't here by tomorrow, we'll draw straws and send two men back to look for them," a man said.

"Let's get some grub going," another man said.

"Hey, you don't suppose something happened to those old men?" a man said.

"Better not. They promised each of us ten thousand in gold," another man said.

"This jug's empty, get another," a man said.

Murphy took note of the paths leading down the canyon slope, then stood and backed away from the cliff. He walked several hundred feet to where Boyle was tethered to a tree limb. He rubbed Boyle's massive neck.

"We have some work to do before we go home," he said.

Murphy mounted the saddle and rode Boyle about a quarter mile away, then dismounted and made camp. He built a fire and put on a pan of beans with bacon and a pot of coffee. He wasn't worried that the smoke and smell would reach the encampment well below his own camp.

While supper cooked, Murphy fed and groomed Boyle. "They're well on their way to a good drunk," Murphy said.

Boyle turned his head and looked at Murphy.

"Because a man who is drunk makes an easier target and can't shoot straight, that's why," Murphy said. "Now be quiet and let me eat my supper."

Murphy made enough for seconds and ate two plates of food, washing the food down with cups of coffee.

Then he smoked his pipe and waited for the moon to rise. There was one cup of coffee left in the pot. He mixed it with an ounce of whiskey.

As he smoked and sipped, Murphy cleaned and loaded his Colt with fresh ammunition. He kept a spare Colt in his saddlebags and made sure it was in working order.

Slowly, several hours after dark, the moon rose and the ground glowed and lightened.

Murphy broke camp and saddled Boyle.

"You know what to do," Murphy said as he rubbed Boyle's neck. "It's not much different than the old days."

Murphy mounted the saddle and rode to the place on the cliff where he earlier watched the encampment below.

He dismounted, held the reins, and squatted down for a few minutes.

A large campfire burned brightly. Most of the men were asleep or passed out drunk. Two were passing a jug and talking.

Murphy stood, mounted, and gently rubbed Boyle's neck. "Nice and easy," he said. "Just like the old days."

Murphy held the reins in his left hand and the Colt in his right as he gently guided Boyle down the side of the cliff.

The trek took several minutes. Murphy guided Boyle out of the gorge to the flat ground where the encampment was well lit by a campfire and moonlight.

Two men were seated in front of the fire and were pulling on a jug. They looked at Murphy in disbelief as he rode Boyle directly at them. They weren't sure if they were actually seeing Murphy or if, in their drunken condition, they were seeing spirits in the dark.

Murphy cocked the Colt in his right hand.

"Toss your weapons," Murphy said. "Do it."

Both men jumped to their feet and pulled their sidearms.

Murphy shot them both where they stood.

The remaining five men bolted awake and tossed their bedrolls. They drew pistols and grabbed rifles, but, still drunk and in the dark, they were little more than targets for

Murphy.

A man fired a wild shot at Murphy.

Boyle, calm under fire, responded to Murphy's gentle tug and turned to the left. Murphy shot the man dead.

"Assassins and paid mercenaries, the lot of you," Murphy said.

The remaining four men, panicked and still drunk, fired upon Murphy, but Murphy charged Boyle directly at them and killed three more.

The last man standing turned and ran away from the fire.

Murphy followed on Boyle. "You tried to kill Grant so you could kidnap a young girl to finance your resurrection," Murphy said. "But you're nothing more than cheap hired killers."

"Stay away from me," the man cried in the dark.

"You killed five secret service agents and a young girl, and now I'm here to kill you," Murphy said.

The man tripped and fell in the dark.

Murphy stopped Boyle, dismounted, holstered the Colt, and walked to the fallen man.

"Look at your executioner, you coward," Murphy said.

The man got to his knees, turned, and

looked up at Murphy. "You," he said.

Murphy stared in disbelief at the face of Christopher, Burke's carriage driver and the man who had violated Sally Orr two years earlier.

Hatred for Christopher boiled inside Murphy until it reached the breaking point. He grabbed Christopher by the shirt and yanked him to his feet.

Murphy slapped Christopher several times across the face.

"You violated and ruined a woman who never did you any harm," Murphy said. "You caused her death carrying your child and for what? For what?"

Christopher spat blood onto Murphy's shirt.

Murphy tossed Christopher to the ground and kicked him several times. "It doesn't surprise me none the likes of you is mixed up with the Klan, you miserable son of a bitch."

Christopher got to his knees. "Kill me and you won't . . ." he said.

Murphy pummeled Christopher with his fists, knocking Christopher to the ground once again.

"It's time for you to die in the dirt like the coward you are," Murphy said.

He drew the spare Colt and cocked it. "I

doubt God has any use for any last words you might have to say, but go ahead and say them," Murphy said.

"The girl is alive," Christopher said.

"What?" Murphy said.

"The kidnapped girl, she's alive," Christopher said. "Kill me, and you'll never find her, alive or dead."

Murphy de-cocked the Colt and stuck it in his belt. "Get up," he said and yanked Christopher to his feet.

Murphy sipped coffee as he looked at Christopher.

"These ropes are too tight," Christopher said of the ropes that bound his wrists and ankles.

"I can put one around your neck even tighter," Murphy said. "Now tell me what you know about everything."

"I was riding with two of those men you just killed," Christopher said. "One of them is related to a man named Westbrook. He said we could make some quick money, some real money, by helping them with this plan they had to bring back the Klan. They said they needed someone who knows Washington."

"And that would be you?" Murphy said.

"Every square inch," Christopher said. "It

339

didn't take me long to figure out how to grab the ambassador's niece."

"Did you know I would be guarding Grant?" Murphy asked.

"No, but it doesn't surprise me none," Christopher said.

"Why the niece?"

"The old men figured an international incident would carry more weight with President Arthur," Christopher said. "They figured right."

"Go on."

"After we got the first shipment, the old men decided they needed more gold," Christopher said. "They figured if Arthur didn't want to pay, they could always tell him the girl was alive and would have to pay for her return."

"I didn't figure you for the Klan," Murphy said.

"I'm not," Christopher said. "But I am for easy money, and I had nothing to do with those five men getting killed. That was all the old men's doing. They gave the orders."

"Maybe they gave the orders, but you went right along with them," Murphy said. "Now where is the girl?"

"It ain't going to be that easy," Christopher said.

"Don't task my patience," Murphy said.

"Right now if that girl lives or dies is up to you, not me," Christopher said.

"How so?"

"Come morning, when I'm completely sober, you let me gather up supplies and what money the dead men have and allow me to ride out of here alive and I'll tell you where the girl is being held captive," Christopher said. "That's how so."

"Do you really expect me to trust you," Murphy said.

"What choice do you have?" Christopher said. "Unless you really want to gamble the girl is already dead. But, what if she ain't dead? You'll never find her."

Murphy, stuffing his pipe, paused and looked at Christopher.

"Right now, where she is, she's safe," Christopher said. "But, if word don't get to the men holding her soon enough, they're going to start treating her different, if you know what I mean."

Murphy struck a match and lit his pipe.

"You let me take my horse, supplies, what money I can dig up. You give me a head start come light, and I'll tell you where the girl is held captive," Christopher said. "Otherwise, she'll wind up a two-dollar whore in Mexico somewhere, never to be heard from again. If they let her live, that is."

"If you lie, I'll spend the rest of my days hunting you," Murphy said.

"I know that. I won't lie," Christopher said. "So do we have a deal or does the girl meet a horrible fate that you will have on your conscience forever?"

"We have a deal," Murphy said. "But do anything foolish, and you'll wish for me to kill you."

"I'm no fool," Christopher said.

Murphy lifted the pot from the fire and filled his cup. "Which horse is yours?"

"The spotted pinto."

Murphy looked at the pinto as he sipped coffee.

"I guess I'll get some shut-eye," Christopher said. "And I guess, since you have to watch me, you won't."

Murphy set his cup aside, stood, and walked to Boyle and removed his rope.

"What are you doing?" Christopher asked.

Murphy looped the rope around Christopher's neck and then tied the other end around Boyle's neck.

"If that rope tightens, my horse will stomp you to death where you lie," Murphy said.

With his hands and legs tied, Christopher was helpless. "You're a son of a bitch, Murphy. You know that?" he said.

"I thought you were going to sleep," Murphy said.

In the morning, Murphy dug six shallow graves and buried the dead. While breakfast cooked, he removed the firing handle from the Gatling gun and then gathered up all the pistols and rifles and loaded them onto Christopher's horse.

He ate breakfast while Christopher watched.

"What about me?" Christopher asked.

"I'm leaving you exactly what you asked for, supplies, money, and your horse," Murphy said. He drew the Colt, cocked it, and aimed it at Christopher. "Now go ahead and lie to me."

Christopher grinned. "I'm no fool. Are you a man of your word?"

"You know I am."

"The old men hired a team of men to watch the girl," Christopher said. "Some are relations, some are not, but all are like the six you killed, men for hire. Right now their job is to hold the girl without harm so she can be returned for ransom. Things will change if word doesn't reach them in a few weeks."

"Where?"

"I have your word."

"Yes, you have my word."

"Adobe Walls in Texas, on the Llano."

Murphy de-cocked the Colt and holstered it. "How many men?"

"Six, but it could be as many as eight."

Murphy stood and walked to the eight horses. He tied the one with the weapons to Boyle's saddle horn. The remaining seven he scattered into the canyon pass with a few shots from the Colt to the ground.

"You gave your word," Christopher said.

"And I'll keep it," Murphy said.

He tossed a knife beside Christopher's boots.

"You'll find your horse a few miles south," Murphy said. "Everything you asked for is loaded on the saddlebags. All you need to do is walk to your pinto."

With both hands tied in front of him, Christopher reached for the knife.

"Enjoy your breakfast," Murphy said.

Murphy mounted Boyle and, with Christopher's horse in tow, he rode up the side of the cliff.

CHAPTER THIRTY-SIX

Burke, Judge Parker, Kai, and six secret service agents met Bass Reeves at the Washington railroad depot. Parker and Burke tried to convince Kai to wait in the hotel, but she insisted on meeting Reeves. After much arguing, they gave in to her will and allowed her to come.

"Judge Parker, Kai, what are you doing here?" Reeves said.

"I could ask you the same," Parker said.

"The president is waiting to be briefed," Burke said.

"Marshal Reeves, where is my husband?" Kai said.

Reeves looked at Parker, and Parker nodded.

"After we captured this bunch, he went after the rest in those canyons in Utah," Reeves said.

"Alone?" Parker said.

"Hell, Judge, I'm bringing them in, but

Murphy is the one who did the capturing, including the Cain boy," Reeves said.

"He's not harmed?" Kai asked.

"Harmed? Hardly," Reeves said. "Murphy is an army by himself, Kai. Just ask this bunch."

Kai nodded. "Thank you, Marshal Reeves," she said.

"Kai, a secret service agent will escort you to the hotel," Burke said. "We'll have dinner together later."

Arthur read Murphy's report concerning Joshua Cain.

"What do you think, William?" he asked.

"I don't see any reason not to grant the pardon as Murphy requested," Burke said.

"Marshal?" Arthur said.

"I go along with Murphy," Reeves said. "The Cain boy isn't like his father. He told Murphy where to find the rest in the canyons. I didn't even need to shackle him on the trip."

Arthur nodded. "I'll agree to the boy's pardon, but the rest will be severely punished," he said. "The ambassador wants them hanged, and I tend to agree with him."

"Yes, sir," Reeves said.

"Mr. President, as this started in Fort Smith, I would like to hold the trial and hang them in my jurisdiction," Parker said.

"I'll agree to that," Arthur said. "What do you think, William?"

"It's cleaner that way, to hold trial outside of Washington," Burke said.

"I'm going to dispatch the army to search for Murphy," Arthur said.

"With all due respect, Mr. President, the army has a better chance of finding Murphy with me along," Reeves said.

Parker looked at Reeves and nodded. "I agree with that, Mr. President."

"I'll be on the first train west in the morning," Reeves said.

"Very well," Arthur said. "William, send a telegram to the post commander at Gunnison. Tell them when the marshal arrives, they are to send out a search party for Murphy."

"Mr. President, I think the marshal might like a hot bath and change of clothing right about now," Parker said.

"He's earned it," Arthur said.

"Why would he go after them alone?" Kai said.

Burke sighed. "As long as I've known him, it's been his way," he said. "I expect he's not about to change now."

"No, he wouldn't, I suppose," Kai said.

"Not for his final assignment."

Burke glanced at Parker for a brief second.

"This was his final assignment, or am I mistaken?" Kai said.

"That was the agreement," Burke said.

"You haven't touched your supper, Kai," Parker said.

"I guess I'm not very hungry," Kai said.

"Where is the marshal?" Burke asked.

"Sleeping," Parker said. "He said he was exhausted."

Kai stared at Burke for a moment. "Are you a man of your word?" she said.

"I am," Burke said. "If I wasn't, your husband would have nothing to do with me."

"Break your word, Mr. Burke, and you shall see the Navajo side of me. You won't like it very much at all."

"I won't break my word," Burke said.

"Mr. Burke, if I'm not needed, Kai and I will return to Fort Smith in the morning," Parker said.

"I'll see you off," Burke said.

Burke and Arthur shared a late-night drink in Arthur's living quarters.

"The son of a bitch went after them alone, why?" Arthur said.

"That was his assignment," Burke said.

"Alone and classified."

"Up to a point," Arthur said.

"You don't know Murphy very well," Burke said.

"I'm afraid I do not," Arthur said.

"You said up to a point," Burke said. "He doesn't know where that point is. That has guided him his entire life."

Arthur smiled and sipped his drink. "I assume his wife is pretty upset," he said.

Burke grinned. "She threatened to show me her Navajo side if anything happens to him," he said.

"Lord," Arthur said. "I hope nothing happens to him."

"That makes two of us, Mr. President," Burke said.

Parker shook hands with Reeves and Burke at the train depot platform.

"Marshal, I need you home and in one piece," Parker said.

"Don't worry, Judge," Reeves said. He looked at Kai. "I'll get word to you as soon as I can."

"Thank you, Marshal," Kai said.

"Now don't worry, Kai," Burke said. "Murphy is like the British empire, a good friend and a bad enemy. He will be fine."

Reeves boarded his train. He waved goodbye and entered a riding car.

"Well, our train doesn't leave for an hour," Parker said. "How about we get a cup of coffee?"

"Will you join us, Mr. Burke?" Kai asked. "I'd like to hear more about the British Empire."

Kai and Parker arrived in Fort Smith around six o'clock in the evening.

"I'll walk you home," Parker said.

As they neared the boarding house, Kai said, "I smell Mrs. Leary's beef stew. As we skipped lunch on the train, why not stay for supper?"

"Beef stew, huh?"

"She makes a good one," Kai said. "And plenty of it."

"You talked me into it," Parker said.

When they entered the house and walked into the dining room, Kai was surprised to see Mr. Grillo at the table.

"Mrs. Murphy, there you are," he said.

"Marshal Reeves, it's after midnight," Captain Jenner said.

"I know that, Captain," Reeves said as he walked his horse to the mess hall. "Any chance of a man getting something decent to eat at this hour."

350

"I'll have a cook awakened and meet you at the mess hall," Jenner said.

"Thank you, Captain," Reeves said.

Unable to sleep, Kai warmed a glass of milk and went outside to the porch. The moon was up, and she didn't bother to light the wall-mounted lantern.

After a few minutes, Mrs. Leary came out, wrapped up in a robe.

"I thought I heard you," Mrs. Leary said.

"I couldn't sleep," Kai said.

Mrs. Leary sat in the chair beside Kai. "Worried about Mr. Murphy?"

"I suppose," Kai said. She sipped milk. "The worst part is not that he could be killed. I've lived through that once. The worst part is not knowing where he is."

"Well, if it eases your mind some, Mr. Murphy is not the kind to go tomcatting around in some bordello somewhere."

Kai smiled. "No. No, he isn't," she said. "And that never entered my mind."

"Come to bed and try to get some sleep," Mrs. Leary said.

The cook prepared six scrambled eggs to go along with a thick steak and a pot of coffee.

While Reeves ate, Captain Jenner drank a cup of coffee and smoked a cigar.

"I received a telegram from the president," Jenner said.

"Yes, sir," Reeves said. "I was there when it was sent."

"A patrol of sixteen men plus yourself should be adequate, I would think," Jenner said. "We'll leave after morning mess."

"We'll?" Reeves said.

"Every patrol requires an officer to lead, and I haven't been on one in a while," Jenner said.

"You lead, Captain, but I guide. Agreed?" Reeves said.

"Agreed," Jenner said.

Burke was having a sleepless night, one of many recently. He left his bed, poured a drink of whiskey, and went to his study to read for a while.

He lit a cigar and tried to read, but the words on the page all ran together and he closed the book.

He sipped whiskey and thought for a while.

Where in the hell was Murphy?

CHAPTER THIRTY-SEVEN

Murphy walked Boyle away from the railroad depot and into the streets of Dodge City. Once a small stop on the cattle rancher's drive to market, Dodge was a lawless and wild town in those days, but things had changed recently.

The population had nearly tripled with the building of the railroad depot. Wyatt Earp and Bat Masterson helped tame the outlaws, and Fort Dodge kept relations between the whites and Comanches civilized.

Murphy had passed through Dodge about a year ago when on assignment. Bat Masterson was temporarily serving as town marshal at the time, but he left shortly afterward.

On that trip, he was surprised to see that Dodge now had an opera house and a four-story hotel called the Dodge House.

The first order of business was to board

Boyle at the livery stable. He told the manager to give Boyle as much grain as he wanted, but not to try to brush him down. Boyle allowed only Murphy to brush him, and he would return later to do so.

He took saddlebags and his Winchester with him to the Dodge House, where he got a room on the top floor facing the street. He ordered a bath and the laundering of his dirty clothes.

Clean, wearing fresh trail clothes, Murphy left the Dodge House and walked several blocks to the largest of three gun stores in town.

"Can I help you?" the clerk behind the counter asked.

Behind the counter was a long row of rifles and shotguns. After Murphy scanned the row he said, "I'm looking for a Sharps with a thirty-four-inch barrel."

The man, much shorter than Murphy, looked up at him. "There hasn't been buffalo around here in ten years," he said.

"I know. Do you have one and ammunition?" Murphy said.

"In the back," the clerk said. "I haven't had anybody ask for one in so long, I took it off the shelf."

"Let me see it," Murphy said.

The clerk went to the back room and

returned a few moments later with the Sharps rifle wrapped in cloth. He set it on the counter.

Murphy removed the cloth wrapping and lifted the massive rifle. He inspected it carefully, checking the barrel for pitting and springs for weakening.

"How much ammunition do you have?" Murphy asked.

"Four boxes of fifty each," the clerk said.

"I'll take the rifle and four boxes," Murphy said.

"Forty for the rifle and twenty for the ammunition," the clerk said.

"I'll throw in an extra ten if you give it a good cleaning," Murphy said.

"In advance," the clerk said.

Murphy counted out seventy dollars and set it on the counter. "Do you have a cleaning brush for it?" he asked.

"An extra two dollars."

Murphy placed the extra two dollars on the counter. "I'll pick it up in the morning," he said.

"Are you some kind of lawman?" the clerk asked.

"Why do you want to know?" Murphy said.

"Dodge has an ordinance against wearing sidearms in public, and you're wearing a

355

fairly expensive Colt," the clerk said.

Murphy removed his wallet and showed his identification to the clerk.

"Is the president coming to Dodge?" the clerk asked.

"No."

Murphy left the gun store and found a large mercantile a few blocks away. He entered and ordered sixty pounds of fresh supplies.

"What time do you open in the morning?" Murphy asked the clerk.

"Ten sharp," the clerk said.

"I'll pick up the supplies at ten. How much?"

"Twenty-five dollars, and we'll call it even."

Murphy paid the clerk and went out to the street. A sheriff and a deputy, both armed with Winchesters, were headed his way.

Murphy stopped and waited for them to arrive.

"Afternoon. I'm Pat Sughrue, Sheriff of Ford County. This is my deputy, Bill Tighman," Sughrue said.

"I'm aware of your no-sidearm-in-public ordinance," Murphy said. "I was here just a year ago."

"Then why are you wearing that Colt?"

Tighman said.

Murphy looked at Tighman. "Son, would you like to find out how fast your life can change?" he said.

"Hold on, mister," Sughrue said. "We have the —"

"I'm going to reach into my pocket and remove my wallet," Murphy said.

"Go ahead," Sughrue said.

Murphy removed his wallet, opened it, and showed Sughrue his identification.

"Is the president coming to Dodge?" Sughrue asked.

"No," Murphy said.

"What is it?" Tighman asked.

"This man is a United States Secret Service Agent," Sughrue said. "His name is Murphy."

"Well, what are you doing here?" Tighman said.

"I'm on assignment," Murphy said. "I needed some supplies. I'm staying at the Dodge House. Why not join me for dinner around seven o'clock?"

"Where are you headed right now?" Sughrue asked.

"Livery, to see to my horse."

"I'll walk with you," Sughrue said. "Bill, go about your rounds."

As Murphy and Sughrue walked to the

livery, Sughrue said, "This assignment, does it have anything to do with Dodge?"

"Not a thing, Sheriff," Murphy said. "Like I said, I needed supplies. I'll be gone in the morning."

They reached the livery. "My horse needs a brushing," Murphy said. "I'll see you at the Dodge House at seven."

"I'll be there."

"Where is your telegraph office? I need to send a wire."

"Same block as my office."

"Obliged."

"They serve a pretty good steak," Murphy said.

"That they do," Sughrue said. "But considering Dodge is a cattle town, I'd be surprised otherwise."

"Last year, Bat Masterson was serving as town marshal," Murphy said.

"He left and went to New York to write about sports for the newspapers," Sughrue said. "My duties as county sheriff take up too much time, so a new town marshal will be elected soon. Young Bill might run for the office, so he said."

"He's young," Murphy said. "He needs to learn to think first with his brain and not his mouth."

"But eager to learn."

"Last time I was here, there was a boxing exhibition at the opera house," Murphy said.

"I remember."

"There was a carnival barker on the street with one of those blow horns," Murphy said.

"I saw that, too," Sughrue said.

"Any idea where I can get one in town?" Murphy asked.

"I suppose at the opera house, but whatever for?"

"You never know when one might come in handy," Murphy said.

Kai sat on the porch with Grillo, each with a cup of after-dinner coffee.

"Tomorrow I'd like you to take a ride with me to inspect the layout," Grillo said. "If you approve the plans, we can start work in a few days."

"All right," Kai said.

"Of course, you'll need to approve certain colors, such as the roof and flooring, but I'm sure you'll be pleased with the choices," Grillo said.

"Neither my husband nor I are picky," Kai said.

"Still, it's nice to have colors you can live with," Grillo said.

A messenger from the telegraph office approached the porch. "Mrs. Murphy?" he said.

"Yes," Kai said.

"Telegram," the messenger said.

Kai took the envelope and said, "Let me get my purse."

"Allow me," Grillo said and tipped the messenger fifty cents.

"Thank you, Mr. Grillo," Kai said.

After the messenger left, Kai opened the envelope. "Could you turn up the lantern, Mr. Grillo?" she said.

Grillo stood and turned up the flame on the lantern. "I'll turn in and see you in the morning," he said.

"Good night, Mr. Grillo," Kai said.

After Grillo entered the house, Kai read the telegram.

Presently in Dodge City. I'm fine and plan to be home soon. I love you. Murphy.

Kai lowered the telegram.

"Dodge City?' she said aloud.

After breakfast in the Dodge Hotel, Murphy, with Boyle in tow, met Sheriff Sughrue at the opera house on Main Street.

The opera house had several blow horns they used to advertise shows and events and agreed to sell a used one to Murphy.

360

"I won't ask you what it's for," Sughrue said.

Sughrue accompanied Murphy to the gun store and then to the mercantile, where Murphy loaded Boyle with supplies.

"Well, Sheriff, if I'm back this way I'll stop in and say hello," Murphy said.

Sughrue looked at the massive Sharps rifle on the side of Boyle's saddle. "I expect you're not after elk," he said.

"No," Murphy said and mounted the saddle.

CHAPTER THIRTY-EIGHT

Led by Reeves, the patrol of soldiers reached the point where Murphy and Reeves had captured the prisoners.

Reeves had no trouble following Murphy's trail into the canyons and the campsite.

"What in God's name happened here?" Captain Jenner said as he inspected the site.

"Captain, the firing handle on the Gatling gun has been removed," a soldier said.

"Who dug these graves?" Jenner said.

"Murphy," Reeves said. "Six graves, but there were seven men. Murphy allowed one to live. Murphy rode out with the man's horse, and the man walked. I know Murphy's horse tracks."

"I don't understand any of this," Jenner said. "Why did he let one man live and then take his horse?"

"I don't know, but he had a reason," Reeves said.

"I don't suppose we can track him?"

Jenner asked.

Reeves grinned. "No, Captain, I expect not," he said.

"Well, some of you men get the Gatling gun ready to move. We're heading back," Jenner said.

The Llano Estacado in northwestern Texas could take weeks to cross, if you were lucky enough to survive the trip. Elevated to three thousand feet, after you crossed the Canadian River there was little to no water to be found and nothing in the way of game to hunt.

Fortunately for Murphy, Adobe Walls was just a short ride south of the Canadian River to the east. Once a large trading post established forty years ago, all that remained now were the crumbling walls of the many buildings that had made up the establishment.

About a thousand yards north of the walls, Murphy dismounted and removed binoculars from the saddlebags.

From a prone position, he zoomed in on the walls. Seven horses were tethered to a long rope suspended between two wood posts in the ground. One horse had recently been ridden and still was saddled. A fire pit had been constructed with a large cauldron resting in a tripod above a fire. Three men were seated against a crumbling wall, drinking whiskey and watching a young woman as she stirred the pot with a large wood spoon. He recognized her from the photograph as Elizabeth Turner.

The young woman's clothing was tattered and filthy. Her blond hair was limp and dirty. Her feet were bare. Elizabeth Turner had been having a rough time of it, for sure.

Murphy lowered the binoculars and stood up. He replaced the binoculars and removed a long rifle scope, the Sharps rifle, and a box of ammunition. Once the scope was mounted onto the Sharps, he inserted a round, and then set the rifle on the ground.

He removed the blow horn from the saddle, held it to his lips, and shouted, "Elizabeth Turner, this is Agent Murphy of the United States Secret Service."

Elizabeth looked up as the three men stood against the wall, and three additional men came out from inside the walls.

Murphy lowered the blow horn. "Six men, seven horses," he said to himself.

The six men huddled closely as they scanned the horizon, but from a thousand yards away and with the sun in their eyes, Murphy was all but invisible.

Murphy placed the blow horn to his lips

again. "Elizabeth Turner, count to ten and get on your belly," he shouted.

Murphy dropped the blow horn, got on his own stomach, and grabbed the Sharps rifle. Through the scope he watched the six men look into the sun as they tried to locate him.

He waited until Elizabeth got on her stomach and then he aimed and fired the Sharps and then ejected the empty shell and loaded another.

The five men looked at the sixth man as he fell dead on the ground. It was confusing to them, because the bullet struck the man three seconds before the sound of the bullet reached them.

Murphy fired again and another man was blown off his feet. Murphy reloaded quickly and shot a third man as he tried to run behind the protection of the walls.

Murphy set the Sharps aside and picked up the blow horn. "Elizabeth Turner, get on the saddled horse and ride north. You three men hiding in the walls, if you stick your heads out, I will shoot them off. Elizabeth Turner, get on the horse now."

Murphy watched through the scope on the Sharps as Elizabeth stood and walked to the saddled horse. As she untied the rope tethering the horse, he fired a shot that struck the wall the three men were hiding behind. He reloaded and fired again as Elizabeth mounted the horse. As she turned the horse and raced it north, Murphy fired three more rounds into the wall.

Then he kept the scope on Elizabeth Turner. The girl knew how to ride and raced the horse toward him. She rode about four hundred yards, and Murphy stood when she was out of range of a Winchester rifle.

Elizabeth kept the horse at a full run.

Murphy placed the Sharps into the sleeve on the saddle and was about to mount Boyle's saddle when Elizabeth's horse tripped, stumbled, threw Elizabeth, and fell to the ground.

Murphy jumped into the saddle and tugged hard on Boyle's reins. Boyle responded by breaking into a hard run.

Elizabeth was about five hundred yards away, and Boyle covered the ground quickly. Murphy kept his eyes on the walls as he rode. The remaining three men were saddling their horses.

Murphy yanked the reins. "You have to give me more, boy," he said.

Boyle responded by flaring his nostrils and opening his gait even wider.

Murphy, close to where Elizabeth had fallen, looked past her to the three men who had mounted their horses and were riding toward him.

Elizabeth was standing up when Murphy raced past her toward the three men. He drew his Colt, cocked it, and waited to close the distance between him and the three men.

They had pistols drawn.

The gap closed.

The men fired at Murphy.

Murphy yanked Boyle hard to the left and returned fire. One of the men fell from his horse as Murphy rode past them and quickly turned Boyle around.

The men also turned their horses, and Murphy shot another from the saddle. The third man turned his horse and ran away.

Murphy slowed Boyle to a stop, holstered the Colt, and removed the Winchester from the sleeve. He cocked the lever, aimed, and shot the fleeing last man in the back.

Once the man was dead on the ground, Murphy replaced the Winchester, turned Boyle, and rode back to Elizabeth.

She was standing, watching him, as Murphy rode to her and dismounted.

"Are you hurt?" Murphy asked.

"A little banged up. Nothing serious. I've taken harder falls," Elizabeth said in her British accent.

"Can you ride?" Murphy said.

"Can you?" Elizabeth said. "Are you aware that you've been shot in the chest?"

"I am, but we can't worry about that at the moment," Murphy said. "We have to put some distance between us and here. There might be others we don't know about."

"There were three others, but they rode off early this morning," Elizabeth said. "I think they went for supplies."

Murphy looked about the dry Llano. "Those horses have scattered, so we'll have to ride double. Get on."

"You're bleeding," Elizabeth said.

"You can stop it later," Murphy said. "We have to cover some ground before those three return and see what's happened."

Burke took the telegram from the White House operator and walked it to the Oval Office.

Arthur was meeting with the Speaker of the House, Joseph Keifer, and Burke had to wait for a few minutes in the hallway.

When Keifer came out, Burke entered the office without knocking and simply handed the envelope to President Arthur.

Arthur opened the envelope, removed the folded paper, and read it quickly.

Murphy returning to Fort Smith according to a telegram he sent to his wife. Judge Parker.

"Fort Smith? Why?" Arthur said.

"We don't know," Burke said.

"When?"

"We don't know that either," Burke said.

Arthur sighed. "William, I'd like you to go to Fort Smith and find out just what the hell is going on."

Burke nodded. "I'll leave in the morning," he said.

After crossing the Canadian River, Murphy rode Boyle east into Oklahoma. An hour before sunset, he stopped and dismounted and then helped Elizabeth down from the saddle.

"They won't be able to track us at night," he said.

"You've lost a lot of blood," Elizabeth said.

"You'll have to take the bullet out and close the wound," Murphy said.

"Me? I'm a political science major with a minor in Elizabethan English," Elizabeth said. "I don't even know how to knit."

"We're a day's ride to a town in any direction," Murphy said. "Even if the bullet doesn't kill me, blood poisoning will."

"What . . . what do I do?" Elizabeth asked.

"Do you know how to make a fire?" Murphy said.

"In the fireplace back home," Elizabeth said.

"Look, it's not that hard," Murphy said. "Gather up some brush and whatever wood you can find and make a pile. Strike a match and toss it on. That's it, you got fire."

Elizabeth nodded. "And then?"

"Make the fire first."

While Elizabeth gathered brush and wood, Murphy removed the saddle from Boyle. He felt light-headed and dizzy and sat with his back against the saddle.

It took her several tries, but finally Elizabeth made a fire.

"Let it get hot, then put my knife in the flames," Murphy said.

He drew the long field knife from its sheath on his belt and handed it to Elizabeth. She took the knife by the handle.

"And then?" she said.

"Then you dig the bullet out, wash the wound with whiskey, and cauterize the skin to stop the bleeding."

"Cauterize the . . . I don't think I can do that," Elizabeth said.

"Then I'll die, and then those men will catch up to you and kill you," Murphy said. "They will kill you because they know their scheme went bad, and you know their faces.

So, do you think you can do this or not?"

Elizabeth nodded and placed the knife in the fire.

"There's whiskey in my saddlebags. Get it," Murphy said.

Elizabeth opened the saddlebags, and removed a sealed bottle of whiskey and handed it to Murphy. He broke the seal and took a long swallow.

"There is another knife in the saddlebags," he said.

While Elizabeth found the knife, Murphy took several more swallows of whiskey.

"What do I do?" Elizabeth asked.

"Hold out the knife," Murphy said.

Elizabeth held out the knife and Murphy poured whiskey over the blade. Then he took several more drinks of whiskey and gave Elizabeth the bottle.

"Pour some over the wound after I open my shirt," Murphy said.

He opened the buttons, carefully removed the shirt, and tossed it aside. "Cut off my undershirt," he said. "I don't think I can lift my left arm."

Elizabeth used the knife to slice open the bloody undershirt and exposed the bullet hole. At the sight of the wound, she gasped.

"It's not that bad," Murphy said. "It's just below the surface. It didn't hit anything vital. Let me have the whiskey, and then I'll tell you what to do."

Elizabeth gave Murphy the bottle and he took a long swallow.

"Are you really a secret service agent?" Elizabeth asked.

"Well, I hope you don't think I do this for a hobby," Murphy said and took another swallow of whiskey.

"How did you know where to find me?"

"That is a very long story," Murphy said. "And one for another day."

"Those men, they wanted ransom money for me," Elizabeth said. "Did they pay?"

"A quarter of a million in gold. They wanted more. Your uncle and President Arthur believed you were dead and said no to the second demand."

"So they sent you?"

"Something like that."

Murphy took two more swallows from the bottle and gave it to Elizabeth.

"Okay, now do exactly as I say," he said. "First, pour more whiskey onto the wound and the knife."

Elizabeth did as instructed and then said, "Now what?"

"Now use the knife to open the wound," Murphy said. "Just a small cut on the top and bottom."

Elizabeth stared at the bullet wound.

"It's going to hurt me worse than you," Murphy said. "Do it now, as I don't fancy a case of blood poisoning."

Elizabeth placed the tip of the knife on the wound and cut a small incision on the top and bottom. As she cut, Murphy gritted his teeth and choked back the pain.

"It's . . . bleeding again," Elizabeth said.

"You just cut into an open wound, so I'm not surprised. Clean it with the whiskey to keep it clean," Murphy said.

Elizabeth poured whiskey onto the bleeding hole.

Murphy winced and said, "Bullet's near the surface. Can you see it?"

"Yes."

"Insert the tip of the knife until it's behind the bullet and then gently pry it out," Murphy said. "Be careful not to break it up into pieces."

Elizabeth slowly moved the tip of the knife to the wound. "My hands are shaking," she said.

"Take a sip of whiskey," Murphy said.

"Whiskey?"

"I'm sorry we don't have any Earl Grey with honey at the moment," Murphy said. "Take a sip of whiskey and steady your hand."

Elizabeth reached for the bottle, placed it to her lips, and took a small sip. She coughed and gagged and said, "It's like drinking coal oil."

"I wouldn't know. I've never drunk coal oil," Murphy said. "Now remove the damned bullet."

"You don't have to shout," Elizabeth said.

"Sorry, but lying in the dirt bleeding to death tends to make me a bit grouchy," Murphy said. "Now, if you don't mind, would you pretty please get the bullet out of me."

Elizabeth placed the tip of the blade against the wound again and slowly inserted the knife until the blade was behind the bullet.

"I got it," she said.

"Now pry it out, but make sure it doesn't break apart," Murphy said.

Slowly, Elizabeth wiggled the bullet until it broke through the surface of the skin.

"I see it," she said.

Gritting his teeth, Murphy said, "Pry it out."

Elizabeth flicked the knife, and the bullet popped out and fell to the ground.

"Is it in one piece?" Murphy said.

Elizabeth picked it up. "Yes."

"Pour some more whiskey into the

wound."

Elizabeth poured whiskey onto the open, bleeding hole.

"Now take the hot knife and hold it against the skin until the bleeding stops," Murphy said. "It should take no more than three or four seconds."

"Do you want to bite on something?" Elizabeth asked.

"Yeah, a thick, juicy steak. You got one?" Murphy said. "Take the knife and do it. Do it quick."

Elizabeth grabbed the knife by the handle from the fire. It was red hot.

"Now?" she said.

"We could wait for snow? Yes, now," Murphy said.

Murphy took a deep breath and looked away as Elizabeth touched the hot knife to the open wound. Flesh and hair burned as she counted to four, and then removed the knife and looked at the skin.

She could smell Murphy's roasted skin.

Then she turned, dropped the knife, and vomited onto the grass.

Gasping in pain, Murphy said, "Don't get any on my boots," and then passed out.

CHAPTER THIRTY-NINE

Murphy opened his eyes to sunlight and the smell of bacon, beans, and coffee. His shirt was on and buttoned. Elizabeth was kneeling beside a fire, stirring the bacon and beans.

"How long was I out?" Murphy asked.

Elizabeth stood. "About twelve hours now. How do you feel?"

"Like a cow that's been branded on the wrong end," Murphy said.

"From all the scars on you, I'd say you've been branded more than once," Elizabeth said.

"Scars seem to be part of the job," Murphy said.

"Do you think you can eat something?"

"Fill me a plate and a cup with coffee and a biscuit or two."

Elizabeth filled a plate and cup and handed them to Murphy. "Sorry, I'm fresh out of Earl Grey with honey," she said with a smile.

"If we make it to Fort Smith, I'll buy you a case of each," Murphy said. "Did you feed Boyle?"

"Your horse?"

"Don't let him hear you call him that. He thinks he's a person."

"I fed him grain from your bags. Why Fort Smith?"

"Why not? Eat. We got to get going," Murphy said.

"You're in no condition to —" Elizabeth said.

"We stay put and they catch us, we die," Murphy said. "I'm too weak at the moment to go three on one. Our safest bet is to put distance between us and them."

"What if they're not after us?" Elizabeth said.

"They're after us, of that you can be sure," Murphy said. "They got paid to hold on to you, and you can identify them. I don't know how much they know about the entire operation, but they know enough to know leaving you alive is a twenty-year stretch at Yuma prison."

Elizabeth nodded. "What if we went to the nearest town?"

"They would track us to that town and

ambush us," Murphy said. "We'd be sitting ducks in a town. No, our best bet is to keep riding, open some distance between us, and reach Fort Smith before they can catch us."

"If that horse hadn't tripped," Elizabeth said.

"But he did, and there's no sense wasting time thinking on it," Murphy said. "Can you saddle a horse?"

"I ride equestrian back home," Elizabeth said.

"Then help me up and let's get started," Murphy said.

"What if you start to bleed again?"

"I'd rather bleed in the saddle than on the ground," Murphy said.

Burke carried a large satchel from the Fort Smith railroad depot to the boarding house. The afternoon streets were crowded with pedestrians and wagons. A town peace officer was directing traffic on Main Street near the courthouse.

He walked to the courthouse, checked in with the marshal on duty, and was escorted to Judge Parker's office.

"Mr. Burke, this is a surprise," Parker said. "Are you here to check the status of the trial for the kidnappers?"

"No, but as long as I'm here, do you have

one?" Burke said.

"It's after four. How about a small drink to wet your beak a bit?"

"What do you have?"

"A bottle of the whiskey Murphy drinks."

"In that case, make it a big drink, and do you mind if I have a cigar?"

"Not at all."

While Parker dug out the bottle and two glasses, Burke lit a cigar.

"A federal prosecutor from Washington is preparing his case against the defendants, and the defendants have hired private counsel for themselves," Parker said. "By the time jury is selected and cases are prepared, we're talking sixty days down the road for opening arguments. I have no doubt a jury will find them guilty. I will hang the lot of them on the same day."

"I'll advise the president," Burke said.

Parker handed Burke a glass of whiskey. Both men sipped.

"I'm here about Murphy's telegram," Burke said.

"I sent you what I know, and there hasn't been another since," Parker said.

"I'm wondering what he was doing in Dodge City," Burke said. "Well, why not be my guest for dinner tonight along with Kai? Seven, and you pick the place."

379

"Delmonico's suit you? They serve up a pretty decent steak," Parker said.

"We'll meet you there," Burke said.

Late in the afternoon, Murphy rested Boyle for about an hour. He and Elizabeth shared a cold snack of water and biscuits.

"Have you always been a secret service agent?" Elizabeth asked.

"Since Grant became president in sixty-nine," Murphy said.

"Back home, my family is involved in politics," Elizabeth said.

"Is that why you're studying political science?"

Elizabeth nodded. "And I hate every boring minute of it," she said.

"Does your uncle know that?"

"He wouldn't care if he did know," Elizabeth said. "I'm supposed to return home and marry a man who is engaged in British politics. It's expected of me, and my family doesn't have room in them for disappointment."

"You are a brave girl, Elizabeth," Murphy said. "Most folks would have cracked after what you've been through. It seems to me you have the stuff to stand up to your family and tell them you want to take a different path."

"They won't agree. If I disobey them, I'll be cut off and on my own," Elizabeth said. "London is a frightening place in which to be poor and on your own."

"How many more years do you have in school?"

"At least three."

"Then you have plenty of time to figure things out," Murphy said. "In the meantime, in my saddlebags you'll find a warm pair of wool socks. Put them on, and let's get moving. We have four hours of daylight left, and we need to make another twenty miles."

"Your horse is carrying two, plus supplies," Elizabeth said.

"Boyle is a draft horse and can pull a building," Murphy said. "He doesn't even notice your weight. Grab the socks and let's get moving."

After meeting with several attorneys concerning pending cases, Parker was about to leave to meet Burke and Kai for dinner, when Marshal Reeves knocked on the office door and entered.

"You're back," Parker said.

"Yes, Judge. I figured you'd want to hear my report right away," Reeves said.

"I do. Proceed," Parker said.

"We tracked Murphy to the hideout in the

canyons," Reeves said. "Seven men and a Gatling gun. Murphy killed six and let one man live. Murphy rode out on his horse, and the seventh man walked. Murphy had such a large lead on us, Captain Jenner decided to return to the outpost. I agreed with him, Judge. Murphy had too big a lead to track."

"Any idea why he allowed the seventh man to live?" Parker asked.

"No, sir, but from what I know of the man, he won't do something unless it's for a good reason," Reeves said.

"Several days ago Kai received a telegram from Murphy in Dodge City," Parker said.

"Dodge City? What's he doing there?"

"I guess we'll have to wait for his return to find out," Parker said. "Go home to your family, Marshal. You've earned a rest."

"Do you ever get sick of beans and bacon?" Elizabeth asked as she stirred the pan.

Murphy was seated against his saddle, smoking his pipe. "Had you ever tasted bourbon whiskey before the other day?" he said.

"I'm allowed only a few sips of champagne on special occasions, usually when a toast is made," Elizabeth said. "That sip of whiskey you gave me was the first time I tasted it. I can't say I enjoyed it much."

Murphy dug the bottle of bourbon out of a saddlebag and opened it. "This will give supper some flavor," he said and poured an ounce into the pan.

Elizabeth stirred the beans and bacon. "Are you married, Agent Murphy?"

"I am."

"Why don't you wear a ring? I've seen many men wear their wedding rings."

"It didn't fit," Murphy said. "My wife went to have it resized, and I never got around to trying it on again."

Elizabeth looked at Murphy's hands. "I can see why it didn't fit. What's her name, your wife?"

"Kai."

"That's an unusual name."

"She's a quarter Navajo," Murphy said. "The rest is Irish, English, with a bit of German. She spent time with the Navajo and the Sioux, and they hung that name on her."

"Is she pretty?"

"The handsomest woman I've ever seen," Murphy said. "Now, how about you load up a few plates and we eat?"

Over dinner at Delmonico's Restaurant, Parker told Kai and Burke about Reeves's report.

"It doesn't surprise me that Murphy would kill those six men," Burke said. "But he must have had a very good reason for allowing one to live."

Kai stared at Burke.

Parker cleared his throat to alert Burke.

"Oh, I am sorry, Kai," Burke said. "I didn't mean to upset you just now."

"You didn't," Kai said. "I'm well aware of who and what my husband is. I don't know why he went to Dodge City, but I would bet it has something to do with letting one man live."

"I agree with you," Burke said. "I'm just curious as to the reason."

"I expect we'll find out soon enough," Parker said.

Murphy tossed his bedroll over Elizabeth and then extinguished the fire. As he settled in against his saddle, he said, "Do you think you can handle Boyle?"

"The reins?"

"Yes."

"He's no equestrian horse, but I think so," Elizabeth said. "Why do you ask?"

"I feel a fever coming on," Murphy said. "That's common after being shot, but I won't be able to handle the reins if I'm burning up with fever."

"Can't we do something to bring it down?" Elizabeth said.

"Afraid not," Murphy said. "It will have to run its course."

"How much farther to Fort Smith?"

"Three full days in the saddle."

"Then I guess I have no choice," Elizabeth said.

CHAPTER FORTY

"We have to rest," Elizabeth said. "You're burning up with fever."

Barely able to hold the reins, Murphy stopped Boyle. "Help me down," he said.

Holding Murphy around the waist, Elizabeth released her grasp and carefully dismounted. "Give me your hand," she said.

Murphy lowered his hand. Elizabeth took it and, slowly, Murphy slid from the saddle and nearly fell flat on his face.

"You are really burning up," Elizabeth said. "You need to rest."

"What time is it?" Murphy asked. "My watch is in my pocket."

Elizabeth removed the watch from Murphy's pocket and checked the time. "A few minutes past noon," she said.

"We'll rest for two hours," Murphy said.

Elizabeth spread out Murphy's bedroll. He was asleep almost immediately. Although they had found several streams along the way and kept the one-gallon canteen filled, she didn't know how many more streams they would encounter the rest of the way to Fort Smith.

She removed a clean neckerchief from one of the saddlebags, wetted it thoroughly with water, and placed it across Murphy's forehead to cool his skin.

Then she took a few sips of water, replaced the cap on the canteen, and set it aside. Even though she'd eaten breakfast, that was six hours ago, and her stomach grumbled. She removed a loaf of cornbread wrapped in waxed paper from the supplies, cut off a slice, and ate it sitting beside Murphy.

He was the most fearless man she had ever met. After she fell off the horse, he'd raced to her rescue without the slightest hesitation or concern for his own safety. She wondered how a man got to be that way.

All the men in her family were always so polite and reserved, with soft hands and bellies. At school in Washington, the male students were about the same, soft and polite and probably never had a callus on their hands in their entire life.

Would any of the men she knew back home or in school have been able to rescue her the way that Murphy had?

She knew the answer was a definite no.

Elizabeth felt Murphy's neckerchief, wet it again, and rubbed Murphy's face. Fever was burning in him, but other than cool his skin, there wasn't much else she could do.

She gathered up some wood and made a fire. She wasn't fond of American coffee, but she made a pot anyway. Then she gave Boyle some feed and tried to brush him, but he wouldn't allow it.

The bond between Boyle and Murphy was strong. Elizabeth sensed Boyle wouldn't break that bond for anybody.

When the coffee boiled, she filled a cup and took a sip. "Dreadful stuff," she said aloud.

She remembered the bourbon and how a small amount made the food taste so much better. She dug out the bottle, added a splash to the cup, and tasted it again.

"Better," she said.

Burke and Kai sat on the porch of the boarding house after lunch and drank coffee. Burke lit one of his cigars.

"How long do you plan to stay?" Kai asked.

"Until Murphy returns," Burke said.

"You saw his telegram," Kai said. "The word 'soon' to my husband could mean tomorrow or a month from now."

"I've known Murphy for a number of years now," Burke said. "He can be hard-headed and stubborn, but there isn't any man I trust more when he gives his word. And besides, as remarkable as it may sound, Murphy is my friend."

"If you are really his friend, when he does return, you'll keep your word and won't ask any more of him," Kai said.

"My word is as good as his," Burke said.

Kai nodded. "I'll tell Mrs. Leary you'll be staying awhile."

After dark, Murphy's fever grew worse, and he started talking in his sleep. Elizabeth kept wetting his face with the neckerchief, but it didn't seem to do any good. As he said, the fever would have to run its course.

She didn't know what else to do when Murphy started shaking from the chills caused by the fever. She built up the fire and then lay down next to him and wrapped them up in the bedroll to give his body some warmth.

After a while, Elizabeth fell asleep.

Murphy opened his eyes and immediately knew his fever had broken. His shirt was drenched with sweat, but his skin felt cool. He sat up in the bedroll and looked around for Elizabeth.

A pan of beans and bacon was cooking on a fire along with a pot of coffee, but Elizabeth was gone. He checked his pocket watch. He'd been asleep almost twenty hours. He gave the watch a few winds and put it away.

Murphy sat up and then slowly stood. He was slightly dizzy and stood still for a few moments to let it pass. Once he was steady on his feet, he knelt and stirred the pan.

Behind him, Elizabeth arrived with an armload of wood.

"I didn't know how long you would be out, so I gathered extra wood," she said.

"We'd best eat and get moving," Murphy said. "I've caused us enough lost time as it is."

Murphy dished out two plates of food and cups of coffee, and they ate seated beside the fire.

"Who is Christopher?" Elizabeth asked.

"The worst sort," Murphy said. "A criminal and a coward to boot."

"And Sally?"

"I see I did some talking in my sleep," Murphy said. "Fever will do that."

"Tell me, please. I'm interested," Sally said.

While they ate, Murphy told Elizabeth

390

about Sally Orr and Christopher right up to the point he let Christopher go in exchange for information concerning Elizabeth's whereabouts in Adobe Walls.

"So you let him go to find me?" Elizabeth said. "What if he lied to you?"

"I would have known," Murphy said. "And I would have tortured him into telling the truth."

"Would you have killed him after he talked?" Elizabeth said.

"Yes, because of what he did to Sally," Murphy said.

"Was Sally anything like Kai?"

"No. Now finish up so we can get moving," Murphy said.

With Murphy at the reins, they were able to make up some lost time. Late in the afternoon, as they passed through a green pasture with good tree cover and brush, he stopped and dismounted.

"Why did we stop?" Elizabeth said as she got down from the saddle.

"Wild prairie chickens," Murphy said.

Elizabeth looked about one hundred yards away at a group of wild chickens pecking the ground near some thick brush.

Murphy removed the Winchester from the saddle and cocked the lever. "They will scatter at the first shot, but maybe I can get two before they take cover," he said.

Murphy selected a plump hen as his target, aimed the Winchester, and killed the bird with one shot. At the crack of the bullet, the chickens scattered, some into the brush. A few took flight.

Murphy quickly cocked the lever, aimed, and was lucky to take down a second bird.

"Supper and breakfast," Murphy said.

"Breakfast?" Elizabeth said.

Murphy replaced the Winchester into the sleeve and then removed an undershirt from the saddlebags. He tied the shirt into a pouch and handed it to Elizabeth.

"Let's go shopping," Murphy said.

"I don't understand," Elizabeth said.

Murphy walked to the thick brush and Elizabeth followed.

"Farm or the wild, chickens are all the same," Murphy said. "They nest. While I gather up our supper, you hunt around in the brush for some eggs."

With two chickens and thirteen eggs loaded onto the saddle, Murphy and Elizabeth rode until dark and then made camp.

At the fire, Murphy plucked the chickens.

"You leave the feathers on until you're ready to cook the bird," he said. "It keeps

392

the bird fresher."

Once he cleaned and dressed the chickens, Murphy fastened spits from sticks and roasted the birds over the fire.

"You've lived off the land," Elizabeth said.

"Many times."

"Those chickens will be a welcome change from beans," Elizabeth said.

"They are that," Murphy said. "Now you turn the birds every few minutes while I see to Boyle."

About an hour later, Murphy and Elizabeth feasted on roasted chicken. There was salt and pepper in the supplies and condensed milk for the coffee.

"My family has taken me to the finest restaurants in London and Washington, but this bird tastes better than any other meal I've ever had," Elizabeth said.

"After a week of beans anything is a welcome change," Murphy said. "But don't worry; you'll be dining on the Hill in Washington in no time."

Elizabeth stared at Murphy for a few moments. "Is that what you think of me, that I'm a spoiled rich brat from England?"

"No. No, I don't," Murphy said. "Most girls would have cracked after what you've been through. That you didn't shows real character. You remind me of my wife in that regard. She's fearless and has true character."

Elizabeth smiled. "That pleases me greatly," she said. "I hope to meet her one day."

"Sooner than you think," Murphy said. "She'll be in Fort Smith."

"What is Fort Smith like?"

"A town."

"Will I be able to get some clothes?"

"Whatever you need."

"How much longer to get there?"

"If we keep up the pace we're moving at, three days," Murphy said.

"I could use a bath," Elizabeth said.

"Tomorrow some time we'll cross a stream," Murphy said. "I have a bar of soap in my bags."

"That will give me that chance to check your wound," Elizabeth said.

"It's fine. A little tender, but fine," Murphy said.

After supper, Murphy gave Boyle a second brushing and extra grain.

"Tomorrow, I'm going to ask you for forty miles," Murphy said.

Boyle turned his head to look at Murphy.

"I know you're carrying two," Murphy said. "But she doesn't weigh more than a hundred pounds soaking wet."

Boyle snorted.

"I know it's your back, but if you get us to Fort Smith in one piece, the both of us can retire to a life of leisure," Murphy said.

Boyle snorted again.

"Yes, you can have some sugar cubes," Murphy said.

Seated beside the fire, Elizabeth said, "It's almost as if he understands you."

"That's because he does," Murphy said. "And I understand him."

In the morning, Murphy coated the fry pan with a bit of condensed milk and then scrambled the eggs. With some cornbread and coffee, the eggs made for a decent breakfast.

Boyle gave Murphy twenty miles before one in the afternoon. He rested him for one hour, and Murphy and Elizabeth ate a cold lunch of cornbread with water.

An hour before sunset, Murphy stopped and made camp for the night. Boyle had given him forty miles and a bit more.

"There wasn't time to stop and hunt today," he said as he put on beans and bacon and coffee to cook.

"Maybe you could add a little extra flavor?" Elizabeth said.

"About what I was thinking," Murphy said

as he reached into the saddlebags for the bottle of whiskey.

After eating, Murphy put the fire out and sat with his back against the saddle. The moon rose early and was bright.

He lit his pipe.

Exhausted, Elizabeth relaxed inside the bedroll.

Murphy, facing west, spotted a red dot on the otherwise dark horizon.

CHAPTER FORTY-ONE

"No time for breakfast," Murphy said as he saddled Boyle at daybreak.

"Why?" Elizabeth asked.

"Last night I saw a fire in the distance," Murphy said. "In open country like this, a fire can be seen up to ten miles. They're close, and we need to move before they get closer."

"Maybe it isn't them?"

"And maybe we can't chance it is," Murphy said.

Elizabeth stared at Murphy.

"Let's go," Murphy said. "Right now."

Murphy mounted the saddle and then pulled Elizabeth up behind him. "Maybe we can make the Ozarks before they catch us," he said.

Murphy pushed Boyle hard for four hours until they reached the foothills, then dismounted and helped Elizabeth down.

"We'll give him thirty minutes' rest," Murphy said. "He still has to carry us another two days, and I've ridden him hard for hundreds of miles."

"Can they catch us?" Elizabeth asked.

"A tired horse carrying two? They can catch us," Murphy said. "And it won't be pretty if they do."

Elizabeth stared at Murphy. He could see the worry and fear building in her eyes.

"I won't allow that to happen," Murphy said. "I give you my word on that."

Boyle gave everything he had left, but the massive horse was exhausted and slowed considerably.

They reached the high foothills of the Ozarks by early afternoon. Some of the hills reached a thousand feet high or more. Murphy dismounted and helped Elizabeth down.

"He can't go any farther," Murphy said. "He's been too good a horse for me to allow him to go out this way."

Murphy removed the Sharps rifle and a box of ammunition from the saddle, then removed the saddle from Boyle and set it on the ground.

"You rest now, boy, and I'll handle it from here," Murphy said. He looked up at a hill that reached a thousand feet high. "Grab the canteen, the binoculars, and some of the biscuits," he said to Elizabeth.

"Where are we going?" Elizabeth asked.

"Up."

The climb to the top of the hill took about thirty minutes. It was steep, and Elizabeth had to make the climb wearing just Murphy's socks. Once they reached flat ground, Murphy selected a clear line of sight to the trail below.

"The sun will be at our backs soon," he said. "Might as well get comfortable."

They ate a few biscuits and drank sips of water as they waited.

"Are you sure they're coming?" Elizabeth asked.

"They're coming," Murphy said. "They can't afford not to. When you were captive, did they violate you in any way?"

"No, nobody touched me," Elizabeth said. "They were mean and treated me badly, but none of them physically touched me."

"Because there was a big payday in it for them," Murphy said. "But now all you are is somebody who can identify them. They will rape you and then murder you, given the chance."

Elizabeth stared at Murphy.

"Remember that when the time comes to get mean," Murphy said.

A slow hour passed. The sun moved

behind them on the cliff. Shadows started to creep across the ground below them.

"I see three riders coming in the distance," Murphy said. "Give them a while to get closer, and then use the binoculars to see their faces."

After about fifteen minutes, the riders were in range of the binoculars. Elizabeth used them to study the men's faces.

She lowered the binoculars and looked at Murphy.

"It's them," she said.

"You're positive?"

"Yes. I'll never forget their faces. Ever."

Murphy opened the box of Sharps ammunition, removed a cartridge, and fed it into the chamber. "Let them get a bit closer," he said.

"Are you a religious man?" Elizabeth asked.

"That isn't the question you're asking," Murphy said as he cocked the hammer on the Sharps. "You want to know if I'm worried I'll be condemned to hell for the men I've killed? The answer is no, I am not worried."

Murphy held the Sharps and took careful aim through the scope.

"Are you familiar with Psalm Twenty-Three?" he said.

"I'm afraid not," Elizabeth said.

"Take out two bullets and hold them for me," Murphy said.

Elizabeth removed two bullets from the box.

"What is Psalm Twenty-Three?" Elizabeth said.

"The Lord is my shepherd, I shall not want," Murphy said. "And I will dwell in the house of the Lord."

Murphy pulled the trigger. Three seconds later, a rider fell off his horse. The shot echoed loudly throughout the hills.

Murphy ejected the spent round and Elizabeth handed him a fresh one. He loaded and took aim at the remaining two riders below. They had panicked and were frozen in place, trying to search the hills.

Murphy pulled the trigger. Three seconds later another rider fell off his horse.

The third rider turned his horse and raced away.

Elizabeth handed Murphy a third round and he loaded and aimed the Sharps rifle. He pulled the trigger, and the third man fell from his horse.

"Well, let's go down and have a look," Murphy said.

Elizabeth's face was pale as she stared at Murphy.

"It's over," Murphy said. "You're safe."

"Stay with Boyle," Murphy said.

"I want to come with you," Elizabeth said.

"This won't be pretty," Murphy said. "Stay with Boyle."

He replaced the Sharps rifle onto the saddle and walked toward the three fallen men. The first rider had died from a head shot, and there wasn't much left of his face. The second rider had died from a massive chest wound.

The third rider was hit in the back.

As Murphy approached the man, he turned suddenly and fired his pistol at Murphy. The bullet was off the mark and struck Murphy a glancing blow on the left side of his forehead.

The force of the bullet knocked Murphy to the ground, where he lay for several dizzying moments.

When his head cleared, Murphy slowly stood, pulled his Colt, and walked to the third man. He was seriously wounded and dying, but he had just enough sand left in him to cock his pistol a second time.

Murphy cocked the Colt and aimed it at the man. "I have had more than enough of you," he said and shot the man.

When Murphy holstered the Colt and

turned around, Boyle was running toward him with Elizabeth giving chase.

When Boyle reached Murphy, he nuzzled Murphy's face with his massive nose.

"I'm all right, boy. I'm all right," Murphy said.

Winded, Elizabeth arrived behind Boyle.

"Your head is bleeding, and so is the wound on your chest," she said.

"Let's find a place to make camp in case someone happens along," Murphy said. "Then we can deal with the bleeding."

"A fraction of an inch more, and that bullet would have killed you," Elizabeth said.

"But it didn't," Murphy said. "I'm just a little dizzy, is all."

Elizabeth washed the cut on Murphy's head with a wet neckerchief and then wiped a little whiskey on it.

"Open your shirt so I can see," she said.

"The bleeding has stopped," Murphy said.

"Open it anyway."

Murphy unbuttoned his shirt and Elizabeth inspected the wound. "You tore the skin a bit, but I don't think it's serious."

Murphy buttoned his shirt. "Let's get some supper going so I can tend to Boyle."

"I couldn't contain him when that man shot

at you," Elizabeth said.

With his back against the saddle, Murphy looked at Boyle. "We've been together a lot of years and covered a lot of ground, for sure."

Elizabeth spooned beans and bacon onto two plates along with hunks of cornbread. "Mr. Murphy, you've taught me a great deal this past week and I am grateful," she said. "I believe I have the courage to tell my family I don't wish to marry a man for the sake of family politics. In fact, I think I just might take a year off from school and travel America and see what I've been missing."

"Fort Smith is as good a place as any to start," Murphy said. He tasted supper and said, "I see you flavored the beans a bit."

"Try the coffee," Elizabeth said.

Murphy took a sip of bourbon-laced coffee.

"You have learned a thing or two," he said.

"I'm afraid that was the last of it," Elizabeth said. "The bottle is empty."

Murphy opened a saddlebag and removed an eight-ounce silver flask.

"For the after-supper cup of coffee," he said.

Elizabeth grinned. "I shall miss you a great deal, Agent Murphy," she said.

"Well, before you go to missing me too

404

much, we have to get where we're going first," Murphy said.

Chapter Forty-Two

Judge Parker was meeting with Marshals Cal Witson and Bass Reeves in his office when the noise of a crowd gathering on the street caught his attention.

"Bass, see what that commotion is," Parker said.

Reeves went to the window and looked out. "Judge, best have a look at this," he said.

Parker and Witson went to the window.

Both sides of the street leading to the courthouse were filling with people. Centered in the street, Murphy rode his massive horse toward the courthouse.

"He's got someone with him," Reeves said. He looked at Parker. "A girl."

"Good Lord," Parker said.

Kai and Burke were in the dry goods store when they noticed people rushing along the street.

"Something is going on at the courthouse," Burke said.

Kai and Burke went to the street and followed the crowd. As they neared the courthouse, Kai said, "Oh, my God," when she saw the fuss was centered on Murphy.

"Oh, my God is right," Burke said. "That's the Turner girl, the kidnapped girl, riding behind him."

Burke took Kai's hand and pushed his way through the crowds gathering on the street to the courthouse where Judge Parker, Reeves, and Witson stood on the steps.

"Judge! Judge Parker, it's Burke, and I have Kai with me," Burke shouted.

"Bass, Witson, make a hole in the crowd for Kai and Mr. Burke," Parker said.

Reeves and Witson descended the steps, parted the crowd for Burke and Kai, and led them up to Parker.

"Do you know what you're looking at?" Parker asked Kai.

Murphy was just a few hundred feet away now, and she could see the cut on his forehead, the filth and blood on his trail clothes, and the exhaustion on his face. Boyle appeared weary and weak, but still proud and spirited. The girl holding Murphy about the waist was wearing a dirty, tattered dress and a pair of Murphy's socks.

Her weariness showed in her eyes.

"Yes, Judge, I know what I'm looking at," Kai said and to her own surprise, her voice was filled with pride. "I'm looking at a lawman."

Boyle reached the bottom of the courthouse steps. The gathered crowd grew quiet as Murphy dismounted and then helped Elizabeth from the saddle.

"Burke, this is Elizabeth Turner, niece of Ambassador Turner," Murphy said. "And I owe her a cup of Earl Grey."

ABOUT THE AUTHOR

Ethan J. Wolfe is the author of the western novels *The Last Ride, The Regulator, The Range War of '82, Murphy's Law, Silver Moon Rising, All the Queen's Men, The Cattle Drive, The Devil's Waltz,* and *Lawman.*

The employees of Thorndike Press hope you have enjoyed this Large Print book. All our Thorndike, Wheeler, and Kennebec Large Print titles are designed for easy reading, and all our books are made to last. Other Thorndike Press Large Print books are available at your library, through selected bookstores, or directly from us.

For information about titles, please call:
  (800) 223-1244

or visit our Web site at:
  http://gale.com/thorndike

To share your comments, please write:
  Publisher
  Thorndike Press
  10 Water St., Suite 310
  Waterville, ME 04901